A Soul Undiminished

Robin Ray

ISBN 9781919615820 (Paperback)

ISBN 9781919615813 (E-book)

Editing, cover art, and book design by PaperTrue Ltd.

Printed in the United States of America

First edition August 2021

Published by PaperTrue Ltd.

Contents

Contents

Summary

Set in the bewitching world of the renowned Harry Potter series, the plot of *A Soul Undiminished* is set in motion when Severus Snape happens upon the protagonist, Sirana Cadogen, in Malfoy Manor. Having found Sirana on his lawn with apparently no memory of how she got there, Lucius Malfoy had been torturing the infiltrator to retrieve information when Severus arrives. Severus is inexplicably but undeniably drawn to the fiery woman he sees, and takes over responsibility for her, despite the risk it poses toward exposing his double-cross. Once he takes the mysterious woman to Hogwarts, he is unable to hide his curiosity. She is surprisingly much more cooperative with his inquisition. What's more, she admits that she too is drawn to him! A whirlwind passion ensues. We follow Sirana as she navigates and assimilates into her new reality, while understanding her bond with Severus. As he tutors Sirana on the magical world and its many differences, Snape simultaneously learns to open up and accept the love that he never thought he would get, or deserved, after Lily's death. Sirana's natural ability and determination have her joining the Hogwarts faculty as a teacher. It is soon discovered that she, in fact, has magical blood in her through her grandfather, Kane Cadogen, a renowned member of the Order of the Phoenix.

This discovery provides the clues as to her mysterious arrival at Malfoy Manor. As the story progresses, her connection to Severus is revealed to begin from before her first meeting with him. She was present the night the Dark Lord attacked the Potters. Lily, in all her selflessness, protects Sirana and through the use of powerful magic, transports her to Severus, so that he may heal from the wound of Lily's demise. This tale of acceptance and love follows the events of the series while centering on the relationship between Severus and Sirana, offering an alternative to his heart-breaking death in the original series.

Author Profile

Robin Ray, both as an author and an individual, has always strived to call into question the undeclared social norms that restrict women. She was inspired to begin writing after watching an interview with her favourite actor Alan Rickman, in which he advocates for strength in oneself and in one's dreams. Her first novel, *Psycho Therapist*, embodies this very message. Her second work, *A Soul Undiminished*, is set in the magical world of Harry Potter and expertly introduces a more mature tone to the celebrated children's series. While she has a successful career, Robin's primary focus has always been her family. She enjoys reading and writing romance, science fiction, and fantasy fanfiction.

Chapter 1

Malfoy Manor

Severus Snape entered Malfoy Manor by Apparating directly into the main hall, having been invited there by Lucius Malfoy himself. If he hadn't been expected, his way would have been blocked by protective spells, and the result would have been a painful rejection to outside the gates of the Manor. What he didn't expect to see was a woman hanging above the large fireplace, as if standing atop the mantle, with her hands tied at the wrists behind her back. Her long, dark blonde hair was tangled with sweat. Her gown was in the same state as her hair, and clung to her body and legs.

Lucius Malfoy entered the room, which was otherwise empty, and greeted Severus more warmly than was his nature.

"I see you have a new plaything, Lucius. Is she the reason you asked to see me, or an attempt to add to the ambiance?" Severus asked in a disapproving tone that he softened with a small quirk of a smile. Despite being a professor at Hogwarts School of Witchcraft and Wizardry, Severus had to uphold his reputation as a Death Eater among those who trusted him to do anything for the Dark Lord.

Lucius laughed and looked at the woman, then sheepishly back at Severus. "No, no. Although I will admit that she is quite the mystery. My staff found her on the lawn. She was unconscious and seemed close to death. I suspected she is a spy, so I have been conducting an inquiry with her. She has not been willing to cooperate, so it has come to this. Her story is one of ignorance, and as much as I have enjoyed using *almost* any means necessary to relieve her of her truth, I am growing weary of her obstinance."

Lucius started to brush off the subject, getting to why he had asked for Severus in the first place, when Severus realized something strange and asked, "Is she a Muggle?"

"I believed so at first," Lucius replied quietly. "However, she has a very strong mind, so much so that I am inclined to believe that she is part witch." He hesitated, then continued, almost embarrassedly, "She has thwarted my attempts to enter her mind completely, and I simply cannot seem to break her. I am now using a spell that is quite insidious, one that mixes pain with pleasure, and although she seems to be finally weakening, she resists me still."

Severus knew of the spell, as it was dark magic that the Dark Lord often used. He wasn't overly surprised, especially since Lucius was envious of the Dark Lord's power, and it was not beneath him to imitate the Dark Lord's magic. He was surprised that anyone, let alone a Muggle, could resist the almost tortuous effect of it. He was more curious than he wanted to admit and tried to reach into the woman's mind himself but was met with a wall of stone and fire. Just as he pulled back, he suddenly felt the wall drop and so halted his retreat. He moved deeper into her mind. His breath was almost taken away when his mind reached out—fire threatened to consume him as the flames licked at his brain in a way that was painful yet enticing. He realized she had let him into her mind enough to share her experience, and he was immediately aghast at the thought of her being subjected to any more of it. He knew nothing of this woman, and yet, there was something that inexplicably drew him to her. Of course, he let none of this reach his expression, and instead, turned away to have his talk with Lucius.

"I'm sure it will come to light eventually," Severus said, waving off the subject as if it were none of his concern. Lucius shared the reason for the meeting, and from Severus's experience, the request for him was not going to be pleasant. Severus agreed to the mission that was given him, supposedly directly from the Dark Lord, and assured Lucius in his most dangerous tone that he need not worry about anything being missed. Lucius smiled and clapped Severus on the arm, keeping up pretenses of being good friends, both knowing that the trust between them was no longer there. Lucius carried a suspicion of Severus, fueled by jealousy and contempt, as he knew the Dark Lord held Severus in high esteem. Severus knew of Lucius's suspicion of him, knowing him therefore to be terribly dangerous to Severus's secret allegiances. He also knew Lucius had his weaknesses, which perhaps made him even more dangerous. Severus nonchalantly turned his attention back to the woman, who was quiet, except for her breathing, which gave away her discomfort.

"Perhaps, when you are done with her, if there is anything left worth sharing, you can send her my way. I have been a bit bored as of late, and I could use a distraction," Severus stated with an eyebrow raised.

Lucius gave him a knowing grin, considering the proposal for a long moment. "Actually, Narcissa is returning this weekend from a trip, and I'm not completely certain if she would think highly of a beautiful virgin decorating our mantle," he said wryly, and maybe a little regretfully. "I have had more than my share of virgin sacrifices thrown my way and have found them to be overrated. So, if you are willing to take her with you, I see no harm in sharing her misfortune with a friend," he said magnanimously.

Severus looked more closely at the woman, noting her to be not so old, and not so young either. For the first time, he realized that she was indeed beautiful, even as dirty and tattered as she first appeared. This made him wonder at what Lucius had said about her being a virgin, and why Lucius would even share that bit of information. He had no illusion that Lucius could have easily used his considerable skills at magic to find out. That was of no real concern to him though, and the desperate desire to save this woman from suffering any more at the hands of Lucius drove him to action now. He did not want Lucius to sense any of this, so he quickly accepted the offer and removed his wand from the sleeve of his long overcoat, using his own magic to release the woman from the spell, lowering her to stand next to his side. Her legs looked a little wobbly, so he reached behind her to grasp her by the clasps holding her wrists to steady her without giving Lucius the impression that he cared one way or the other if she were to fall. The woman stood straight, raising her head to cast a look of seething hatred towards Lucius. Lucius stepped forward, raising his hand as if to wrap it around her throat, stopping just short.

"You dare meet my eyes again knowing I can crush you into a pile of flesh and bone?" Lucius spat menacingly. "I almost envy you Severus," he continued, speaking to Severus while not taking his eyes off her, "as you will have the pleasure of breaking her down, and hopefully, tearing her apart."

This woman obviously had some power in her to trigger so much fury within Lucius. Severus smirked at Lucius, not daring to look down at the woman in his grasp. She was standing against his side as if to steady herself against Lucius, projecting rebellious hatred towards him. Severus felt a strange feeling of needing to ally himself with this woman. He did not want Lucius to have any inkling of his thoughts, otherwise the wizard would see her as a tool to use against him.

"Well, you can take comfort in knowing I will share any information of the mystery I am inheriting." Severus's slight smile did not reach his dark eyes. He then Apparated back to his rooms at Hogwarts with his prize in tow. He looked down at the woman and was surprised to see her looking at him intently, without a speck of the intense hatred she had held for Lucius.

Why the bloody hell did I involve myself in this woman's life? he thought to himself.

One thing didn't escape him though—even with the news of his mission from the Dark Lord, his mood felt less tired and dark than it had in ages.

Chapter 2

Fantasy

Confusion and nausea came in a wave over her as she found herself whisked away from the terror of Malfoy Manor with her new captor. He was dressed in layers of black, his long, straight, black hair just brushing the top of his shoulders. He was tall and looked well-built, but it wasn't only his physical nature that made him appear strangely intimidating; there was a powerful presence about him that filled the room with an almost overpowering current of pulsing energy. Sirana felt a strange curiosity about him as he let go of her wrists and stepped back to draw his wand. He asked her to turn away from him in a low voice. She looked up at the imposing man for a moment, meeting his eyes. He had dark, possibly even black eyes, which looked like pools of shiny, black tar, and although his face showed no emotion, she found something deep in his eyes that contradicted his outward stoicism. She held his eyes for a long moment. There was a familiarity that she couldn't quite put her finger on, and she felt drawn by an almost palpable magnetism pulling her to him. She suddenly moved back a step, reminding herself that this man in front of her was somehow associated with Lucius, and that she should be more careful to not underestimate his intentions. His expression changed at her action, appearing to her as if he regretted the fear his presence had elicited from her. Deciding to save resistance for when she knew it was her last option, she turned away from the stranger without comment, and was a bit shocked and relieved when the clasps around her wrists disappeared. She turned back to the man that Lucius had called Severus, stubbornly resisting the urge to rub her painfully raw wrists. Severus met her eyes again, and she saw something in them, maybe even a look of approval.

"Follow me," he said as he turned sharply on his heel, his long coat and robes whipping around dramatically. He led her to the facilities of his quarters and proceeded to start a hot bath. Suddenly, she felt a little less brave and a lot more vulnerable. She had no qualms about resisting the likes of Lucius and would have fought him tooth and nail to her own death if needed. This situation made her feel more unsure of herself. She didn't know if she was supposed to try to fight or to flee, and she surely didn't know what to think of the unexpectedly compelling, yet dangerous-looking man in black. So far, he had treated her in a manner that was completely opposite to that of Lucius...so far. But she knew that she was practically defenseless against the strange power that these men seemed to wield. Everything up to this point had felt like a fantasy—a terrible, frightening fantasy. Everything felt so real, and yet, nothing was what she would consider to be within the realm of reality. She resolved that there would be plenty of time to figure it all out, as this nightmare seemed to drag on for eternity.

She was brought back from her thoughts with a low cough from Severus. He motioned around the room to her with a sweep of his arm. "You are welcome to the privacy of this room to relieve yourself and to bathe. I wouldn't recommend falling asleep in the tub though. As comfortable as it is, the water tends to cool quickly." He momentarily met her eyes, and then abruptly left the room, closing the door behind him.

Sirana let out the breath that she seemed to have been holding, realizing she had been standing as rigidly as possible, battling against the weakness she felt throughout her body. She gratefully made use of the facilities, and hurriedly removed the damp cotton gown she had been wearing for too many days, ridding herself of the foul garment that Lucius had ostensibly gifted her as a gesture of his concern for her modesty. Sirana looked back at the closed door for reassurance, then stepped into the warm, steaming bath, stretching out until her entire body and head were submerged. She waited until she was almost out of breath, enjoying the quiet warmth encompassing her, then pushed herself up to gasp for air. She dove under and back up once more, leaning back to allow her long, tangled hair to cascade wetly behind her. She found everything she needed in a metal tray hanging on the side of the tub, and was most grateful to comb out her hair. The wounds she had almost forgotten about started to sting even more, but the longer she laid in the warm water, the better she began to feel. She laid back and almost started to drift off when she heard the door open and footsteps softly approach. There was a low cough, and she assumed he was gently warning her of his approach. She sat up and covered herself with her arms, not overly worried any longer of her modesty. Considering the hell she had been through the last week, she was only slightly embarrassed at the situation she was in, especially knowing it was through no fault of her own.

Severus approached from behind her, setting down fresh clothes for her on the chair beside the tub, then withdrew his wand from his sleeve. She wasn't going to crane her neck to see what he was doing or turn in the tub to reveal more of her nudity, so she settled on turning her face towards where she could see his black-booted feet. He pointed the wand at the tub, and said a few quiet words, then spoke directly to her, "It is a common spell. It will charm the water to provide cleanliness for at least a month. You will find it is very helpful, unless you happen to be the sort who enjoys bathing daily, as many Muggles do." She could hear the slight sneer in his voice at that last part and wondered what the word she had heard said a few times already today really meant. She was hoping at that point that he would leave her to dry herself and dress but noticed his feet didn't move from their place.

"I will turn around if your modesty requires it, so that you can remove yourself from the tub," Severus said with all seriousness.

She nodded, and saw his feet move to face the other way. She dipped her head down into the water once more, just in case what he said about the charm working to keep her clean that long actually worked, then stood up to gingerly climb out of the tub. She winced when the towel she was using to dry off found fresh bruises and cuts she had acquired. At that, Severus turned around unexpectedly to look directly at her, scanning her entire body. She was suddenly shy as she felt herself flush, and she covered herself with the towel as he scrutinized her body.

Chapter 3

Mettle

S everus had seriously intended to face away from this woman to give her privacy until she was dried and dressed, but the sharp sound of pain from her startled him into turning to look at her. He noticed the obvious reason for her discomfort, feeling a twinge of pain in his own body at the thought of how she had acquired all the injuries he could see in spite of the towel covering her. He drew his wand out of his sleeve again, noticing how she held her head up as if to steel herself against whatever was coming. He hesitated, acknowledging momentarily the admiration he had for this woman's will, then flashed his wand. Her wounds faded, leaving only traces of her abuse at Lucius's hands. He would find the healing potions to completely remove any sign of scars and any trace of pain, but this would have to do for the time being.

He lurched forward as he saw her start to collapse, realizing that the relief from the pain she was carrying was almost unbearable in its swiftness. He reached out and caught her, then in one fluid motion, swung her legs up to carry her out of the room. He sat her in a chair in the living room, and seeing her secure her towel around herself, turned and went back to retrieve the fresh clothes for her. When he returned, he motioned to the small tray of food and drink on the table next to her chair. He saw her glimpse up at him with a grateful smile as she accepted the clean garments. Severus then turned to leave to the study to again offer her privacy while she donned the fresh clothes and ate. He was sure it had been too long a time since she had either.

He sat down at his desk and wiped his large hands over his face, leaning back in his chair exasperatedly. Absently looking at the wall of books in his study, he wondered how he could possibly explain any of this to Headmaster Dumbledore. He had avoided scrutinizing his feelings since he left Malfoy Manor with this mystery of a Muggle woman…or perhaps she was more than meets the eye, as Lucius had suspected. Severus held his own suspicions though, as he had sensed something about her that he couldn't put his finger on. He was not a fearful man, and his time as a Death Eater, as well as the devastating loss of his dear Lily, had robbed him of most of his gentler emotions, but something about this woman had evoked a sense of fear…maybe of losing her. He had lost Lily to their arrogant classmate, James Potter, which utterly devastated him, only to find what utter devastation meant when he lost her again, and finally, to death. He put those memories aside for now—he had relived them a lifetime's worth in his mind over the years. He turned his thoughts back to the present, and the woman who was presently in the very next room. There was something about her that seemed to stir something in him that he had not considered for many years. He felt more than pity for her, or even compassion, which were still in his thoughts. He felt an intense attraction to her, more than to her physical appearance—something about her whole being that he felt deep into his own. He scoffed at himself, sitting upright in his chair, chastising himself for his sudden flights of fancy. Surely all of this was just a reaction to having a lost, helpless, beautiful woman in his home…he revised that thought in his mind—no, not helpless. She had already proved her mettle against Lucius, and was not in a heap on the floor, wailing and sobbing as any other Muggle, or even witch for that matter, would be doing at this very moment. He felt the need rising again in him to protect this woman from further harm. He suddenly vowed to follow through with whatever this mystery held, and to see it to its ending, for good or bad.

Severus rose quickly from his chair to go face the person who caused more uncertainty and fear than he had felt for a long time, knowing that he had passed the point of being able to turn away from her and return to his solitude without knowing—*what*, he thought. *Without knowing what?!* He refused to let that thought bloom. He would not even consider the preposterous chance of finding love again. Whatever the future held with this woman, he would not allow himself the hope of anyone ever loving him. He had written that thought off long ago, and he would not be so foolish again to open his heart to the possibility. He stormed into the living room in a much darker mood than he had started off in.

Sirana started a little as Severus barged into the room. She had finished dressing and gratefully helped herself to the food and wine he had provided. There was a little of each, and she thought it was most likely intentional to keep her from getting sick after having gone so long without. He glanced briefly at her when he entered the room—to make sure she was clothed and awake, she assumed—then asked her to follow him in that strange yet deep, alluring voice of his.

He led her to the bedroom and motioned to the bed. "I apologize that my rooms include only one bed. You are welcome to it, or at least, one side of it. I'm sure you are quite tired after your ordeal."

She lowered the hood of her outer robe, doffing it to lay it on the large reading chair. She then quickly slid under the covers, rolled to her side, and adjusted the pillow under her head. She looked up briefly to lock eyes with Severus, and sleepily said, "Thank you," before falling fast asleep.

Severus knew that she must be exhausted, wondering how she had managed to make it this far without collapsing, but he felt something gently tug on his heart when she said 'thank you' to him. For all she knew, Severus considered, he could treat her as badly as Lucius had, maybe even worse, and yet, she had put enough trust in him—a complete stranger—to fall asleep in his bed, as if...as if they were lovers...? He thought about what Lucius had said about her being pure and changed his thought—as if they were in love. That sounded better. He winced inwardly as that thought had crept unintentionally into his mind again, and he lingered for a moment in his bedroom, looking at this woman he had already developed an appreciation of. He remembered then that he didn't even know her name. He sat up for a while with a glass of brandy, determined to learn at least that information tomorrow before he finally decided he thought about the what-ifs and whens long enough before heading to bed himself. He was tired. It had been a long day. And yet, he didn't feel tired to the soul as he had the past years. He disrobed before climbing in bed on the opposite side of his enchantress. He almost took his own bait to consider the possibility that she was indeed an enchantress, sent by Lucius or even by the Dark Lord himself, but stopped short of attributing her presence to sorcery. She was still in a fetal position, laying on her side, cradling her pillow under her head. She looked completely peaceful, and he was almost jealous of her for finding something he rarely could—peaceful sleep. He closed his eyes with a sigh and was only slightly aware of his surprise as a peaceful sleep claimed him as well.

Chapter 4

Sirana

Sirana woke in the most comfortable bed she could ever imagine. She felt completely and utterly healed from the events that led her here. She decided to linger in comfort a while longer before getting up and wrapping the robe from the chair around her to ease the chill of the room on her shoulders. She found a small washroom in the corner, which she used to freshen up before heading out to meet whatever this fantasy had in store for her. She stopped briefly before opening the door, fully accepting that this could turn into a nightmare as it had the previous week, then opened to door to find a comfortable room. The room appeared a little dark even though the light of dawn filtered in from the high window. She recognized this room from last night, but she hadn't really looked around much. It was a large room, with a comfortable seating area and a dining room. It was more modest than the elaborate Malfoy Manor had been, but it was not small or cramped by any means. She saw Severus sitting at the dining table and stepped further into the room as he looked up from his book. He put his book down and stood up long enough to wordlessly motion for her to join him at the table.

She sat at the other end from him and noticed that there was food in front of her, but only a cup in front of him. He hadn't picked up his book again and was looking at her almost expressionlessly.

She mustered the confidence to speak first and asked, "Aren't you going to be eating?" Besides a soft crack in her voice, she sounded almost familiar in her tone, as if they were known to each other, sharing a casual moment at the breakfast table.

He smiled wryly and answered, "I have already eaten, thank you, and brought you back some food from breakfast."

She thanked him politely and thought about that small piece of information. Where had he gone where there was breakfast being served? What sort of place was this? She ate heartily this time, appreciating the chance to renourish her body after such a long time.

When she finally wiped her mouth and put her napkin down, Severus asked pointedly, "What is your name?"

She wondered if he had been watching her eat and realized she had been so absorbed by the enjoyment of her meal that she hadn't even let concern or fear of her new captor enter her mind. Why did she feel so at ease with him? She quickly tucked that question away in case things took a turn for the worse.

"Sirana," she answered.

He paused and looked at her more closely. "Sirana. Is that all?"

"That is all I'm willing to offer at this moment. I hope it is agreeable with you," she said with as amiable a tone as she could muster for such a cross response.

He nodded, and it seemed like he was allowing that one to slide—for now. She saw in his eyes that he may not continue to be agreeable if she attempted to be as sly with more of her answers. She gathered the courage to look at him more closely than she had in the darkness the night before. He was tall; his shoulders and chest looked broad in his tailored black clothes, and even though he was no longer wearing his long overcoat, he looked just as imposing as he had the previous night. But he was also strikingly handsome. Not good-looking in the sense of boyish good looks, but the rugged, defined look of a mature man. There was a power about him that had nothing to do with magic. She thought with a grin that if she was in a fantasy world, this man would surely fit her fantasy. She suddenly caught herself and was embarrassed to notice that he was watching her looking at him so thoroughly.

Severus's mood had started to lighten a little as he watched her enjoy her food silently. He noticed that they shared the time without any of the awkwardness expected from two strangers sitting together at the breakfast table. He didn't want to interrupt her obvious enjoyment of the meal, so he had waited until she was finished before asking her his first question. She had answered with 'Sirana'. He liked the sound of it, registering the subtle similarity to his own before asking her whole name. She answered so politely that it took him a moment to realize that she hadn't really answered him at all. Somehow, that made him immediately think of Lucius. Had she been so polite to his questioning? Had she driven him to madness by meeting his interrogation with sugarcoated defiance? *What if she were to drive me to the same fate?* he thought, slightly amused. But Lucius was already mad, in his opinion. She probably just wounded his insecurities with her cunning intelligence. He started to wonder for a minute why he was making such complimentary assumptions about someone he'd just met. He stopped short of fully considering this when he noticed her looking at him—not really looking him in the eyes, but looking him over, almost appraisingly…his face, his hair, his clothes, his whole person. Then, he saw the exact moment she caught herself doing so. She looked down quickly and he almost smiled at her—almost.

"What were you doing at the Malfoy Manor?!" he asked abruptly, not really meaning to sound so harsh. This brought them both out of their own thoughts and into the present.

She looked up and answered straightforwardly, "I told him everything I know. He refused to believe me, and I refused to offer inaccurate information to appease him, which ultimately led to the situation in which you found me."

Severus quietly acknowledged that her response was again not a direct answer to his question. He considered that perhaps she was hesitant to risk him reacting in the same manner as Lucius had. He decided not to push her, choosing instead to look at her expectantly. She met his gaze, and he saw her lower her shoulders and heard her sigh in what would appear to be a decision to elaborate.

"From what I overheard Lucius say to you, he probably knows more than I can remember from that night. I vaguely remember waking up in a forest and stumbling through what seemed like an impossible distance before I lost consciousness. I was so cold.

I don't remember anyone finding me on his property, or how I ended up in his house…except that I was…transformed."

He was puzzled with this last part and asked her what she meant by 'transformed'.

"It was almost as if I was the same person but renewed. My scars, from injuries from where I played sports, were gone. It was like I was stripped of any imperfections and given a brand-new body, but still my own. It was so confusing, and I just remember Lucius being so nice at first, but then, the more I spoke, the angrier he became with me. He became violent, and that's when I saw the impossible—the magical power that he possessed. Really, that's when I decided I was either in an equally improbable parallel universe or some insane delusional fantasy."

He was careful to leave his face expressionless so as not to risk her becoming fearful that he would react with anger as Lucius had.

She seemed a little timid about proceeding, perhaps not wanting to relive the memories. "I fought him when he became violent, and that's when he used his magic against me. I really thought I was either going to wake up from that nightmare—or die. And then, you appeared." She trailed off, and he considered all that she had said before proceeded with his own interrogation, not completely sure of the meaning behind such an unexpected story, although he sensed she was telling the truth so far.

"Where are you from?" he asked, a little less forcefully this time.

She laughed a little, with the slightest tinge of hysteria in her voice. "Originally? New England? United States? Earth? I moved to England a couple years ago, but I don't even know where I am in relation to that! Since he had assumed I was lying, he refused to answer my questions about where I am now!"

Severus saw her face shut down at that point. He could understand her trepidation, especially considering how she had been treated by Lucius. It all sounded a bit implausible, but he didn't want her to stop being open with him, so he pressed her further.

"And you are being completely truthful with me now? To your own knowledge at least?" He added the last question as a caveat, because he had still not ruled out the possibility of someone putting her up to all of this, with her knowledge or not.

"Yes!" she said confidently, although he thought he caught a glimpse of tears threatening to well up in her eyes, giving away the possibility that she was not completely fearless of him. "Everything is the truth…except for me being a virgin, which is not something I said but that he said about me. I was married before, and I am a widow. So, unless that was also somehow transformed, he was mistaken or lying about that."

He considered that for a solid minute before resuming his questions. He wondered what would prompt her to actually be so honest with him as to assure that there was no untruth to be found.

She looked at him directly this time, and continued in a voice that sounded genuine, if not a bit naïve, "I am not a deceptive person. I would not choose to lie to you—unless you left me no choice."

He heard the caveat at the end of her comment as well and wondered if she had felt she had no choice but to lie to him now. Maybe she was fearful of him and had been simply trying to avoid the truth to protect herself. Severus was not gullible by any stretch, so he decided to test her assertion of complete honesty with a question—and he would never admit to himself how self-serving the question was.

"Do you find me attractive?"

He saw her jaw drop open slightly before she recovered and took a moment to answer him. "Yes," she said hesitantly, not meeting his eyes, and he saw that she had started to continue with something else before resolutely closing her mouth before she said more.

Severus was immediately suspicious now of everything she had said to him up to this point. He knew that he was not an attractive person, his looks being harsh and intimidating to most people, and he took her unwillingness to finish what she was going to say as either dishonesty or fear of angering him by being truthful. Either reason hurt him more than he would admit to himself. He thought for sure she would answer with a 'no' to prove her honesty, because he knew surely and deeply that a woman so beautiful, or almost any woman for that matter, would not find him attractive, and now his self-doubt mixed with his distrust of her words sparked his anger. His eyes narrowed, and he stood up from his chair, approaching her in two long strides to look down into her wide eyes.

"And what were you going to say? A lie, followed by another lie, or a lie, followed by a truth?" he asked, in a low, almost dangerous voice. Maybe deep down, he was starving to know the truth—*her* truth.

Chapter 5

Honesty

Sirana had answered him honestly, stopping short of finishing her sentence with what she really felt—"Yes, I find you very attractive." She was not a forward person— honest, yes, but not forward in the way of talking to men about her romantic notions. She could almost kick herself for not being more careful with her words and felt a surprised twinge of fear in her stomach when he approached her so quickly to stand over her. It was the question itself that had thrown her. Had he sensed her thoughts? Maybe he would use that information against her somehow. Maybe he was playing a cruel game as Lucius had, with just a different angle. She had decided to be honest anyway and suddenly felt naïve for not being willing to lie to protect herself. It just wasn't in her nature to play games. She would have to try harder to keep her honesty a little closer to her chest. She did not consider withholding information as being dishonest if the reason wasn't based on deception.

He must have sensed the argument in her, and without touching her, his hands clasped behind his back, and he lowered his head so that she could feel his warm breath as he whispered in her ear, "It would be in your best interest to answer me truthfully. *Now.*"

It sounded like a veiled threat to her. She had told him she would not be deceptive to him, and she meant it. Now, she was perturbed by his insinuation that she was lying, and yet, she couldn't help but notice the warmth creeping up from inside her at the realness of his body being so close to her, his warm breath on her face…

As he rose up to await her answer, she pushed back her chair and stood in one motion, her eyes meeting his with fire in them, "I was going to say, 'Yes, I find you very attractive.' And if you ever doubt my honesty again, you can rest assured that I will not answer any more of your stupid questions!" Her face was flush with the anger and embarrassment of such raw emotions. So much for keeping her thoughts from reaching her mouth…

She saw him freeze and felt a hint of fear that her outburst would set him off. She stood her ground though, as she felt a hot tear fall down her face. She decided at that moment that she would not be afraid of anything, or anyone, ever again.

Severus was taken aback. He felt the raw honesty of her, and he almost let the revelation of her words, and what they meant to him, enter his mind. Before he got that far in his thinking, he felt immediately regretful that he had been so forceful with her, especially considering her answer, which had unexpectedly shaken him a little. Why had he even asked her the question? It seemed foolish now that it was out there, and he wished he could withdraw it. He stepped forward to her, closing the already short distance in between them, and placed his hands on her shoulders. It didn't get past him that her shoulders were shaking almost imperceptibly with emotion, or that the tears he had noticed earlier had lost their tenuous hold, and a couple made it down her flushed cheeks.

The words "I'm sorry" slipped out of his mouth as he looked down into her eyes. She seemed unwilling to lower her eyes, or even to soften the emotion in them. He had wanted to protect this woman, and yet, he had started off by hurting her. He took one small step back, leaving his hands on her shoulders, and said again, "I really am sorry for this. I'm sorry that I pushed you to answer. I never..." he paused for a minute, not wanting to reveal his own vulnerability to her, and yet, wanting to lessen the sting he knew his actions had inflicted. He really didn't want to hurt her. He sighed and continued, "I never would have considered your initial answer to be an honest one. Not that I thought you would not answer honestly...just that I had not considered that as a possibility of an honest answer." He realized that may have sounded like a riddle, but he saw her eyes soften and she nodded, almost as if to accept his apology while acknowledging his own honesty. He still regretted having insisted that she had been lying, but that feeling was replaced by the realization of the admission of her attraction to him. 'Very attractive' ran a circuit through his mind, and he couldn't resist the sudden powerful urge to kiss her. Not to try again to test the honesty of her assertion, but because it was the only thing that seemed to make sense in this moment. He slowly lowered his head, his eyes locked with hers until the moment he met her mouth with his, knowing he would have pulled back if he felt her expected resistance. Instead, he felt her respond to him, and heard her breath catch in her throat as she returned his gentle kiss. It was all more than he could even fathom as he felt her lean into him, her hands grasping his arms, and he deepened the kiss until they both pulled away breathlessly. He didn't understand how any of this could make sense, and yet, he was reassured that his instincts had not failed him. This time, she did lower her eyes, dropping her gaze in what he imagined was a sudden wave of shyness and embarrassment. He reached with his hand to gently grab her chin to bring her face up to his and said in the gentlest voice he had ever heard from himself, "I am willing to concede that one of us is in an alternate reality, or a parallel universe, but I am not convinced yet that it is not myself that is in the delusional fantasy. I am, however, willing to stay here for the time being, as this fantasy, if it is such, is quite compelling."

Sirana felt like molten lava was running through her body, and both the heat and weight of the sensation made it almost impossible for her to move. Yet, she had moved, as if pulled by an unknown source of gravity towards this man. Finally, they reluctantly pulled apart from the most impassioned kiss she had ever even imagined, and she found that she could not meet his eyes. She was embarrassed at her passionate response to him, a man who was a stranger to her, and she didn't know how she could ever look in his eyes again. Maybe this was how her new captor would wield his magic against her, and it seemed equally as dangerous as any she had seen since arriving in this strange place. As he lifted her chin, she heard his words, surprised to hear something so tender coming from such a severe, intimidating-looking man. She couldn't explain why, but she no longer had any fear that he would hurt her, but she did have a fear of the intense feelings that he evoked in her.

She remembered that she had promised herself only minutes ago that she was no longer going to fear anything or anyone, and she knew that this was poetic justice that something so unexpected had presented itself to challenge that promise. She couldn't help but smile a little at that thought, and she saw a brief glimpse of something in Severus's eyes before he stepped back abruptly, breaking the contact between them. His expression hardened again, and he left the room without looking back at her. She wasn't sure what had just happened. Maybe he may have thought her smile was mocking him, or maybe, he suddenly had the same reservations about what had just transpired between them as she herself had felt. Her emotions and the nerves in her body were still so raw from the days prior, and she felt so tired and emotionally drained that she wanted to do nothing else but shut her brain off and sleep. She didn't want to return to his bedroom. Even though he wasn't in there, it felt like such an intimate space, so she proceeded to almost fall into the nearest chair in the living room, covering herself with her outer robe and hood, before falling off into a restless sleep.

Chapter 6

Wonder

Severus retreated into his study once again. He wondered what had come over him. He thought about the day, and realized that his wonderment at his own actions, all of them, had begun the moment he decided to help this woman. Sirana... he felt like he knew her somehow, like he was closer to her than his one day of time with her. He had heard people speak of soulmates, and he had considered it nonsense... until he met Lily. He was then sure that she was his soulmate, destined to be together forever. That cruel illusion was very short-lived, and he was once again cynical of the concept of a soulmate, until today. He had felt drawn to Sirana when he entered Malfoy Manor that night. Every moment thereafter seemed to strengthen the powerful gravity he imagined pulling him to her. From her reaction in the dining room, he thought for a minute that she had felt the same pull. Then his doubt had taken over, and he cursed himself for allowing the sweet smile he saw on her lips fool him into thinking he was anything other than detestable to the opposite sex. He inwardly admitted that he was being a bit hard on himself and was uncharacteristically allowing himself to indulge in self-pity. He knew 'detestable' was a strong word, even for himself.

There were other women in his past who had considered him attractive, or were at least attracted to his power, or even his position as a Death Eater. But to consider this woman as attracted to him was difficult to believe—she was beautiful, there was no denying it, along with a tough-as-nails will, all bundled up in a lovely package, one that willingly admitted her own attraction for him, by her words and by her actions. Whatever the true reason behind her mysterious appearance in his world, in his life, no longer mattered. He was ready to take the risk of falling hard even if it was, in fact, an elaborate illusion.

With that understanding, he decided to stop hiding out in his study and to face the only person he wanted to see. He found her curled up in his favorite chair in the living room. He stood over her for a while, just looking at her, being close to her. He saw her start to breath faster, as her body twitched, her eyes tightening. He heard a muted moan coming from her, as if she was screaming within a dream. He decided to break the spell of her nightmare and gently lifted her up in his arms. Then, turning to sit in the chair, he held her in his lap. She was surprisingly light, especially considering that she was not a delicate-looking woman. She looked well-toned and healthy, almost athletic, but he knew her recent ordeal, first being lost in the forest for who knows how long, and then being held at Malfoy Manor for the last week or so, had taken its toll, and he could feel her ribs too close to her skin. His concern for her well-being welled up, as she recovered from the nightmare without waking, and began to sleep more calmly in his arms. She felt so warm and soft that he felt a bit of guilt for the feelings that holding her against him stirred up in him. However, he remained content to hold her while she slept and found himself dropping off to a warm, comfortable sleep himself.

Severus woke to find Sirana still coiled up on his lap sound asleep. He gently tucked her head under his chin, thinking of the dark solitude he had expected for himself, and silently wished for things to be different. He had loved before…Lily, and his love for her was like a wound that could never be healed. But that love was not mutual, at least to his knowledge, and he craved in his soul a mutual love that would give and not just take. There was something familiar about Sirana, but also something very compelling. She was soft and hard, she was bold and shy, she was innocent and passionate, she was fiery and gentle. Maybe the duality of her nature suited the duality in his own. A contradiction that somehow found a balance. She didn't know him yet though. If she discovered his own true nature, would she be repulsed by him?

As if by more than mere coincidence, he felt his Dark Mark begin to move, and he knew that the Dark Lord was summoning him. It was still early in the day, and Severus regretted having to leave Sirana. He rose from the chair, gently lifting and carrying her into his bedchamber. He laid her on the bed, tucking the blanket in around her. The sensation from Dark Mark on his arm was beginning to grow more uncomfortable, reminding him of the painful choices of his past. He slowly leaned down to place a kiss on Sirana's forehead, stubbornly refusing to give in to the urgency of the call from Voldemort, however; he knew it was not wise to delay answering to the Dark Lord, and he strode from the room with the resoluteness of a man determined forge a new path.

Chapter 7

Pitch Dark

Sirana woke to find herself in his bed. She knew that this wasn't where she had fallen asleep earlier and was very curious to how she ended up here. The room was dark. She wondered how long she had been sleeping—surely not since this morning. She couldn't see if there was anyone next to her in the bed. The room was pitch black so she couldn't see her own hand in front of her face even if she tried, which she did. Curiosity took over any sense she had, and she slowly slid her arm across the cool sheets. Her motion was suddenly stopped when her hand met the warm body lying on the other side of the bed. She didn't want to startle him awake, so she slowly withdrew her hand. She let out a gasp of surprise when he quickly rolled towards her, grasping her hand in his. His roll brought him close enough to her that she could feel the heat of his body radiating under the covers, but he did not touch anything but her hand.

"Is there something you need?" Severus drawled, and she heard a tinge of humor there, suspecting he was teasing her a little. She could imagine a mischievous smile on his face, although there was not enough light in the room for her eyes to even start to adapt to seeing anything. She pulled her hand back gently, removing it from his grasp, and assured him that she was fine. He didn't make any move to roll back away from her, and she could hear his low, slow breaths in the otherwise quiet room. She almost imagined she could hear his heartbeat as well, and then realized it was her own, pulsing hard and fast. She could no longer keep up the pretense that she was breathing calmly and drew in a deep breath, letting it back out again slowly. She suddenly felt panic rise in her. She did not know this man, or his intentions. *In fact, I don't even know my own intentions*, she thought dryly. She was not repulsed by the closeness of this stranger, and she had already admitted her attraction for him. Her body was so tense now, trying not to move and risk touching him, either accidentally or intentionally. She tried to relax, as surely she could trust herself not to maul the stranger next to her, and realized she was indeed holding herself back from the urge to reach out. What was she trying to protect? She could not find an answer to her own question. She had nothing to lose in this reality, no reputation to uphold, no ties to anyone or anything. She finally closed her eyes and gave herself into everything around her. She felt like she was deep in a dream, seeing nothing, but hearing and feeling everything. She slowly reached out again, and this time, allowed her hand to find his again, right where she had left it.

Severus wasn't sleeping when he felt her hand touch his side. He noticed the change in her breathing and knew that she had awakened. He felt her hand move across the sheets toward him and he lay perfectly still until she withdrew her touch. He was feeling mischievous when he rolled over to ask her if she needed anything. He knew what he wanted from her but wasn't under any illusion that she would admit to wanting or needing anything from him. Now that he was so close to her, he didn't want to move away, and even though he resisted making more contact than her hand, he was satisfied with that connection. He had almost retreated to his side of the bed when she had slipped her hand out of his—until he heard her breath become quicker and deeper. He saw through her effort to hide the feelings she must have also felt, and although he was still surprised by her attraction to him, he knew he wasn't the only one feeling the almost magnetic force drawing them together. His suspicion was validated when he felt her hand find his again. His own pulse quickened as he felt her hand move from his, softly caressing his arm up to where it rested on his shoulder. His breath caught in his throat. He was keenly aware of the duality of his thoughts—part of him was deeply touched at her timid attempt at reinitiating the contact between them, the other part of him fully absorbed the intensity of the tantalizing touch of her hand on his arm. He felt the need to rush to find out the direction this was going, to force the hand to be played, but he didn't want to risk an early ending if she rejected him. Severus was initially surprised by his body's intense reaction, cursing himself as being weak. He was not an inexperienced youth, unable to control his carnal desires, and he quietly steeled himself. He brought his hand up to rest on top of hers, then slowly traced the same path on her arm that she had on his. His hand reached her shoulder, and they both froze, content for a moment to enjoy the unexpected closeness of the mutual contact.

The pressing silence of the room was broken by Sirana's hesitant whisper, "Will—Will you hold me?" He was almost undone by her gentle request and breached the distance between them by swiftly moving to pull her in towards him. One would think that there would have been the sound of thunder crashing when their bodies crossed the plain of heat radiating between them. He felt her arm wrap around him and heard a soft "Mmmm…" coming from the darkness. Any doubt he had was drowned out by the sheer magnitude of his desire, and he heard a low, throaty moan come from deep within himself. He lowered his head towards her, unable to see anything in the darkness, and felt a sweet sense of gratitude as his mouth found her soft, willing lips ready for his. There were no walls between them then, and he felt her melt into him, meeting his passion with her own. He had nothing to compare this experience to, and although he had known young, innocent love for Lily, and wanton lust for women later in his life, this was on another plain of reality in its fierce intensity of emotion and sensation. He openly let himself register the raw emotions he was feeling, remembering his determination to never allow this woman to come to any harm—even from himself. He recognized that they were approaching the point where they may no longer be willing to put a stop to an inevitable end, and he made a concerted effort to slow the pace of their passionate kiss.

Sirana was utterly shaken, her breath deep and ragged, her entire body quivering with the effort of pulling herself away from the powerful spell this wizard had put her under. She immediately conceded to herself that this powerful feeling had nothing to do with magic but seemed instead to radiate from each of them. She felt as if she was immerging from a deep abyss of swirling sensations, sounds, and emotions to slowly regain conscious, lucid thought. No longer bewitched, she became keenly aware that Severus had pulled them both back from the brink. She felt a twinge of shame at her lack of control but was unwilling to chastise herself for the most euphoric experience that she had never even imagined to be possible. It was just a kiss—*just*. She had realized that the impassioned kiss from earlier was just a starter in comparison.

Severus Snape was a powerful wizard, a powerful man, and this moment took every bit of his concentrated power to resist his own dark side, which was telling him that stopping now was folly. He didn't consider that he was using his will to fight not only against his dark side, that craved the need to consume this woman with lust and savage desire but also the part of his being that sought love and acceptance, and even whispered promises of the healing of wounds. There was another part of him though that was fiercely determined to protect this woman, and this part won the battle that would even defend her against his own passion, his own emotions, his own desire to be rid of the painful wounds so deep that they slowly seeped out anything good and light, threatening to diminish even his own soul.

Severus did not pull away from Sirana, even though their passion was quieted, leaving only the sound of ragged breathing coming from each of them. In fact, he pulled her even closer to him as if to envelop her entirely with his body. His mind pictured himself as a bat, wrapping her up with large, black wings, and he would have felt fortunate to have that capability now to completely encapsulate her with himself, warding off any that would penetrate his defenses.

Chapter 8

Familiarity

Sirana woke up to the feeling of a chill creeping into her body. Her eyes flew open widely, trying to find any light to help her find her bearings. The memory of the night slowly came back into her mind, which warmed her body enough to take the edge off of the chill. Evidently, the reason she was so cold is that sometime in the night, after they had fallen asleep, they had moved to their own sides of the bed, naturally finding their own comfort. Severus must have rolled the blanket right off the top of her when he moved to his side. She resisted the urge to giggle—some things were universal, even the humor that comes with sharing a blanket. She reached over and found the edge of the blanket and tried to gently pull some of it her way. The blanket was most decidedly wedged under the sleeping figure on the other side of the bed. She heard his peaceful breathing, and not wanting to wake him, she moved over to lay lightly against him, finding there was enough of the blanket available that way to drape over the back of her. She relished in the comfort and warmth, hoping the chill of her own skin wouldn't wake him, before sleepily falling back into a dream.

Severus Snape had no illusions about his own duplicitous nature. He had moved past the notion that he would ever atone for the atrocities dealt by his own hand as a former Death Eater and a member of Voldemort's legion. He was, therefore, surprised at the twinge of guilt he felt for rolling the blanket off his willing enchantress in hopes that she would come searching again for his warmth. When he felt Sirana move over to unshyly lay her body against his, he pursed his lips in a contented smile, the ends of his mouth turning both up and down in their unique configuration. Unbeknownst to him, Sirana had found his unique and rare smile quite seductive. Had he been a cat, he would have purred in comfortable contentment. He had another two entire days before he had to resume his duties as Professor Snape, and he would not waste any moments of the enjoyment of this strange and unexpected situation.

He thought once again of his dark past. It haunted his present, and he had felt only brief moments of light since losing Lily. His passion for his career as a professor at Hogwarts had provided a way to pass his time in a meaningful way. Only those closest to him, both enemies and allies, knew of his continued dealings with Voldemort, however; there was only one who knew the whole truth. His thoughts turned to Albus. Albus Dumbledore knew Severus Snape, perhaps better than anyone—alive—knew him, but even Dumbledore did not know the depth of him. His love for Lily had both driven him and Albus apart, and then, forced them back together as unexpected cohorts towards a greater ending than either of them could find within themselves. The loyalty Severus had for Albus was tainted with regretful blame and unforgivable shame. Snape's trust had been broken when Albus failed to protect Lily from death at Voldemort's hands, not considering his own plea to Voldemort to spare Lily when he came for her son was farthest from what Lily would have wanted. Protecting the only thing left of Lily, Harry Potter, had forced an alliance between himself and Albus that overshadowed any bitterness they may still harbor.

The dark direction his thoughts had taken would not allow him to drift back off into sleep. He thought once more of Lily—not her soul-tearing end, but the time when they were friends, happy to pass their days together, uncomplicated by the weight of the world. He felt a warm feeling come over his body, and as his thoughts brushed past the memory of her loss, he felt a comforting wave, as if someone had rubbed a healing salve over his deepest wound. He rebelled against it for an instant, not willing to give away any of the still sharp sting of this most painfully cruel memory. He relented slightly as he felt a familiarity pass over him, and he groaned softly, feeling as if this wound had been touched at its deepest core, then had been set to healing. He drifted off into sleep before he could put a finger on the source of the warm familiarity he felt, and the magic that would not show itself until the proper time.

Chapter 9

Dream

Sirana woke to find that she was the alone in the bed. She wasn't chilled though, as it seemed that the covers had been tucked in around her. She smiled softly and wondered how she had come to be in this place—not just this room, or this world, but in what seemed to be the second chapter of her life. Actually, her own life had had many chapters already, and she had lived an almost ordinary, yet fulfilling life. This was more like a second life—not an after-life, but like she had been reincarnated while retaining her own self.

She had already ruled out that this place was a delusional fantasy, as it was just too real in every way. As for the magic and the unfamiliar ambiance of this place, as if she was in a medieval, Victorian, wizardly world, she considered for a moment that maybe the world held more mysteries than she had ever dared to believe were possible. She had seen things over her lifetime that were strange, but she had always found a way to categorize them using a scientific explanation, even though some were a stretch. Her adoring husband had always jokingly accused her of being a witch, and often complained of the spell she had over him. Handel, who she lovingly called Handy, especially since he could fix almost anything, was a mild, good-spirited man with warm hazel eyes that matched his sandy blonde hair. She lost him much too soon, and the unrealized plans they had made together had felt like a thick, heavy cloud hanging over her life. His diagnosis of cancer had caught them all off guard, and she had spent the last year of his life helping him accomplish all of the items on his bucket list. They had traveled the world and spent time with loved ones, and then she had stayed by his side until the end. He had made her swear to him that she would follow her dreams and live her life to the fullest, for both of them. After he passed, she no longer felt settled, the contentment she felt with him suddenly gone from her life. She had decided to move overseas to be with her dear grandfather, who needed her in his elder years...not forever, as she had assured friends and family in the States. Regardless, she had settled down in the quaint town where her grandfather had lived for what seemed like forever.

It felt like a lifetime ago...a lifetime...and she was a little sad that her memories had started to fade. Even the pain of loss was softened to a dull ache. For the first time since she came to be here—finding herself in the forest, alone, renewed—she tried to remember what had happened before that could have brought her here. She knew that she had dreamed of it the other day, and the nightmare was lost to her when she had woken, leaving only flashes of images. She saw the face of her grandfather, his usually good-natured face drawn into rage. She saw him, his nightrobes flying out behind him, as he ran faster than looked natural for an elder man towards their neighbors' house. She saw strong flashes of light in their windows, as if a bolt of lightning had found its way into their house and was desperately trying to escape. Her dream had been interrupted at that point, and she had a sudden foreboding that the events that had transpired that night would reveal themselves to be more than her heart could bear. She brought her hand up to her face, finding it wet with tears. Wiping them away with her gown, she rose from the bed, resolutely deciding she would uphold her promise, and she would make the most of this new life.

Chapter 10

Intentions

Professor Snape sat across from Headmaster Dumbledore as they sipped on the brandy that the latter produced after searching through the numerous items that filled the shelves of his room. He blew a thick layer of dust off the ancient-looking bottle and poured them both a generous drink in their goblets.

Severus raised his brow in appreciation after taking a first taste of the robust liquor.

"Special occasion, Albus?" Severus asked, unaware of how long it had been since he and Dumbledore had shared a drink.

"You tell me, Severus," Dumbledore asked in return. "Is there a special occasion that we could raise our glasses to?"

Severus thought there was a look of humor in his eyes and answered in a surly voice, "None that I can possibly imagine."

Dumbledore took another slow sip, then leaned forward to set down his glass before adopting a more serious tone, "What are your intentions, Severus?"

Severus began to open his mouth in reply, not yet meeting Dumbledore's gaze, and wisely thought better than to feign ignorance and answer the question with a question. He was

A Soul Undiminished—Severus Snape

distinctly aware that not much got past the Headmaster of Hogwarts, and he knew Sirana was the subject of his inquiry. Despite the gravity of the question, his words hung in the air.

"Intentions…" Severus repeated, staring off at some far point in the room, but not really seeing.

He leaned back in his chair, crossing one leg over the other, his casual pose contradicted by the intensity of his voice. "I have been presented with a mystery, and I feel that I must solve it." He brought his eyes back to Dumbledore's, perhaps looking for an answer.

Dumbledore spoke ominously. "You know that there is no path that is before you that would bring a favorable ending." He hesitated thoughtfully before continuing more gently, "You know it is beyond my position to ask you to make another sacrifice, as the time comes swiftly for each of us to give perhaps our last pound of flesh."

Severus sat his own half-empty glass next to Dumbledore's, looking at them for a moment before standing to leave. "I have long suspected that my flesh is not a sufficient offering, and if there is even a pound left of my soul, it will be the requisite recompence."

Dumbledore stood as if to dismiss Severus, but stepped towards him instead, standing only a breath away, and spoke above a whisper. "Perhaps, Severus, your soul has more value than you ascribe to it."

Severus closed his eyes and let his head tilt softly back, letting a breath out slowly.

Dumbledore continued, "I have found that, while it is true that life is rarely equitable, it is once and again known to be merciful."

When Severus finally opened his eyes, Albus was no longer present in the room.

Severus left the Headmaster's chambers in a pensive mood, brooding on the unfortunate events that had recently transpired at Hogwarts as he walked through its familiar halls. He was keenly aware of the growing threat of the Dark Lord, and he had been tasked by Albus Dumbledore to strengthen the Potter boy's mind against the Dark Lord's, which seemed dangerously intertwined. Harry Potter was a constant reminder of his painful past; however, he was also the only real tie he had left to his dear Lily.

Severus had already begun the lessons with Potter, so far finding the power of Occlumency to be out of the boy's capacity to fully grasp. He did not, however, intend to disappoint Dumbledore's expectations of either of them.

Severus was pulled from his thoughts as he spotted the trio of students, who always seemed to be inseparable, and they appeared to be up to something. Harry Potter approached him while the other two students, Hermione Granger and Ronald Weasley looked on timidly. "Professor Snape, I was wondering if you could help us with something," Potter said.

"Yes?" Severus drawled, immediately suspicious of what they could possibly need his assistance with.

"You see, we've been trying to work on something," Harry Potter said, and Severus was immensely curious as to what they would possibly need that they would come to him in particular. Perhaps his time working with the Potter boy on Legilimency and Occlumency had bolstered their trust in him.

"Yes?" Severus drawled out even longer, waiting for the boy to get to the point of his inquiry.

"As you know, Professor Lupin taught us about the Patronus Charm, and we were hoping you might have some insight…for those who might find it…difficult to cast a Patronus," Potter said, as if it pained him to have to ask.

Severus thought about the request. Even as an undeniable master of potions, his current position as Potions Professor did not take full advantage of his invaluable expertise in other areas. Severus had always had a predilection for Dark Arts defense, and the question that Harry Potter now posed only worked to validate Severus's certainty that he should have been rightly granted the position of Defense Against Dark Arts Professor long ago.

"First and foremost, one must avail oneself of a powerful memory," Severus said, looking to see each of them staring at him wide-eyed, as if hanging on his every word. He continued, trusting that they were indeed interested in the value of his lesson, "Secondly, the memory must be a happy memory…the happiest you can conjure from your young lives. Thirdly, you must allow this memory to fill you, to suffuse your mind, to pervade your entire being. Lastly, you must combine this with the proper use of your wand and the appropriate incantation… which I am certain Professor Lupin provided you with."

Severus said the last part with a hint of a sneer, knowing Professor Lupin to have very different teaching techniques than his own. "Perhaps when you have the opportunity, I can instruct you in the finer points," Severus said, his eyebrow raising inquisitively.

"Thank you, Professor Snape, I think we've got it from here," Harry Potter said, and Severus was again reminded of Harry's resemblance to his father, James, and how both seemed to share an unfounded pretentiousness about themselves. Severus silently hoped that he could instill a bit of humility in his lessons with Harry Potter, and perhaps help him to avoid the same arrogance that Severus believed to contribute to the unfortunate fate that befell Harry's father. As Severus watched the three of them go on their way, talking to each other as if his lesson had held the key to their lives, his thoughts turned to Sirana, hoping wistfully that she held the key to his own.

Chapter 11

Optimism

S everus felt a sliver of trepidation about returning to the dungeons where he kept his residence while at Hogwarts, afraid for a moment that it had all been an elaborate fantasy, and he would find himself, once again, truly alone. He couldn't allow his courage to fail him so early in the hour. He felt a rush of uncommon optimism and assumed the effects of Dumbledore's brandy had finally taken hold. He marched in as if to boldly meet his fate.

Sirana was sitting once again is his favorite chair, her legs drawn up beneath her, her nose in one of his books. She jumped, startled at his abrupt entrance, standing quickly, turning only a moment to lay the book in the chair before looking at him, nervously adjusting her gown. It reminded him of one of his students being caught in the act of breaking a rule, and he strode over closer, closing the distance between them in swift strides. He resisted the urge to ask her if she was up to something and settled on reaching behind her to pick up the book from the chair to inspect the object of her attention, only slightly brushing her as he did so. He looked at her oddly as he saw that the book was a manual on the rules of Quidditch. He felt a twinge of guilt for assuming she was snooping and wondered about the reason for her skittish reaction to his return. He chose to avoid the subject entirely for the moment and asked if she found the breakfast he left for her.

"Yes, thank you," she replied and proceeded to blush. It dawned on him the reason for her seemingly nervous discomfort at being in his presence. The comfortable familiarity they had shared yesterday was before they had shared the passionately intimate moments last night. He sadly realized they were still strangers to each other really, and decided to remedy that post-haste. He handed the book back to her, moving to sit in the adjoining chair as she sat back down. She did not look as comfortable as she had when he had entered, and sat a bit stiffly in the seat.

"You are welcome to peruse any of the books here. You might find most quite boring," he said.

She smiled, and he could see that she had relaxed a little.

"However," he continued, "There is a problem I need to rectify."

She looked at him expectedly, as if worried at his serious tone.

"You happen to be sitting in my chair," he said, as he raised both his eyebrows, waiting for her reply.

"Oh!" she gasped, and jumped up quickly, holding the book against her chest. "I'm so sorry!"

Severus looked up at her, not rising from his own seat, and then uncrossed his leg. His suddenly impish grin, and the almost imperceptible shift in his chair, subtly hinted that he was offering his lap as an alternate seat. He had no clue where his suddenly gamesome mood had come from, and he almost relished in her embarrassed distress.

It took Sirana a moment to recognize the game he was playing. He was teasing her, enjoying watching her fidget at the awkwardness of the moment, silently daring her to have a seat on his lap, knowing that she wouldn't dare. He was at the disadvantage of not knowing her, or the streak in her that would not turn away from a challenge, and she did dare. As she stepped quickly over and curled up in his lap, she briefly saw the look of complete shock on his face, his eyes widening, knowing he must have fought to keep his mouth from dropping open. She had called his bluff, breaking the air of the uneasiness she felt in his presence by doing something completely out of her nature.

She reopened her book, her own impish grin tugging at the corners of her mouth. She felt like she had won a match—until she realized that this was not a game, and that she was sitting in the lap of the man whom she had anxiously dreaded the return of all morning. She knew that she wouldn't know how to face the dangerously alluring man who had evoked such a strong reaction, and she felt the shyness in the daytime that had been stripped away under the cover of darkness. She felt him recover from his initial shock as he moved his arms to gently hold her, settling into a position that was comfortable for them both. She couldn't deny that she felt at ease in his arms, and she snuggled in with a wiggle.

Chapter 12

Unforeseen

Severus sat quietly, watching Sirana page through the Quidditch manual, which was sparsely illustrated, as if she was deeply immersed in an enthralling novel, until he could no longer hold back his curiosity.

"What could a Muggle possibly find so interesting about the game of Quidditch?"

She looked up from the book for the first time since she sat with him and smiled a little, answering almost merrily, "From what I can make out so far, this is a sport, and a quite challenging one at that. I can only imagine how exhilarating it would be to watch, much less participate in."

His lips pulled up into an amused, almost affectionate grin. "Yes, it is. You are correct. It is both a sport and quite challenging, although I have only found it to be exhilarating on rare occasions. Perhaps one day I could..." He stopped himself from continuing the sentence, realizing suddenly how complicated this unforeseen arrangement was, and he couldn't imagine how he could explain the presence of his new companion at a Quidditch match, much less to Lucius, if he were to hear that she had not met the fate he had portended for her. He couldn't leave the unfinished sentence hanging, and finished differently than his original thought, "... explain the finer intricacies of the game to you."

She continued as if she hadn't noticed his hesitation and replied as if genuinely interested, "I would like that."

Severus was touched by the innocent curiosity of her answer, her eager interest in learning something from him, albeit a subject as bland as Quidditch. He felt the deep need to learn more about her.

"Tell me more of your life before you came here, " Severus said, and although it was not a question, his inquiry did not sound the least bit demanding.

Sirana wasn't sure where to begin, so she decided on continuing with the subject of the day.

"Quidditch reminds me a bit of a game called lacrosse, although I've never actually played it myself surprisingly..." she mused. "I've played my fair share of sports though, and I've always loved a challenging competition."

Severus seemed content to let her ramble, waiting patiently for her to take the conversation in her own direction.

"I suppose that's what led me to choose my profession. I'm a teacher. Or at least, I was." There was a tinge of regret in her voice.

"A teacher? Really?" Severus asked, a bit of surprise in his voice. "What subject do you teach?"

She laughed a little embarrassingly before admitting, "I'm a physical education teacher—an athletics coach. Don't laugh! I know some people look down their nose at my chosen profession, but I was very proud to share with young people my love for sports and fitness."

"I can assure you, I wouldn't dare to laugh at such a worthy profession," Severus replied seriously.

She had to look up to see if his expression was a mocking one, wondering if his statement was laced with sarcasm, but he continued, "I have found that a teacher who is not only passionate about their subject, but willing and able to successfully pass their knowledge on, is an invaluable treasure."

She was flattered by his sincerity and asked, "What is your profession?"

She saw a sheepish grin form on his face before he answered, "I…am a professor. Although I often question whether it was my true calling. Let's just say that my chosen subject deals with matters of…science…and nature."

She could hear his hesitation and the vagueness of his reply, but she did not want to spoil the light mood by pressing for more specifics. She continued instead.

"I didn't want to give up my job. I loved my students and my school, but I was sent word that my grandfather was ailing, and needed more care, and after my husband had passed, the ties that had kept me there before were no longer strong enough to keep me from going to my grandfather. I had only been overseas once before to see him when I was very young, but we kept in contact through letters. I was very fond of him, as he was of me."

She stopped for a moment, as if in brief pensive thought before continuing. "It wasn't too long thereafter before I found myself here. I spent only a few short seasons caring for him in his lovely home full of old books and his eccentric collection of souvenirs."

She was pulled from the warm memory by his response. "I'm sorry for your loss," he replied thoughtfully.

She knew it was her own fault that he had misunderstood her words, and she corrected her own error. "Oh no! Thank you, but he didn't pass away. He is still living."

She stopped suddenly, a terrifying thought suddenly hitting her, and she shook her head quickly in confusion. "Actually, I don't know...I'm sorry, I...have only dreams of the last time I saw him, and I'm still not sure if they are real memories or just part of a nightmare I can't seem to shake."

Severus could hear the sudden distress in her voice, and although he didn't want their conversation to turn unpleasant, he had a foreboding that this may be a window into the mystery of her arrival into his life.

"Can you tell me about it...your nightmare?" he asked gently, hoping that talking about it might relieve some of her distress as well as open the window further into her world.

"I'm sorry," she said a little shakily. "I..." She almost said she didn't remember, but then, she thought of her promise to be completely truthful with this man. "I see my grandfather's face in the dream, his expression one of rage and anguish. He is running towards our neighbor's house, and I'm running after him. Dear friends of ours live there, and I know there is something happening there, something very bad, and I'm worried because I don't know what could be so dangerous as to make my grandfather so desperate to try and stop it."

She abruptly uncoiled from his lap and stood, walking to slide the Quidditch book back into the only empty spot in his bookcase. He felt a twinge of regret, already missing the closeness they were sharing. She was standing in front of his bookcase, her eyes closed in thought. He rose from his chair, and slowly approached from behind. Part of him was afraid she might reject his attempt at comforting her, but he was willing to risk the sting of rejection, gently placing his hands on her shoulders, leaning his head down to lightly rest his chin on her head. She did not reject his closeness and reached to place her hand on top of his. They stood like this for a while, each to their own thoughts, simply comforted by each other's presence.

Chapter 13

Muggle

Severus dreaded the next day, which had nothing to do with teaching his classes. He usually found his job as a professor at Hogwarts eventful, and could usually find some pleasure in tormenting his students, trying to drill something into some of their thick skulls. Some skulls were thicker than others, and he doubted that Ronald Weasley had much besides solid bone sitting on his shoulders.

Professor Snape began each semester at Hogwarts vowing to himself that he would teach each of his students at least one useful thing—as among the many things they might learn, there could be that one thing that would be useful in the dangerous times he knew were coming.

He did not hold much affection for his students, and he knew he was often reviled by most students at Hogwarts—except for those in his own house, Slytherin. Even those students often did not like their stern taskmaster, but they relished in his extensive knowledge and power and jockeyed for their chance to move up in the ranks of the magical community.

Although he would not admit to having an affinity for any of his students, there were those who were...*more important* to him than others. The likes of Harry Potter was like a festering thorn in his side—and yet, he could see a part of Lily in the boy's eyes and knew that he would give all of himself to protect him. In fact, Severus knew that he would protect them all till his own ending, whether they were aware of it or not. No, he did not dread his days of teaching, but tomorrow, he must begin the tasks that the Dark Lord had laid out before him, and that would take all of his focused determination whilst hovering above the precarious precipice that lay between his sworn allegiances. If he failed to succeed in performing this macabre balancing act, it would put in motion the ending of Hogwarts, and perhaps devastation even beyond its walls.

Severus's dark thoughts were broken when Sirana lowered her hand from his and turned to face him, almost shyly. Perhaps she had felt the dropping in temperature as the icy chill of his thoughts permeated his stoic form.

"There are things I would like to—well, that we need to talk about," Sirana said, unsure of how to begin.

She had felt the shift in mood and remembered that there were things she must address about this unlikely situation she found herself in. Sirana knew that the current pretense of having all the time in the world to, she tried unsuccessfully to reject the expression, 'play house,' was not realistic, even in this surreal existence. She would, however, remain affable to this man while he continued to do so to her. She found that she enjoyed his company, noticing he was a quiet, solemn man, and so, she found herself enjoying the few words he did say. Finding herself fixating on his resonate voice, his intonation, the way his lips seemed to caress each word, and when he did rarely give the hint of a smile, she felt her middle warm deep within. She chided herself for thinking like some lovesick schoolgirl. Yes, she probably could stay here indefinitely, living in a charade of blissful ignorance, but it went so much against her character of being in complete control of her own life that her mind forcefully rejected the mere concept. She had been given the opportunity to recover herself from the cruelty she had endured at the hands of Lucius Malfoy, and she was ready to confront whatever truth was laid out before her.

Severus raised an eyebrow, and replied in a serious, almost regretful tone, "Indeed." He held his hand out towards the dining table, "Please, join me," he said courteously, holding his hand out towards the dining table. "I have some bread and wine that we can share while we talk."

He knew it would have to come down to this. He could not expect to keep her as his prisoner, nor would he imagine her willingness to live as a consenting captive, playing mistress of his house, willfully accepting whatever he doled out to her without question. He had seen the fire in her eyes and her mind, and he acknowledged the choice of her own fate.

He served them both a plate of bread and poured them each an ample glass of wine. As they ate and drank, he noticed her watching him through veiled lids, and realized he was doing the same to her. Each of them had multitudes to say, and yet, it would seem that neither wanted to begin. Perhaps they were both hesitant to break the pleasant mystique that had surrounded them since her arrival. Finally, he gathered his goblet and bottle of wine, moving to sit adjacent to Sirana at the table. He topped off his own glass, noting she had hardly touched hers.

"Is the wine not to your liking? I have others if you would prefer," he asked, wanting to assure her comfort.

"Oh, no, thank you. It's lovely," she answered pleasantly, lifting her glass and taking a longer sip reassuringly.

"You have been a most welcome guest," he began slowly, "although an unexpected one. I would like to imagine that your stay has been...agreeable..." he drawled slowly, attempting to read her responses in real time before continuing, "I hope that you have at least found my accommodations more pleasant than those previously..." He was not one to look past finding a humorous dialog even in the most somber of circumstances, and he was rewarded at seeing a small smile turn up at the corner of Sirana's lips, even though she timidly looked down at her wine.

He was relieved to see that Lucius had not wounded her so deeply as to cause her continued discomfort at the remembrance. He pressed on. "I would like to share with you my intentions, however; they have not revealed themselves—even to me. In honor of the honesty that we promised, I will tell you that I did not deliver you from an unfortunate fate at Lucius's hands because I am a saintly benefactor. Although my intentions towards you are not malevolent, I will not dissimulate the presumption of innocence." He paused as he took in her response, observing her intently, then slowly continued, "As much as I would like to keep you here as my...*guest*, I must first provide you with answers to any inquiries you may have to ensure that you are able to make your decision based upon an adequate understanding of your... situation."

Sirana took another sip of her wine, trying not to drink too much as her tolerance had always been low. Her face was already beginning to feel pleasantly warm. Although she appreciated that it took the edge off the conversation, she needed to keep her wits about her now. There were so many questions she needed to ask. There was so much she needed to learn about where she was and how she got here.

"What is a Muggle?" She was a little surprised that that was the first question that jumped in queue past the more important questions, skipping right out of her mouth.

The same surprise registered on his face as he answered, "A Muggle...A Muggle is a person who is not of magical bloodlines—one who does not possess any magical abilities. As you may have already surmised, those who reside here are not Muggles."

He paused, and she asked, "If you are not Muggles, what exactly are you? And where exactly is 'here'?"

He replied in measured tones, "'Here' would be Hogwarts School of Witchcraft and Wizardry, and 'we' are wizards and witches."

Sirana absorbed that information with as open a mind as she could muster. She took another long sip of wine, reflecting with amusement that perhaps she should have imbibed more heartily from the beginning.

"Was Lucius's home also at Hogwarts School, or was that another place?" she asked, trying to piece all of it together.

"No, the Malfoys live in Wiltshire, and although they are obviously not Muggles, their home is located outside the grounds of Hogwarts," he explained.

Sirana could tell that she would need to ask each specific question in turn, seeing that he was not the type to elaborate voluntarily. "So, are Muggles welcomed here? Are there others like me?"

She could see a smile turn one corner of his mouth, and he replied with a tinge of irony, "No, there are no others like you…" he said in a low, silky voice, looking down at his own glass.

She could feel her face suddenly get even warmer than the wine could excuse, and her embarrassment that he may notice ramped up the temperature even more so. Anyone who really knew her considered her to be tough as nails—a strong, confident, resilient woman. And yet, she had always known that one of her biggest weaknesses was that her face couldn't hide anything, and those who knew her as such lovingly delighted in this trait.

Chapter 14

Blush

Severus looked back up from his wine, swearing he could feel the heat radiating from the lovely woman's face, which had turned several deeper shades of red. He felt a little wicked when he pointed it out to her.

"Are you not feeling well? Perhaps the wine was not to your liking after all..." he smirked in mock concern. Severus saw her place the back of her hand on her cheeks and forehead as if to cool them, and he wondered if perhaps she were feeling faint.

"No," she insisted. "Really, I'm just not accustomed to drinking so much wine. I'm just a little flushed. I'll be fine," she continued as she absently took another drink.

He smirked. "Wonderful. Perhaps a recess is in order, regardless. It would appear that you are as much a mystery to me as I am to you. And as much as I would like to...*rectify* that, we have all day to do so."

Sirana's face was on fire now—or at least she thought she could smell smoke coming from her ears. She could see through his banter easily enough, as it was skillfully humorous and teasingly suggestive, but it still both delighted and embarrassed her. She was no delicate flower, wilting in the sunlight, and admittedly, she had always been a passionate woman, drawn to the passions of others—professionally and personally. She felt that draw to Severus, and wondered how such a quiet, almost expressionless man could exude so much passion, as if it radiated from his aura.

Her late husband had been a sweet, loving soul, and although he seemed to thrive under her passionate demeanor, he lacked much of his own. He was content to pass the days in each other's company as contented companions, while lovingly offering her unwavering support for her own passions, she thought reverently. This man in front of her was a different sort of animal…a horse of a different color, she mused. She could feel her passion equally matched, if not exceeded, in his nature.

"Yes, a break would be nice, but one thing first…you said that we have all day to figure out my mystery…Does that mean we 'only' have today?" she asked. She thought that she could imagine seeing his face blush almost imperceptibly at that, and wondered briefly why, until she thought about the possible interpretation of her own question. She took another sip of wine.

Severus thought about her last question, and he knew what she meant, but a part of him imagined she was asking in a way that meant that she longed for them to retain each other's company for even more time. After he saw her take another sip of wine, thinking she must have realized her unintentional innuendo, he refilled her glass without asking, topping off his own. He rose and offered her his hand formally. She took his hand, looking a little unsteady as she rose, and he was grateful that he had made the offer to assist her standing before she actually required it. He smiled inwardly, finding it endearing that she was so unaccustomed to a single glass of wine.

He escorted her over to the living room, each with their full goblets in hand, and he was a bit intrigued as to what the second glass might do for her mood. She was smiling warmly up at him, and she asked him in good humor, "So, you might need to remind me where it is that I should sit, as I may have forgotten the agreed-upon arrangement."

Cheeky devil, Severus thought, reminded that the last time they sat in his living room she was on his lap. He couldn't help but adore her flirtatious mood, and as they reached the sitting area, he sat his glass down on the small side table. He then took her glass from her and sat it down as well, all the while holding her hand, unwilling to break contact. He used his now free hand to wrap it around her waist, pulling her to him.

He almost lost his control in not letting a laugh escape when she asked him, tongue-in-cheek, "How are we supposed to dance if there is no music?"

He released her, stepped back, and retrieved her glass of wine, handing it back to her. "Please, wait here for just one moment."

With that, he left to his study, returning with what appeared to be a small record player. He arranged it on a corner table, turning it on, and carefully set the needle to a specific groove in the disk. He turned and retrieved her glass, once again setting it down next to his, then resumed the position they were in before her question.

Chapter 15

Dance

S irana knew she had deserved this turn of events. "Her comeuppance," as her grandfather would say. She had enjoyed teasing Severus, for a minute forgetting that he had already proved himself to be a formidable match.

"Ask, and it shall be granted to you," Severus said prophetically, before sweeping her in to motion. There was adequate floor between the living and dining room for their dance. Her soft-slippered shoes padded gracefully across the hard floor as he confidently led her in a formal dance in tune with the music. She was a bit astonished that he was such an accomplished dancer. She was equally grateful that she was a studied ballroom dancer herself. She didn't know this particular music or dance, but he was adept at leading her flawlessly into each move. She felt giddy and light, and her partner appeared to be commensurately enjoying himself, his expression as light as she had seen it since their meeting. The song ended, as did their dance, but instead of releasing her from his hold, he drew her closer to him, bringing their joined hands in closer. The tempo of the next song was slower and stronger, and she felt his heated breath on her face as he lowered his head next to hers, and they danced a hypnotically sensual dance unto its stormy crescendo.

As the song and their dance came to an end, Severus observed that Sirana's face was no longer alarmingly red, but he could still see the rosy flush that had settled in her cheeks. They both breathed heavily from more than the exertion from their dance. He didn't release her though, and instead, freed his hand from hers, first tracing her cheek with the back of his fingers, then more fervently moving his hand to her hair, his fingers splayed, to pull her towards him. He paused to look at her through heavy, veiled eyes. He stopped his mouth only a breath away from hers, assuring his own control over himself, before consuming her with a scorching fierceness. He felt her hand land firmly on his chest, and instead of pushing away as he first feared, she moved her hand up his chest to the back of his neck, grasping the collar of his jacket to bring him in to deepen the already impossibly deep kiss. He moaned lowly, almost a growl, as he felt her body press into his. When the moment felt right, he slowed the pace momentarily, then shifting his head over hers, still cradling her head in his hand, slipped his tongue into her mouth. She stopped all motion as if momentarily stunned before accepting his offering with her soft, warm mouth, and he heard a low moan from her. He slid her outer gown off her shoulders and down her back, pulling the fabric to bring her in closer to him. Bending her down and back, he trailed hot flames with his mouth down into her neck. He heard her ragged breath and he pressed himself harder against her, trailing hard kisses back to her mouth. He didn't know if he could endure another moment, and it was a test of his will to withstand the storm that was driving him to lose the last hold he had on his control. He finally broke their hold to grab her shoulders to face him. He saw the flames of desire in his own eyes reflected in hers, and his mind reached into hers none too gently to feel the heat of her own inferno.

"Please, Sirana," Severus said in a desperately low tone. "Come with me to my bed. I want to know you...*all* of you... and I have never been so certain about anything before in my lifetime."

Chapter 16

Innocence

Sirana was past the point of coherent thought, and she knew she couldn't blame the wine for the heat she was feeling this time. There was too much leading up to this point that she hadn't been fully prepared for—his confident humor, the sensual masculinity of his dance, the fierceness balanced by the tenderness, the eagerness to please and be pleased. There was a deep ache tightening inside her, and every touch of his mouth, hands, and body worked against easing it, yet sending her to look for more.

"Yes," she exclaimed breathlessly, "Even if the walls were burning down around us, I would not try to stop this."

"Are you certain?" Severus asked, as if he was in disbelief that it had come to this, that this beautiful woman somehow saw the same beauty in him.

"I am more certain of this than of anything," she reassured him, and with the look in her eyes, she knew he didn't dare question her complete honesty.

She squealed a little in surprise as he managed to swing her up and into his arms with seemingly no effort, carrying her as if she were a bride into his bedroom. She suddenly felt a nervous rush threatening to overwhelm her. The break in their passion was enough for her senses to return momentarily, and she suddenly felt the vivid reality of the intimacy they were about to share.

Severus felt her almost imperceptibly tense in his arms. His mind gently brushed against hers, and he felt it—the strange, nervous innocence. He looked down into her face and smiled reassuringly. He was warmed by the naïve trust her mind revealed, which was mirrored in her timid, unguarded smile. He was reminded of Lucius's declaration of her purity, and despite her contrary assertations, what he found in her mind contained no indication to dispute Lucius's claim. He delved a little deeper into her mind, wanting to know which was truth, finding faded memories made of misty shadows and tender reverence. Whatever magic had brought her here must have truly renewed certain aspects of her body and mind, and he felt no deception within her. His desire for her exploded as he suddenly felt another emotion seep in and take hold in his own mind, and he knew that his heart may not survive this unmarked.

Chapter 17

Whisper

Severus set Sirana down on her feet at the side of his bed. He placed his hands on the sides of her face, holding her gently to look down into her trusting face.

"Sirana," he said in low, even tones. "We have more than just today. I will be here tomorrow; I will be here as long as you need me here. As much as I want you, I want *all* of you, not just this. You need simply say 'wait', and I will wait for you."

Sirana heard his tender words and her heart melted. Her nervousness faded, and she realized that she wanted nothing more than to know the whole depth of this man. She suddenly felt that a lifetime would not be long enough.

She reached up and placed her hands on his, softly smiling. "I would not ask to wait for what I equally desire. By intention or not, I have felt you touch my mind. Touch it now and you will see the truth in my mind and my body."

Severus was surprised that she had known he had entered her mind, but he willingly obeyed and entered now to find fire again, but instead of pain, the flames were those of passion, desire, and...love? All of it engulfed him, and he could feel himself being willingly consumed. He heard her gasp as he met her inferno with his own. When he emerged from her mind, he lowered his head again to kiss her, knowing there were no more words needed.

Severus slid his hands down her silky shoulders, this time to completely rid her of her outer robe, letting it fall to her feet. He started to loosen the ties on her gown, but she gently brushed his hands aside to reach up and remove his outer jacket in turn, unbuttoning his multitude of buttons. She felt his broad chest through his white shirt and felt the urgent need to touch his skin. She had never seen an ascot before in person and fumbled a bit with it. She saw his mouth turn up in smile, and he replaced her hands with his to remove it in a flourish. She started to reach for the buttons of his shirt, but since it was his turn, he went back for her gown. His hands worked quickly to loosen her ties, and let her gown fall to join her robe on the floor at her feet. She saw the look of lustful appreciation in his eyes and might have blushed if she were to actually have any coherent thoughts left in her. She reached up to the top of the row of the numerous buttons on his shirt, working as quickly as she could manage, wishing to herself that there was a hidden zipper.

They were both breathing heavily with anticipation, and as if he could no longer wait, Severus pulled his shirt out of his trousers and started to quickly work on the buttons from the bottom up. At the last one, he removed his shirt hastily, tossing it to the side along with any plans of waiting for any more turns. He saw the appreciation in her eyes now as she spread her hands flat against his chest and then moved them down his torso to the soft, black hair on his lower stomach. When she began unfastening the clasp of his pants, he could no longer hold back from reaching for her, quickly removing her undergarments. As soon as he shed his trousers, he scooped her up and followed her down into the bed, covering her open lips with his own. He raised up on one side to look down into her eyes, which were darkened with their own passion.

Sirana felt her body shaking now, not with fear, but with anticipation and lustful need building in her. She looked back into his eyes as he caressed the soft skin of her breast. He moved his mouth down and kissed her other breast, moving closer and closer towards her nipple, which was tightening into a hard peak. Her body was starting to writhe with anticipation. He finally moved his hot mouth onto her nipple, and she couldn't help but arch her body and moan as he moved his tongue around her nipple and rubbed her other nipple between his fingers at the same time. She could feel the pleasure run a line down her stomach to settle in her core, and she breathed out his name, "…Severus…"

When she felt she couldn't take anymore, he moved his mouth back up to hers. She knew the intensity of his desire matched hers as she could feel the hardness of him pressing against her through his boxers. She ran her fingers into his long hair, grasping onto him desperately.

Severus raised up again, looking down at her beautiful face, which was made even more lovely with her desire for him. Her eyes were closed with inner passion, and he kissed her lips softly once more before moving his hand down her body to caress her soft, downy curls. His own desperate need was building, and he felt the tightness that ached with hard desire. Severus watched her expression as he slid his finger into her warm slit. He was almost undone when he felt her body tremor and heard the sounds of surprised pleasure come from her. He began moving his fingers in a slow rhythm over her but was careful not to delve too deep as he wanted to save that pleasure for when he entered her completely.

"Please...Severus..." she pleaded breathlessly as she grasped at his shoulders. He could take no more of this sweet agony, and he removed the constrictive underwear in one swift motion.

Severus lowered onto her, and she instinctively moved her legs apart. He embraced her in a final passionate kiss, leaning his head down to her ear, his voice deep and dark with the desire he fought to hold in check just a moment longer, whispering as if not to break the spell, "Sirana...I do not wish to hurt you, yet I cannot hold back from you any longer."

She nodded as if quietly steeling herself. Severus reached down, grabbing her soft hips to bring her up to meet him, his body quaking with the effort of restraint, then slid the length of himself inside her with one swift motion. She cried out, and he saw her eyes flash open. He stopped all movement until she made it past the initial shock of his entry. He could feel her hot and tight around him, and his own resolve almost broke, his own throaty cry escaping, "Sirana..." Her breath slowed as the pain eased and he saw her expression deepen to show her mutual need, hearing her reassuring whisper.

Chapter 18

Ecstasy

The exquisite madness of it...sharp pain mixed with intense pleasure...the feeling of him, all of him, filling her to the brink of her limit...the impossible intimacy of it...Sirana cried out with the shock of it all. Her eyes met Severus's, and she wouldn't trade the world for the sight before her now—the deep, powerful need in his dark eyes, the expression of loving concern for her, his sultry mouth slightly open in passion. She could feel his body quaking, and she knew the effort he must be exerting to wait for her, to hold back his impassioned need until she was ready. She felt the brief pain pass, leaving nothing but the powerful need to continue, to completely give herself into this rapture, and she let him know she was ready. He started again slowly, sliding out almost completely, and the relief of him leaving the depth of her brought out a gasp from her. A low, almost feral groan came from him before driving back deeply into her, and he continued thrusting into her in a maddeningly slow rhythm. Her cries were now from pleasure, and she felt a fire growing within her that he stoked with every stroke. She wrapped her legs around him wildly, the movement opening herself to allow him to find a depth of herself she didn't know was possible, and she cried out his name.

Severus had never known this sweet ecstasy. When Sirana wrapped her legs around him, it almost sent him over the edge of control. He slowed the pace, relishing in every moment of each sensation, and was vividly aware of the heat rising within Sirana, which was matched with the fire building within himself. He would see her to this inevitable end, and he let his mind slip into hers once more. He was met with a white-hot flash of burning pleasure and he gasped from the intensity of it. There was no barrier between them now, of their body or mind, and he felt enraptured in the euphoric sensations. His long thrusts shortened to a quicker pace, still driving deeply into the core of her. He felt her erupt into her sweet release, setting off the spark to ignite his own explosion, rocking him hard, and he could no longer tell where he ended and where she began, as if their beings had merged into one glorious culmination. He knew that any magic that he had ever experienced could not compare, and he wished for a magic capable of keeping them in this moment eternally.

Chapter 19

Merciful

"I have found that, while it is true that life is rarely equitable, it is once and again known to be merciful."

Severus thought of the words Albus had said to him as he dressed in preparation to teach his classes at Hogwarts as he had a thousand times before. Today, nothing felt the same. The routine of getting dressed for the day—buttoning his jacket and sleeves; donning his black, flowing robe; combing through his long, black hair…it was all familiar, but different.

Severus looked in the mirror—*he* was different. He looked back to the bed where Sirana was still sleeping. He wished he could stay. After last night, he didn't want her to wake up alone. He thought about leaving her a note, and he smirked at the thought of what he could possibly write that would match what was in himself, what he couldn't even find words to speak that would come close to telling. He withdrew his wand and produced a single flower, a daisy, and laid it on his pillow next to her.

To new beginnings, he thought wistfully, *and to innocence.*

He gathered the books he planned to use for his classes and left to meet the day. Severus knew his heart felt softer, but he was keenly aware that he must not let that change his hardened resolve to see the events to come to their as yet uncertain end. He had much to do, besides just leading his classes, and it would take his unwavering focus to see them through.

Professor Snape burst through the doors to his classroom, walking in long strides, his robes billowing behind him. He didn't meet the eyes of any of his students before gruffly commanding, "Has any of you NOT successfully completed the assignment I gave you for the weekend?"

He inwardly pitied whoever was going to raise their hand, because he was in a right foul mood for being in the classroom when he had so many other places he would rather be today, needed to be. Two students raised their hands warily, a boy and a girl.

"Fine. I have two volunteers for today's subject matter. Please make your way to the front of the class expeditiously." He knew that he had the reputation of being a bit of a bully. He also knew that life was not kind, and what adversity his students may face from him would not even begin to match what they would face out in the real world. He refused to coddle them to their own detriment. He thought of Sirana then. What kind of teacher had she been? He could almost imagine adoring students being nurtured by her tough but fair sensibility. One corner of his mouth crept up in a smile, and he heard Ronald Weasley whisper to Harry Potter, "Look, he enjoys torturing kids so much, it's the only time he smiles."

Severus shot him a stare so menacing that the poor boy practically shriveled in his seat. "You! Mr. Weasley, I just realized

I need a third volunteer." He met eyes with Harry Potter, and the boy wisely refrained from commenting, however, Potter's glare did not go unnoticed by him, and he was once again reminded of his disdain for Potter's hubristic nature. Severus heard snickers throughout the classroom, but everyone stopped and sat alert in their seats as he glared across the room looking for more volunteers.

The rest of the morning went equally well, and it was finally time for lunch in the Grand Hall. Severus sat in his usual spot up on the elevated platform. He greeted each of his fellow colleagues with a curt nod. Headmaster Dumbledore caught his eye as he passed, and he could feel his face start to warm. Dumbledore grinned conspiratorially, taking his own seat in the center of the table. Suddenly, Severus realized that he had left nothing for Sirana to eat. There was some food in his rooms, but not in an obvious place where she might find it. He had planned on staying away for most of the day, as he had tasks to achieve today that exceeded those of his teaching duties. He gathered his lunch and hurriedly made his apologies before leaving.

Dumbledore stopped him before he could make his exit, casually asking as he passed, "Professor Snape, all is well I hope?"

"Yes, thank you. I have simply forgotten something back in my rooms that I require for my teachings," Severus replied coolly.

"Ah, very well, carry on," Dumbledore replied with an odd look and a dismissive wave.

Severus found himself walking more briskly than he could account to himself for. He knew he had plenty of time before his next class as he never had a class scheduled following the midday meal. He slowed his pace and self-consciously wondered why he was breathing so laboriously. He was not in the mood to examine his feelings, and promptly pushed his anxiousness to the side as he opened the door. Sirana was sitting in 'her' chair, curled up like a kitten with a book in her hands. He noted that she had half a dozen more waiting on the arm of her chair. His mood softened perceptibly when she smiled up warmly to him. He noticed that she had placed the daisy in her hair over her ear and thought pleasantly how it suited her.

"Well, hello," Sirana said happily as Severus entered. He looked quite debonair in his formal clothes.

"I apologize for not giving you notice that I would be leaving to resume my teaching duties today," Severus said matter-of-factly.

Sirana noticed his formal tone and understood that his demeanor naturally did not show the warmth that she knew was in him. She also knew that her own personality was not as malleable as to hide her warm nature in order to conform. Although she had been envious of those women who were naturally mysterious, her own attempts at emulating them in her youth were embarrassingly comical. She had decided that being herself was much easier to manage.

"It's alright. I'm sorry for sleeping so late. I'm not usually one to sleep in, but I was especially tired this morning," she said, instantly kicking herself for her word choices considering last night. It seemed her athletic abilities crossed over nicely into her talent at sticking her foot in her mouth, in which she was quite adept.

"Indeed," Severus replied, locking eyes with hers as if challenging her not to look down in embarrassment. She met the challenge, but her face betrayed her once again by blushing hotly.

He seemed satisfied with that and continued, "I also apologize for not setting out something for your meal. I have been a neglectful host. It would seem I'm out of practice."

She smiled at that, "I wouldn't say that. I think you've been a *very* attentive host," and decided to kick herself later for all of her unintentional, but humorously appropriate, innuendos. She was at least glad she hadn't said anything flippant about him being out of practice. She could almost swear his face gained some color at that, but he turned quickly to the table, setting down the bundle he was carrying.

"I brought lunch with me. I thought my earlier oversight could become a welcome opportunity to share it with you," he said without giving away any emotions.

"That's lovely. Thank you, " Sirana replied, joining him eagerly at the table.

They sat at the table together, and Severus noticed that the mood between them was noticcably different. There was once again no awkwardness in the room, but neither was there a sense that they were strangers. It was warm, comfortable, amiable… with a pervading sense of electric excitement. He had spoken before of magic that could 'ensnare the senses,' and that magic paled to the ensnarement that he felt by merely being in her presence. He promptly branded himself a foolish schoolboy, fawning over a crush. He portioned out their lunch and retrieved a bottle of wine and glasses, knowing that performing tasks usually gave him the opportunity to bring discipline back to his emotions.

He noted that she gingerly sipped on the wine, and he smiled inwardly. "Might I inquire as to your choice of reading material? I hope you've found something to interest you in the sparse collection I keep here?"

"Sparse?" Sirana replied. "I would have loved to have such a nice collection. My grandfather had a wonderful collection of books himself that I always wanted to explore. But he was always very private about the items he kept in his study, and I would only sometimes get a glimpse when he passed in or out of the doors. He would often bring a book out to lend to me that he thought I might enjoy."

Severus noticed she hadn't directly answered his question—once again—and he thought that she was quite good at that. He would get back to that though, as he was more interested in pursuing the subject at hand.

"Tell me about your grandfather. Have you suffered any more nightmares about him?" Severus asked, leading the conversation. There was something about her nightmare that had piqued his interest.

"Yes. I did have a dream last night. But it wasn't a nightmare," she said, and he noticed that she blushed again.

He almost felt a twinge of sympathy for her adorable awkwardness, and showed her more pity this time by not pointing it out to her, asking instead, "What was your grandfather's profession?"

Grateful to return to the conversation, she answered, "He was a professor as well, funnily enough. He taught history. I'm embarrassed to say I don't know where he taught. I guess the subject never came up. He was the most interesting person I've ever talked to—present company excluded." The last part must have slipped out past her censor, which had obviously taken the day off.

"Quite the flattery, miss...?" Severus left the question hanging in the air. He really was flattered by her words, and even wondered what had prompted her to say them. He hoped she would take the nudge to answer the question she had left unanswered the other day.

"*Mrs.* Trahern. I kept my husband's name of course, after he passed," she explained.

"And what was your maiden name?" Severus asked curiously.

"Cadogen," she supplied. "I'm told it means 'glory in battle,' although I've never thought to look it up to verify. It is my mother's maiden name too, oddly enough. She insisted on keeping her maiden name, and that I take it as well. Maybe it had to do with my father's last name...it is said that its history was unfortunate. My grandfather, Kane Cadogen, said his first name actually means 'warrior.' And my name means 'born with blue eyes.'" She smiled shyly at that.

Yes, he had noticed her beautiful eyes and their unusual shade of blue. He stared into them now, feeling some sort of recognition of her maiden name that she shared with her grandfather. Surely he'd heard it before. Maybe he'd read it somewhere. Perhaps it would come to him once his mind was clearer. Now, he brought the conversation back to his initial question. "What books have you found to read here? I see you have quite the queue on your chair."

He knew that all of the books in the common area were appropriate for her to read. Any books that he wouldn't want her to have access to were in his study, which he kept locked in his absence. He felt a momentary twinge of regret at that. He didn't want to hide anything from her, but he put that out of his mind, acknowledging the necessity.

"Ha!" She answered with a quick smile. "I'm embarrassed to admit that I've chosen most based on whether or not they are illustrated. Although I wouldn't call them picture books…"

His mood always seemed lighter in her presence, and he found it difficult to keep up his stony façade. He let a small smile reach his mouth. "I will be sure to keep a look out for more…*illustrated* books…to add to my collection. And perhaps those dealing with physical education and athletics," he said with a hint of teasing. "My collection at home is a hundredfold in comparison."

Her eyes widened at that. "That's impressive. I could spend a lifetime there!" she exclaimed.

He raised an eyebrow at that and saw her face flush once again. He was beginning to rather enjoy this game and had a wish for himself that it too would last a lifetime.

Chapter 20

Gossamer

"So, are you done for the day, or will you need to go back to school?" Sirana asked, feeling him warm up to the conversation, not wanting it to end.

"I must return for my afternoon classes, and regrettably, I may not be returning until late in the evening as I have other duties that I must see to." Severus sounded genuinely saddened by that. "I hope that you can find ample books to keep your interest until I return. I must apologize again for being a neglectful host."

She smiled warmly. "Please, don't worry about me. I love reading. I will be as snug as a bug in a rug."

She saw his face soften at her expression. Something crossed her mind that she'd meant to bring up with him this evening. Since he may not return until later, she needed to address it now, although grudgingly. "I am embarrassed to ask, but I'm afraid that, well, um…"

"I have found that the best way to say something is to use words to form a sentence," Severus replied tongue-in-cheek, at her hesitation.

She chuckled, some of her trepidation fading with his humorous jab. "You're right. I'm afraid that the sheets need laundering—well, the bedding," she coughed nervously and continued. "I would have done so already, but I couldn't find anything to do so with."

Severus suddenly realized why she was hesitant to share the dilemma with him. He had known from their lovemaking that she was indeed a virgin, and although the charm of the bath would have worked for themselves, the bedding would show the telltale signs.

"Ah, yes, another oversight I have failed to perform as your host—a bit of housekeeping," he replied in good humor. He rose and removed his wand from his robe, walking to the entrance to the bedroom before casting his spell to clean and arrange the room. He returned to her at the table, stepping up behind her chair.

"Thank you," she said, smiling up to him gratefully.

"You are more than welcome," he said, then leaned down to whisper in her ear. "Never be embarrassed to ask me for anything you need—or want."

Some things are more easily said as a whisper. He saw her small nod, and heard her breath catch, as if she didn't trust herself to speak. He could smell the daisy that was still in her hair, and he kissed her ear just below it, hearing her draw in a quick breath. He swore to himself. He would give his eye teeth to have a spell to slow down time so he could spend it here, but he mused that he would be too old and withered to fulfill his obligations before he would want to end the spell. The visual image that thought conjured was both sublime and somber, as he knew that the morrow would not see him to be a graying old man, passing peacefully in his bed. But he would not let his pensiveness spoil this time he had with Sirana, and he gently brushed her hair aside with his hand, lowering to kiss the side of her neck. He stepped to the side of her chair, lowering down to one knee beside her, almost even with her now, and moving his hand to her face, brought her gently to him in a kiss.

Sirana's amazement at this enigma of a man was seemingly never ending. He had kissed her soundly, leaving no doubt of his feelings for her, foretelling of promises of things to come. When they finally broke the kiss, she placed her hand gently on the side of his face. He gathered her hand in his and kissed it. Kissing the inside of her palm and her wrist.

He stood, pulling her up with him. "I will return to you with all possible haste," Severus said huskily.

Sirana smiled, "Please do, and don't spare the horses." They shared a smile at that. She watched as he left like he didn't want to risk lingering too long and changing his mind. She had a feeling of foreboding, as if he was going away to a battle. The room was suddenly empty as never before, but then, she felt it, as if there was a gossamer thread of silver light connecting them, and she felt the internal courage that it fortified in each of them.

Severus had tried to avoid Professor Umbridge all semester, but the tyrannical Professor had made his attempt almost impossible. He had immediately seen past her sickly-sweet persona and was aware of her obsessive hunger for power. He had been careful to not let her know that he had been covertly working with the Potter boy or that he was aware that students had been meeting in the Room of Requirements to learn Dark Arts defenses. After Harry Potter and his friends had ask for assistance with the Patronus Charm, he had been curious, and was now working to assist them in keeping their secret hidden… without their awareness, of course.

Now, he found himself trapped in the hallway by the pink-clothed abomination who was spouting to him how well her lessons in the Dark Arts were going, and how Severus could perhaps sit in on one of her classes to take notes. He stared at the brick wall behind her, not wanting to look at her cloyingly sweet smile. He successfully resisted the urge to speak, knowing it would only delay his escape. Harry Potter would be waiting for by now for their lesson in Occlumency, and as much as Severus was beginning to dread the task, he knew the necessity of his efforts.

"Certainly, Professor Snape, since I too was in Slytherin when I was a student at Hogwarts, we have a mutual understanding of the need for extraordinary measures when it comes to discipline. I'm sure the students of Slytherin wouldn't mind assisting with enforcing those measures, and I would expect nothing less than your eager cooperation," Professor Umbridge said, her shrill voice growing louder with each word. Severus raised is eyebrow in silent response, unwilling to offer her his endorsement.

Professor Umbridge must have finally felt satisfied with her parting message, shooing him away with a dismissive gesture. She obviously had no idea of his reputation as a formidable wizard, or of his ties to the Dark Lord, or perhaps she was so singularly focused on her own quest to aggrandize herself that she simply didn't care. If he was fortunate, he would be presented the opportunity in the future to serve her a slice of his homemade humble pie. That sublime thought brought a smug smile to his face, and he saw her take a quick doubletake, eyeing him warily before he turned on his heel to make his abrupt exit.

Severus found Harry Potter waiting for his arrival, sitting with his elbows on his knees, his head in his hands as if he was preparing himself for the lesson to come. "Tell me Potter, do you intend to apply yourself this evening, or do you plan on subjecting me to more mediocrity?" Severus said, hoping to goad some semblance of ardor for his instruction from the boy. "I can assure you; the Dark Lord will cut through your mind like warm butter if you do not learn to focus your thoughts," Severus warned as he prepared his implements for his instruction.

"Let's just get on with it, Professor. I'm sure the Dark Lord would no doubt find that your butter wouldn't even melt in his mouth," Harry replied, his insolent tone an obvious attempt to counter the cold countenance of the Potions Professor.

Severus bit back a spiteful reply, encouraged at least that he had elicited at least some emotion from Potter, even if it was impudence. Perhaps he would incorporate the importance of exercising prudence in this evening's lesson.

Chapter 21

Bath

Severus was not yet ready to return to his home at Hogwarts. He had endeavored to prepare Harry Potter for what was to come—to strengthen his mind against the threat of Lord Voldemort. It had been an odious task that always seemed to leave them both in a foul mood. Severus walked through the dark halls, trying to clear his mind of the unpleasantries of the day, feeling his dark thoughts being replaced by the more pleasant anticipation of seeing Sirana.

It was late now, and he was tired to the bone. He entered quietly, knowing Sirana was most likely asleep. He was glad that there was enough left of their shared lunch that he left for her earlier, otherwise he would be apologizing again to her. He poured himself some wine, planning to stay up a bit to prepare his lesson plan for the following day. Suddenly, he heard a noise, and it was not coming from the bedroom where he assumed Sirana would be. He drew his wand and stealthily followed the sound. The door to the bathroom was closed. Surely, she wouldn't be in there since there were adequate facilities in the bedroom. He opened the door and stepped in quickly, prepared for anything—almost anything. Sirana was sitting in a steaming bath, holding a book in one hand and a glass of wine in the other. His abrupt entrance had startled her, and he found it quite amusing that she was in a quandary as to how to place the items she was holding down to cover her nudeness. Severus wondered at her shyness, since they had shared exquisitely intimate moments already. They were still new to each other in many ways though, and although he longed for the day they would no longer be, a part of him enjoyed the journey of discovery.

She choked out a 'hello' as he walked to the side of the tub. "As I predicted, taking a bath for the sake of bathing. A very Muggle thing to do," he said, not revealing in his voice if he was just teasing her.

She managed to sit up and gently dropped the book to the floor, but she couldn't set down the wine glass without raising herself out of the water. As much as he was enjoying the sight, he didn't want to add to her discomfort. He pulled out his wand, and with a quick word, there was now a thick layer of bubbles to protect her modesty.

"Thank you, Severus," Sirana said, more at ease now with the blanket of bubbles. "I'd slept so late this morning that I wasn't tired," she explained. She looked up at him. He looked tired, and it looked like the exhaustion reached deep into his eyes. "Won't you join me? I just ran it, so it's still quite warm," she said with unexpected boldness, mostly teasing…mostly.

When he started to unbutton his jacket, she couldn't stop her mouth from dropping open. She quickly shut it when she realized it.

Bluff—called, she thought. She seriously did not know where to look. She didn't want to look away, but she felt herself blushing from her ears to her toes. His own gaze was unrelenting as he shed his jacket and proceeded to work on his shirt. He was quite impressive, his body standing over her, and she found she could no longer meet his eyes, instead taking in the whole glorious vision of him. She took a sip of her wine, her mouth suddenly parched. He reached out and took her wine glass, taking a long drink for himself, then sat it down on the floor to join her book. He stepped behind her, and she slid forward, taking the cue that he was going to sit behind her. He settled in behind her, his long legs stretching along beside her, and wrapped his arms around her, drawing her in tightly to him. It felt like nothing she had experienced before; he was a dangerously handsome man, and the closeness of him touching her was exciting in a way that was a bit overwhelming, but he also felt familiarly warm and comfortable, wrapped around her, like a favorite blanket. She laid her arms atop his and relaxed into his body.

Severus felt the trials from the day seep out of his body, the hot water working to relieve the tension in his muscles, the feel of her in his arms working to relieve the tension in his mind. He heard her light snore and kissed her lightly on the top of her head. He hadn't realized he had fallen asleep himself until he started to feel the chill of the water on his body. They must have slept there for at least an hour for the water to be so cold. He reached down to grab his wand, which he had placed on top of her book before he had gotten in the bath. He quietly charmed the water, and it slowly started warming up again. Severus felt Sirana stir, and she woke with a yawn, her arms stretching out high above her. The lovely sight and the unintentionally sensuous movement succeeded in rousing him from any tiredness left in him. He wrapped her with his arms once again, then leaned down to kiss her bare shoulder. Severus was rewarded with the sound of a contented purr. He kissed across her shoulders, gently moving her damp hair to make a trail of kisses to the other side of her neck, where he settled in with a deep, hot kiss. He kissed her neck down into her collarbone, then as she turned her face to meet him, he consumed her mouth in a fiery kiss. He grabbed her hips and pulled her up against him, and she moaned in his mouth. When he started moving her against him, seductively grinding her against his hardness, she pulled her mouth away from his, leaning her head back against his shoulder. He reached one hand across her to grab her breast and ran his other hand down the front of her, diving it down into the water to slide between her legs. Severus slid his fingers deep into her, and he groaned his satisfaction when he found her slick with desire for him. He felt her stomach tighten, and she curled forward, a throaty gasp coming from her. Feeling her response to him heightened his already hot-blooded desire. Severus leaned forward with her, maintaining his grasp on her, and drove his fingers in deep, pushing them in hard with each stroke, unrelenting until he felt her warm wetness gush over him, her tight sleeve squeezing over and over in the shockwaves of her orgasm. Severus closed his eyes, his mouth open, his mind relishing in the pleasure he was able to elicit from her. The sounds escaping her lips were glorious, and he did not give her time to recover before spinning her around and lifting her on top of him, then sliding her down onto him.

She cried out his name in a breathy whisper, her breath catching as he grabbed her waist with his hands and drove her down onto him. He pulled her up and down onto him, again and again, in long, hard strokes, the water churning in the tub. Severus watched her lustfully as she leaned forward into him, grasping at his chest, pleading in sounds and words that it was too much for her. In one last thrust, he found his release, releasing his own deep throaty cry of pleasure. They lay heaving together in the still warm bath, unwilling to unjoin. When the water finally started to cool, she raised up and brushed his long, damp hair back from his face, then kissed his nose and forehead tenderly. Severus grabbed her tightly, then in one swift move, lifted them both up and out of the tub. She had only brought one towel, and he used it to dry off her beautifully quivering body, then handed it to her for her to follow suit, appreciating the intimacy of her attention. He swung her up in his arms, and again carried her to his bed. Whatever had transpired that day was no longer weighing on his mind, and he fell asleep in her warm embrace.

Chapter 22

Grandfather

Severus dressed as quietly as he could, hearing Sirana snoring lightly, not wanting to wake her. As he buttoned up his jacket, he looked over to her, and saw her quietly watching him, smiling like a cat that had just eaten the mouse.

"I hope you slept well," he said, walking over to the side of the bed.

"Yes, I slept wonderfully, thank you. And you?" she asked in return.

"I've never slept so well," he said, reaching down to lightly brush her cheek with the back of his fingers. He looked at her lovely face, her body wrapped up to the chin in the blankets, seeing no worries in her eyes. He wished things could stay like this forever, untouched by the events transpiring outside of this room. Severus wondered if he could keep her happy, contented to wait for him to come home to her every day. He knew that wouldn't be fair to her. He was sure that her current contentment was from the sense of safety from the dangers she had already found, and maybe even gratitude from his unwitting rescue of her from Lucius. He had seen and felt the fire within her. Eventually, she would want to continue her own life, whatever life she chose. He could only hope that he would be in her future. The spells he placed on his rooms were undetectable, yet powerful, but there were still risks. As long as Lucius knew of her existence, there were considerations he must address.

His tone became more serious. "You must know by now that you are not my prisoner. However, I must ask that you do not leave these rooms…at least for now. There are dangers outside of these walls that you have only had a glimpse of. There are events already set into motion in which I am grievously intwined." Severus's eyes darkened, and he said with a fierceness, "I will not see you wounded by my complicity." He felt this into his soul. He would die to protect her—even kill. He did not say the words, but he felt in her mind that she knew this to be true into the depth of her as well.

Severus felt something else, almost unexpected—Sirana's own resolve to protect him with all that she is, and the hard iron strength of her that steeled them, combining with his own to safeguard against any who would try to challenge their defenses. Severus thought of Albus Dumbledore's prophetic words—"You know that there is no path that is before you that would bring a favorable ending." Yes, he knew. But he also knew that even unto death, they would not be torn asunder. He had never felt so sure of anything, and he strode boldly towards his course.

Severus left the midday meal early again this afternoon. He knew he could not risk raising suspicion by returning to his rooms, so he had set out plenty of food for Sirana for the day. Instead, he headed to the library. He had a hunch, something he could not drag to the front of his mind, and he thought the library might hold some clues. *Cadogen*…that name. He didn't want to ask around and risk opening inquiries as to why he wanted to know. He couldn't even trust to ask Dumbledore until he knew more. Severus searched in the section that held books on the history of Hogwarts. It took all his lunch time and almost all of the period following. He'd scanned through book after book, making sure to put each back in its place so that no one could follow up and find a trail of his research. He finally found it. It was in a yearbook that went back to the midcentury. There he was, his picture alongside his name, sitting in his teaching robes with his hand placed atop an ornate globe—Professor Kane Cadogen. His sandy blonde hair spilled out from under his hat. His goatee was long and braided. Most telling of all, his blazing blue eyes sparkled with each movement of the picture. Severus felt a heavy stone settle in the pit of his stomach. It was but one piece of her puzzle, but the implications shook him.

He followed the lead and found that Professor Cadogen had held the post of Professor of History of Magic. He was a major player in the First Wizarding War, until the mid 70s, when he was replaced by Professor Binns. He was noted as leading a victorious battle during the war, but there was nothing he could find about his departure from Hogwarts.

Curious indeed, he thought. If Professor Kane was truly Sirana's grandfather, she was more than who she appeared to be. It was confirmation of what he had felt since he had found her. There were signs that he hadn't fully explored, not suspecting a revelation of this degree of significance. Severus touched at the thread connecting them still. They were joined, a bond that was greater than any connection attainable from a non-magic Muggle. He would consider going to Professor Dumbledore, but not as of yet. He had put Lily in Dumbledore's trust, and he has lost her. The thought of losing Sirana was gut-wrenching. There was a truth about Severus Snape that was unknown to many, perhaps even to his own self, and that undeniable truth was that he was not a coward, perhaps the furthest from it, and he would have the courage even to love again, even staring in the face of certain doom.

Chapter 23

Fair Play

Sirana knew that Severus would be late. He'd warned her as much. She wished she could help him with whatever he was up against. She had been reading—a lot. She had a talent of being able to scan through text, as if she was watching a movie, and she would retain most of what she'd seen—as if her mind sorted and categorized all the information into neat, little bins. She wished there was more. She wanted to be prepared to be at Severus's elbow when he needed her most. She knew Severus had more books in his study, but he'd locked them away from her. She knew he must have a reason. His words and actions as well as his very thoughts foretold of a perilous time to come. He did not truly know her if he thought she would shirk at danger—if he thought she would hide away in his rooms while he faced his trials alone. For now, she would obey his request, but she wouldn't sit idly. She would learn as much as possible from his books, and whether he was with her or away, she would be unwavering; she would be his helpmeet, his champion. It drove her spirit, and she felt more alive than she'd ever felt.

Severus was hoping she would be awake when he returned. He had to tell her, had to ask her. He knew she wasn't intentionally hiding anything from him, but he suspected all was not known to her. The sky was darkening upon his return to Hogwarts. He'd had duties outside of its walls that would keep up appearances for Lucius, and, therefore, Lord Voldemort. The sniveling worm didn't have the stomach for the more intricate tasks. Subtlety was not in his nature. He never knew what Narcissa saw in him. She had twice the testicular fortitude than he could ever hope for. Severus tried to shrug off the unpleasantries from the day before he entered his rooms in the dungeons of Hogwarts. He found two Slytherin students, outside their dorms past curfew. They were hiding in the shadows, and from the sound of it, they were snogging. He crept up slowly, becoming visible to them only when he was towering above them.

"Perhaps you haven't been given enough homework to occupy your evenings," he said slowly.

At the first word, they jumped up at attention, hoping not to encourage his wrath.

"Tomorrow I expect a hundred lines from each of you on what potion you think I would use on you if I were to find you again in similar circumstances. Now, off with you." He felt in better spirits now as he made it to his rooms quickly, hoping to find Sirana still awake.

Severus found her in her usual spot, curled up in her chair with a book—actually, about a dozen books. He noticed that they were all different books than she'd had out before. She most likely didn't know he was paying attention to which books she had read. Even though she had carefully placed each book back into its original spot, he knew she was now reading them in order, from top to bottom of the bookcase. She'd almost exhausted his supply.

Curious, he thought. *Surely, she hadn't read them all.*

He also noticed that she had beads of sweat on her forehead.

Even more curious, he thought.

He walked up to her and kissed her on her forehead. *Salty*, he thought.

"You look a little flushed. Have the books you've found tonight been exceptionally exhilarating?" he asked as he sat in his own chair.

She laughed at that. "No. I've just been exercising. I can't risk withering away to nothing by sitting in a chair all day. Your spells have kept the place clean and tidy. So, I try to balance my day between my mental and physical well-being."

He was a bit impressed at that. "I thought to bring you some more clothes. As much as I enjoy seeing you in your robes and gowns, I realized you might not find them practical for daytime," he said.

"Thank you, Severus," she replied, smiling, "It seems you are getting more practice at hosting after all."

There it is, he thought to himself. That warmth that grew from his middle and made his mood lighter.

He stood, asking. "Speaking of which, would you like something to drink? I feel a taste for brandy, but I assume from your tolerance, you may prefer wine?"

She laughed at that, knowing he was teasing her. "Yes, wine will do nicely, thank you," she replied with a conspiratorial smile.

He returned with two glasses and a bottle of each. "I hurried home in hopes of sharing a drink with you," he said as he poured them both a glass, setting down the bottles on the table at the ready.

"To what do we owe the occasion?" Sirana asked, reminding him of a similar conversation starter with Albus. He hoped this conversation would be more productive.

He tried to choose his words carefully. "I have found a piece to place in the puzzle today."

Severus saw her eyebrow raise at that, and he said in an almost warm tone, "Perhaps we can share a glass first before we get to it though, as it is sure to change the tone of the evening, and I would like to bask in your undivided attention for a few moments before we go once more into the breach."

Sirana felt the weight of his exchange, knowing he would impart his information when he was ready. She was a little surprised when he uncrossed his leg, inviting her over to his chair. "Come, sit with me," he said as a request.

She moved to sit comfortably on his lap as he drew her in. They each sipped their drinks while he absently curled her strands of hair around his fingers.

"It is coming upon a holiday and I will be off from teaching for the remainder of the week," he said as an offering of small talk, continuing lightly, "Along with the clothes I brought for you, I have also brought a supply of food to do us through the weekend. Nothing special, I'm afraid. One day, I will have to provide you with a nice meal."

She smiled up at him, saying with mock coyness, "Are you asking me on a date?"

He scoffed, then said in a more serious tone, "Would you say 'yes' if I were?"

She coughed a little in embarrassment. "Of course," she replied a little shyly. "I would be happy to show you off on my arm. We would be the talk of the dance floor." He smiled a little at the vision of that, then regretfully wished for better times. *We would indeed be the talk of Hogwarts and of the Yule Ball, and I would be the one showing* her *off*, he thought wistfully. He leaned forward and kissed the top of her head, and it seemed like for the first time in a while that time wasn't pressing so hard on him.

They sat together quietly enjoying the intimacy of the moment. Sirana rose to refill both of their glasses. Feeling the shift of mood saying that it was time to get to the more serious conversation, she moved back to her own seat. He leaned forward, rolling his glass of brandy between his hands.

"The best way to say something is to use one's words to form sentences. I remember hearing that somewhere," Sirana said in jest.

"I would advise against using my own words against me, Sirana, as I do not play fair in a battle of words or wits," he replied above a whisper.

Sirana was up for the game however, responding, "I believe I read in one of your books that using one's words against them is fair play, and can even be a formidable weapon in battle, however ill-advised in matters of love."

He knew exactly to which text she was referring. "Then, you would also know of the passage that warns that one should not take a bite larger than one has the capacity to consume," he said, raising an eyebrow.

"Ah. Point taken. Maybe we should play chess sometime. Hopefully, I would have a better chance of winning," she replied, conceding the match.

"Doubtful," he replied, half in jest, half in truth.

She raised her own eyebrow at that. "It's a pity I don't remember seeing a version of the expression 'making someone eat his own words,' because that would be quite apropos."

His mouth formed into a dangerous grin. "You should feel fortunate, Sirana, that Hogwarts discourages corporal punishment, otherwise you might find yourself across my knee."

She paused at that, weighing whether he would actually dare. "Checkmate. It would seem you were being honest when you said you don't play fair," she said.

"Yes," he said slowly in agreement. "I would have to disagree with the text on that point though, as one should use *all* the weapons at one's disposal, *especially* in matters of love."

Sirana knew when she was outmatched, even if it was by design, and ignored that the last word had plucked at her heartstrings. "Touché," she said, bowing her head slightly.

Severus suddenly dreaded the need to turn to the more serious subject at hand, not because he wasn't interested in it, but because he was more interested in turning their wordplay into an even more enjoyable play. She had a way of jousting with him that brought out the gamesman in him. He felt like he'd met his match, in wit and passion. It was invigorating, to say the least.

Chapter 24

Connection

Severus took one more sip of his brandy before setting it aside, lacing his fingers together in thought. "When you told me your maiden name the other day, something rang familiar. I did some research in the library and found something of importance. It's about your grandfather—Professor Kane Cadogen. Sirana, this may reveal to you more than you have imagined possible," he said evenly. She nodded, a bit wide-eyed, and he continued, "Your grandfather was a professor at Hogwarts several decades ago. You're right; he was a history teacher—History of Magic, that is. He was noted for leading a battle in the First Wizarding War, and then, I could find nothing else on him."

"Are—are you sure it was my grandfather?" Sirana asked in an unsteady voice.

"There was a picture in one of the books. The resemblance to you is striking. His eyes…" Severus looked into hers now. They were almost like mood stones, and hers were bright aqua-blue at the moment.

"What do you think this means?" Sirana asked finally. She had read enough over the last few days to know some of the implications, but she wanted to hear it from him.

"It means you may not be a Muggle after all," he replied with a tinge of irony in his voice. "Did your grandfather come up in any of your...*conversations*...with Lucius?" He asked with more worry in his voice.

"No, I never mentioned him," she answered, wondering if there was some danger if she had. Maybe if Lucius had known she wasn't exactly a Muggle, things could have been worse. She thought of her grandfather—he was an interesting, eccentric man. She had developed her love of books from him. He had sent her a book for every birthday and Christmas. They would discuss the subject in letters they sent back and forth to each other, their shared insights often going on for months. While her parents had been loving and she adored them, her grandfather was the only one she could really show her mind to who would understand.

She thought she heard Severus breathe a sigh of relief at that. "What about your grandmother?" he asked.

"My grandmother, Katherine, died when my mother was young. It wasn't something my grandfather liked to talk about. He raised my mother on his own. She met my father while at university and moved with him to the States where he was from," she replied, trying to scour her memory for more clues. She continued, a little misty-eyed, "My grandfather and I talked about almost everything, except for his life, or my own, for that matter. There would be snippets of memories we would share, of course, but we mostly 'waxed philosophical', as they say. We understood each other in that way. We didn't have to profess our adoration for each other, or even talk about our feelings.

We knew how much we appreciated one another—without words." She took another sip of wine at that, not wanting to reveal her tears.

Severus saw the glistening on her cheeks. He did not want to leave he alone in her sadness. He stood, holding his hand out to her.

"Come to me," he said. She sat down her glass and took his hand. He pulled her into him, tucking her head under his chin, holding her tightly in his arms.

She felt his warmth envelope her. She reached out gently with her mind and felt him there too—not *in* her mind, but she could feel his presence there as if standing next to her, as real as she felt in his arms now. She finally looked up at him, not completely breaking their embrace, as something dawned on her. "He and I had a connection, like I could always feel him there with me, even when we were a thousand miles apart. In fact, I can still feel the connection—that's why I believe he is still alive. I have never had that connection with anyone else—until recently, with you. It feels different, but it's there."

"I have been aware of it as well," Severus replied. "And I too have only felt it once before. I have reason to believe that you are of magic blood." He hesitated to say 'witch', as he was aware of the connotations of the word in the Muggle world. "You are a mystery. I have no idea how you came to be here, or why. Would you let me look into your mind? Would you open yourself to me? I could try to find a clue as to what brought you to me," he said in a gentle voice, brushing a wisp of hair from her face. He saw her nod bravely.

He grabbed her tightly by the shoulders, moving her to arm's length, looking deep into her. "Don't be afraid."

"I'm not," she replied, inclining her head slightly.

He reached for her mind. He had already been at the door; he merely stepped through. He had probed the minds of others, unwilling captors when he was a Death Eater. It was an unpleasant tool to forcibly take what he needed from them. This was different. He felt like he was walking into a familiar, cozy home, knowing he was warm and welcome. He explored its rooms, leaving private what needed to remain so.

There was a door that was closed. Light shone around it—not a steady light, but flashes, like sparking electricity. He reached out, pushing it open. He saw flashes of images, like she'd described having in her nightmares—he saw the man from the picture, running, barefoot, his robes flying wildly around him as he ran. He tried to direct the images to see what he was running towards, but all he could see was her grandfather, reaching desperately in his sleeve, drawing out a wand. Fire flew from it, and then, blinding light.

"No...too close...I can't..." Severus realized the words were not coming from her grandfather, or from inside the room. He felt himself being pulled back out of the room, and the door closed shut. A wall of fire appeared before it, and he stepped away. He turned and another door opened. It was glowing inside, as if the fire was instead the warm glow of a fireplace. He stepped in. The images were different. Swirling visions of filtered light. He saw himself, and her. They were intertwined with feelings of love, passion, and admiration. The filtered light warmed into a hot glow, and he almost lost himself in the euphoric, burning rapture. He saw himself, like a wall of stone and blade of steel. She was there, encased in shining armor, standing alongside him. It felt prophetic, as if he was looking not at a memory, but at a vision of the future. He suddenly felt their link fading, and he felt his mind move back out of the door. His eyes opened, and he realized that they were wet with tears.

Chapter 25

Free Rein

Sirana looked at Severus. She had seen some of what he saw in her mind. She looked up at his face. It was wet with tears, and she brushed them away with her hand. He reached up and held her hand against his face with his own. Then, he brought her hand to his lips, tenderly kissing each of her fingers and her palm. He leaned forward and kissed away the tears from her own cheeks. He moved his kisses to her mouth, softly kissing across her lips. She could smell the brandy, and she licked her lips, tasting the sweetness of it. She saw his eyes darken, "My witch, if I had not seen your mind myself, I would swear that you were ensnaring me with your magic," he said, his lips parted sensuously.

Her draw to him was palpable. She wanted to feel his lips, knowing it would never be enough to assuage her desire for him. He took her face in his hands, bringing his lips down closer and closer to hers, stopping only when she thought there was no more space between them.

"If you do indeed have me entrapped in your magic, I will not ask you to liberate me, for I believe that I too have captured you in my own spell...and I must warn you, I intend for you to serve a life sentence." She closed her eyes, hearing his low whisper, feeling the breath from it on her lips. Any response she could have tried to articulate was gratefully smothered with his kiss. His hand reached into her robe, wrapping around her side, then sliding to the small of her back. He slowly let his hand drift down her backside, running a line down her middle, pushing into the recess between her thighs. She felt the jolt of shocking pleasure reach up into her stomach, and she gasped hard against his mouth. He suddenly reached in further, grabbing and lifting her up to him, her legs automatically wrapping around his waist. He carried her over to his chair, not breaking their kiss until they were seated. He grabbed the hem of her gown, pulling it up to her waist, freeing her legs to straddle him more easily on the chair. He untied the ties of her gown slowly, then swiftly ripped her gown open to reveal even more of herself to him.

She saw the dangerously roguish look in his eyes as he offered, "We can play chess instead if you think your chances would be better…"

She smiled her own devilish grin. "I think my chances are looking pretty good right here."

Severus let a smile reach his lips as he brought them to take each of her nipples in his mouth, leisurely taking his time with each until she was moaning with desire. He reached one hand to below the small of her back, pushing her into him to rock her back and forth against his lap. She picked up the rhythm herself, grinding hard into him. His own low moan escaped, and he grabbed her head in both hands, bringing her down to kiss him, both breathing heavily with their passion. She began unbuttoning his jacket, but he didn't think he could restrain himself that long. He drew his wand from his sleeve, undoing both his jacket and shirt buttons in one quick flourish. He slid his wand back into his sleeve as she ran her hands over his chest, leaning down to kiss across his chest, licking each of his nipples. That was enough, and he reached down to unfasten his trousers, freeing himself from the restraints. He grabbed her hips then, sliding her across himself, back and forth, feeling her wetness covering him.

She buried her face into his shoulder, and he heard her plead in his ear, "Please…Severus, please…" Her words brought a satisfied smile to his lips. The next stroke he pulled her farther up to his tip and slid her down onto himself hard, pushing her down onto his lap. She cried out and he released her hips to run his hands up her back. Instead of pulling up off him, she ground herself on him, and he let out a low growl. He leaned back in his chair, allowing her free reign.

Her hands flattened out on his stomach, which was quivering uncontrollably with the overwhelming sensation of her. He suddenly noticed her slow down, he saw her eyes close and her mouth open in a silent struggle to reach her climax. He wrapped his arms around her waist, leaning into her, pushing into her harder to help carry her across the threshold to find her release. She finally let out a guttural cry, folding into him, her body shuddering. He couldn't restrain himself any longer, and thrusting hard into her still pulsing sheath, he found his own release, hitting him fast and hard. She fell on his heaving chest, both completely spent. He could feel their connection, and it was fortified, and he knew that nothing could sever the tie binding them together.

Chapter 26

Live

Severus had been dreading this day. He was meeting Lucius at his Manor today. Over the last week, he had carried out everything that Lord Voldemort had asked of him. Fortunately, the Dark Lord was still lying low, weakened. Unfortunately, he was rebuilding his strength, preparing for the day he would re-emerge, perhaps stronger than before. In the meantime, he used the Death Eaters in his ranks to carry out his deeds. Lucius was climbing the ranks in Voldemort's army, hoping to be at his right hand at the end, taking every opportunity to prove his loyalty to the Dark Lord. Severus knew Lucius didn't care if Voldemort would emerge victorious in the end. If Voldemort were to fail, Lucius wanted to be second in line, and then, he would inherit the power he craved. But if Severus knew how weak Lucius really was, he had no doubt that Voldemort knew as well.

Severus Apparated into the Malfoy Manor as he had a week ago. He was not that same man. He must be careful not to reveal anything to Lucius. Lucius was a fool, but he was not stupid. Lucius was waiting for him this time, standing by the fireplace, staring into the blazing fire. Severus wondered what, or who, he saw there.

"Ah, Severus!" Lucius said grandly, waiving his ornate walking stick welcomingly. "I think you were right before...my mantle does look a bit bare since you ran off with my ornament. Do tell—have you disposed of the lovely lass? I hope you were able to glean more information from her than I. You've always had a way with the ladies, haven't you?"

Severus would not be so easily provoked. "Actually, the... lovely lass...is now warming up the ambiance of my own decor. I have not yet discovered any secrets—that you weren't already aware of—but you should know as well as anyone that I am a patient man...and you can rest assured that when I grow bored, I have my ways of making one disappear." He was aware that Lucius knew of his reputation as a Death Eater, and he would also recognize the veiled threat. "More importantly, Lucius, I have finalized the tasks set before me by the Dark Lord. If there are more expectations, I would be most willing to accept his instructions—directly," Severus said, hoping Lucius would be more worried about the reason he wanted to see Voldemort face-to-face, perhaps even challenging his position, and that would distract him from the thought of Sirana.

"He will be pleased to hear that the more...*delicate*...work has been done," Lucius replied. "For now, there are undertakings that I must see to, and I don't believe I will need your...direct assistance." Lucius's smile faded. "However, I will let the Dark Lord know that you stand at the ready."

Lucius had not elaborated on what 'undertakings' he was referring to. Lucius was no doubt unaware that Severus already knew of the plan for the Dark Lord to arrange the mass breakout of prisoners from Azkaban. It was but yet another sign of the building of Voldemort's army. Of course, since Severus knew of it, Albus Dumbledore knew as well.

"Of course," Severus replied. "Please send my regards to the lady of the house."

He chose that moment to Disapparate, having had the last word, knowing Lucius suspected that Narcissa was often more welcoming to Severus than he approved of.

This time, Severus chose to Apparate to his house in Cokeworth. There were several books he had in mind to bring Sirana. She had already read the collection he kept at Hogwarts, except for what he'd kept in his study. He wondered if she actually retained all that she'd read. Even though the books he kept in his library weren't as sensitive in nature as his private collection, there was still a fair amount of knowledge to be acquired from them. He may need to reevaluate his decision to keep his study locked. The potential power of the knowledge those books could impart—to the right person—could prove to be invaluable. If she were to stand at his side as an ally, they could provide a foundation from which to train her up.

He looked around the bleak room. Sirana had said that she could spend a lifetime here among so many books. He would imagine that she would brighten up even these dark walls. He had not foreseen Sirana in his life. Admittedly, he was not a Seer. Severus heard the words from Dumbledore's and his last meeting. He wondered if Albus knew more than he had revealed, as his words seemed almost prophetic now. Perhaps he would find his mercy, perhaps his soul would indeed not be lost. It was too much to ask for, and he would not ask for mercy for himself…but for Sirana. He had offered to lay down his life for Lily, and she had died. Now, he swore, he would do more than die for Sirana and for Lily—he would *live*.

Chapter 27

Elf-Made Wine

It was getting late. It had been a few days since Sirana had seen Severus for more than a few minutes, either when he was falling exhausted into bed, or in the morning when he dressed to face the day. She had used her time alone to its greatest potential—considering the circumstances. Severus had shared some information about the challenges he faced, the evils that threatened to take power, but much of it was vague. She felt that he wanted to protect her, hide her away, but she knew that time was coming to an end. He had told her that he had put a protective spell on the room, so that no sound could escape the walls. She was grateful for that. She made good use of the record player while she worked out, although she preferred complete silence while she read.

She didn't know if she would see him tonight, so she went ahead and had her evening meal alone. She finished her meal and moved to her chair with her wine. She had no new books to read, but she had found some that she wanted to go back through, because now, she had more reference from which to understand them. She wished she had more time to talk with Severus about the implications of what they had learned about her grandfather. She had found some references in the books, however. She wasn't exactly a Muggle after all. She was almost sure her mother wasn't magical, so she wasn't really a half-blood per se, but she now knew that she was magical. It had been lying dormant, mostly. There were events over the years she didn't understand as magic when they happened, but she now suspected it had played a role—like when she had saved one of her students. She had scaled down four stories of the school building to pluck him off the window ledge. She had attributed it to adrenaline and her conditioning. There were other similar incidents, although not as noteworthy. Her grandfather...she wished he had told her. Maybe he was trying to protect her too. And yet, here she was...and she had no idea how or why, but she knew it felt right, like she was where she was meant to be all along. Without rising from her chair, she retrieved another book from the bookcase.

Severus couldn't wait to see her. It had been several days since he had had more than a few words with her. He had brought back some books and a bottle of elf-made wine. As he reached to open his door, he suddenly felt something unfamiliar—jitters. He cursed softly at himself as he entered, and then cursed more loudly at what he saw. Sirana was sitting in her usual spot in her chair, except this time there was a book drifting slowly towards her outstretched hand. When she saw him come through the door, the book hit the floor.

"Uh, I guess I need to work on that," she said as if disappointed in herself for losing focus. She stood to retrieve the book, setting it on the arm of the chair. Severus sat his bundle on the table and, without speaking, took her in his arms, pulling her to him to greet her with a deep kiss, not breaking away until she was flushed and breathless. Any jitters he felt were no longer present.

"Well, that was a pleasant surprise," Sirana said.

"Speaking of surprises, I have a few things for you," Severus said, retrieving his bundle from the table. "I brought you several books from my home and a bottle of elf-made wine." He handed the books over to her, then went to get his two best wine glasses, pouring them each a glass of the deep red wine.

"Mmmm…" Sirana remarked, "I've read in one of your books that it is especially intoxicating to the senses. The book also said that it is prized for its depth in color and flavor."

"Yes, I think you will enjoy it," Severus said, handing her the glass. They stood for a moment, looking in each other's eyes, then each raised their glasses before taking a drink. As a potions master, he had an appreciation for wine, as there were subtleties in each that took a practiced hand. He could feel the unique sensations from the wine almost immediately. He watched Sirana closely. She took the first sip, then closed her eyes; her head tilted back slowly, and her lips parted slightly. He had guessed that he would enjoy her experiencing it for the first time, and he had guessed correctly. Merlin's beard, he wanted to make love to her, here and now. But he would exhibit some control over his own emotions, his own desires. There were things he needed to discuss with her. *And now is the time to practice that which I had preached*, he thought wryly. She opened her eyes. "That's impressive," she said with an embarrassed grin.

He reached out and brushed her mouth gently with his thumb. "Indeed," he said in obvious regard for her, and turned to offer her his arm. She took his arm and he led her towards his study, which she had never entered previously. She looked up at him in surprise.

"Why do I feel like a fly?" she quipped.

Severus cherished her humor. Maybe it played in harmony with his own cynical nature.

"Please, welcome to my parlor," he said, playing along. His study resembled his own home in the sense that books lined all the walls from floor to ceiling. Otherwise, his study was quite warm and welcoming. He watched her as she made a trip around the room, looking at the books, touching some of their bindings.

She looks like a child in a sweet shoppe, he thought.

He thought about how much she would enjoy the Hogwarts library.

*Maybe one day...*he thought with a bit of regret, but at the moment, he suffered from a lack of imagination of how to make that happen.

"It has not gone unnoticed that you seem to have a propensity for magic after all," Severus began. "And I would like to instruct you on its finer points."

Sirana looked like she pondered that for a moment. "Yes, I would like that," she replied in all seriousness.

"I must warn you, I am known to be a hard taskmaster, and I do not intend to employ any other method of teaching," Severus said with a raised eyebrow.

"Duly noted," she replied.

He was pleased with the prospect of teaching her. She was not a child, and yet, she was starting from the beginning. He could see already from what she was able to learn in such a short time that she could catch up quickly, especially if she would tolerate him pushing her to her limits.

Chapter 28

Exquisite

"I have kept you in the dark about many things, Sirana," Severus said as he watched Sirana peruse his extensive collection of books, sipping her wine. He knew the books he kept in his study contained more advanced levels of magical teachings than she had previously had access to. He sat on the edge of his desk, his legs crossed at his ankles, enjoying his own wine. "My allegiances may seem torn; however, that is not truth. I may never atone for my past, as there were choices I made that I fear have stripped away part of my soul. I am no longer a true part of that life, and yet, I cannot deny that that life will always remain a part of me. My path has been chosen for me now, and though I do not desire to willingly submit to my fate, my course is unwavering," Severus said with a conviction that could not be shaken.

Sirana felt what he said down into her own soul. She didn't yet know the course of which he spoke, but she knew she would stand by his side to traverse it, wherever it may lead. She walked to stand in front of him, placing her hand on his chest, and he covered it with his. She wasn't concerned that he had not fully disclosed everything to her. She had felt his mind, and she knew his was not being deceptive with her, as she was not with him. There were things that they would discuss in their own time. Time felt precious to her here in a way that seemed to choreograph their time together, forcing what was important for the now to the forefront. Now, they had some making up to do for the time they had spent apart, and she saw it in his eyes.

Severus traced her cheek with his finger. "We will start your lessons tomorrow. Tonight is for us." He continued in a serious tone, a playful look in his eyes, "After I begin your instruction, you may no longer find me so appealing."

Sirana laughed. "You will never have to worry about that. However, if your teaching methods ever do cause me to find you loathsome, I would suggest that you simply bring home some more elf-made wine. You look absolutely luminous, even more so than usual. I've heard of rose-colored glasses, but I never knew they could be found in a bottle of wine."

Severus leaned forward and lightly kissed her lips. "It can only be a glimpse compared to what I see every time I look at you." He wondered how his feelings so easily escaped him when he was with Sirana. He had always felt deeply, passionately, although his outward stoicism hid his inner fire. Now, all of his fierceness was channeled to her, and he feared that his fire would consume her. Suddenly, he felt her in his mind, a gentle knock on his mind's door, and he opened. He was met with a fiery passion that matched his own, and he no longer worried that his own fire was too much for her, and he willfully met her in their firestorm.

The trail of their clothes started in the study and led all the way into the bedroom. By the time they made it to the bed, neither had any clothes left on their bodies. He laid her down on the end of the bed, following her down to resume their kiss.

He slowed down the pace, wanting to take his time with her. He trailed his kisses to cover all of the parts of her soft skin that he'd been thinking about all week—the hollow of her neck, her shoulders, her breasts, her stomach.

"Mmm…Severus…" he heard Sirana's soft voice. He trailed slow, soft kisses down the line of her center. He could feel her starting to quiver, her breath quickening. He made a roundabout circling her belly button before moving to kiss her soft tummy. He gently rubbed her soft curls with his thumbs, softly kneading, his hands splayed across her hip bones. He moved his mouth to kiss around her mound, his tongue playing with her ringlets of soft hair. He could hear her soft moans, and he inwardly steeled himself to take his time, to savor the anticipation, to relish in her desire for him, to luxuriate in her pleasure. He tasted her wetness, and his lips placed firm kisses on top of her. He could feel that she was swollen slightly with need, could hear her light whimpers growing. He let his hot tongue slip into her wetness, and she gasped. He moaned against her, enveloping her swollen clit with his lips, then let his tongue circle her with exquisite deliberation. She cried out his name lustfully, and it drove him. He softly coaxed her shaking thighs apart with his hand, then rubbed his thumb firmly over her recess. He replaced his thumb with his mouth and pushed his tongue into her. She bucked, surprised by the intensity of the sensations, but he grabbed her by her hips, holding her firmly to him. He moved his mouth back up to her clit, replacing his tongue with his fingers. He slid his fingers in and out slowly as he worked his tongue against her swollen clit in a maddening rhythm. She arched her body, pleading with him in frantic sounds indistinguishable as words.

She wrapped his hair in her hands, not knowing whether to push him away or pull him in. He raised up from her, placing a few gentle kisses on top of her before pulling himself up to kiss her lips and face, kissing her eyes, which were damp with tears from squeezing them closed so tightly.

Between the exotic headiness of the wine, and the slow, exquisite pleasure of Severus, Sirana had never felt such intense sensations in her life. She wanted to hurry towards her merciful release, but she also didn't want the experience to end. She reached down to grab Severus's hardness in her hand and heard his deep moan as he flinched. She pushed his shoulder, rolling him onto his back. She intended to return the favor of trying to drive him mad. She kissed his broad chest, which was one of his features that she found to be very attractive. She kissed his belly, running her fingers through the soft hair on his stomach. She kissed the hollow of his hips, hearing a low growl as he sat up on his elbows, watching her with heavy, passion-filled eyes. She heard him heave out a breathy groan as she took him into her mouth. She worked up and down with her warm, wet mouth, working down lower and lower onto him with each stroke, until she could take no more of him. She grasped what was left of him at the base in her hand, and in unison with her mouth, she moved up and down in a slow, sensuous rhythm. He groaned loudly now, which turned into almost a growl, and he rolled her onto her back as if he couldn't take any more of it. He stood up at the end of the bed and pulled her to him with her legs. The sight of him standing over her with his strikingly handsome form was exhilarating. The power he exuded was almost a bit intimidating, and she felt a twinge in her stomach of nervous excitement.

Severus stood at the end of the bed with Sirana's beautiful figure laid out before him. He pulled her closer to him, holding her legs at his side.

"Severus…" she said, and he heard the anxious catch in her voice. Merlin's pants, he would never get enough of this woman.

He caressed her thighs with his hands, giving her time to regain her courage. "I will never hurt you, Sirana. All you need do is to ask for mercy…and I will give your request careful consideration." She smiled at that.

He wrapped her legs around him, then gripped his manhood to rub himself on her and over her, feeling her begin to bloom, getting warm and wet. The sensations were intoxicating for him as well. There were things about the elf-made wine that he would never reveal to her, things she wouldn't find in books. It had a tantalizing effect that would not only heighten the senses, but also allow them to maintain that level of intensity, longer and sweeter than imaginable. It was well worth whatever bargain he'd struck to acquire it. Sirana started to move sensually now, moaning softly, her hands flat against her stomach, moving as if to ease her building desire. Their eyes met, and he knew she was ready for him. He grabbed her by her hips and slid himself into her slowly, but with such force that she sucked in a loud gasp. He drove into her, over and over, relentlessly. She cried out his name when she finally found the breath for it and reached out her hands against his stomach and hips, trying to hold him back.

"Severus…I can't…it's too much," she begged. He leaned forward, holding up his weight with his arms, allowing himself to grind into her instead. Her eyes closed, and the sounds coming from her changed, and he knew he was in the spot he needed to be to send her over the edge. He set the pace, moving in short, deep, grinding strokes. She was silent except for her labored breathing, and her fingers clinched into his back. He heard a low "Mmmm..." start to come from inside her throat, and he knew she was getting close. Finally, she cried out in passionate release, her whole body shaking with pleasure and relief. He could feel the warmth of her juices cover him. He slowed his pace, allowing her to recover, moving in and out slowly, enjoying the sensation of her warm slickness. He felt his own desire for relief building in him, and he buried himself deeply, gratefully spilling into her.

Severus lay with her for the longest time, holding and being held. He wished he was a master wordsmith so that he could adequately express his love to her. He felt her touch his mind, and a warmth came over him, and it felt as if their warm embrace went further than their bodies, and any spoken words would not compare to the love their connection conveyed.

Chapter 29

Legilimency & Occlumency

S irana woke up earlier than usual. She was excited to start her studies with Severus. She wondered what exactly he had in store for her.

If he is as accomplished a teacher as he is a lover, I'll be a magical genius in no time, she thought with a smile on her face.

Severus must have been watching her from his side of the bed. "You will not likely be smiling by the end of the day. I intend to fully exhaust any energy you may hold until you are completely spent," he said, and she didn't doubt him for a second.

Severus was most impressed by Sirana's skill at both Legilimency and Occlumency. They were rare magical abilities, both of which he himself was quite accomplished in. Lucius had noticed that Sirana possessed the ability to shield her mind from his, but he must have attributed it to mere happenstance or perhaps a drop of magic in her blood to which she was unaware. Severus, however, knew differently. He knew her grandfather had been a powerful wizard, from what he could glean from the books he'd found, and she'd obviously inherited his magical blood. Her own magical powers must have lain dormant for her to have no knowledge of them. He suspected a recent event, perhaps before she came to be at Malfoy's, had triggered its emergence. She was formidable, even to Lucius, in her own way. He knew she was not a lamb, but he would indeed have her be a wolf by the end. There were so many things he wished to teach her, and it would begin today. He'd seen the excitement in Sirana, and he felt it in himself as well. Perhaps his calling did actually lay in teaching. Now, whether to have her call him Professor Snape…

"Snape??!!" Sirana exclaimed. "*That's* your name??? Not that that's a bad thing…but it doesn't roll off of the tongue like Severus. How about I call you Professor Severus? Doesn't that sound better?"

Merlin's…! She is going to drive me mad after all, he thought. He couldn't allow the train to derail before it even left the station.

"Professor Snape will do," he said more sternly, leaving no room for argument.

"Yes, sir," she replied, defeated, and yet, he noticed that she hadn't used his title in a last bit of defiance.

They were in his study, where he'd intended to conduct most of the lessons. He felt it important to keep this part of their lives separated in this manner.

"While I'm away, you will have ample time to read, so while I'm here, we will use that time for practice and direct application. I will prepare your lesson plan so that your reading material will progress in a logical order."

He saw her nod her understanding and proceeded, "From what I've observed, you can read over a dozen books a day. I will check your retention of the material before assigning the next curriculum. There may be days when I am unable to return, so I will set out several days in advance and then perform my assessments upon my return."

She nodded again, and he asked, "How long have you had the ability to…feel someone else's mind?" He was unaware if she knew what the ability was called.

"Since I was young. My grandfather and I have had a connection since we first met. I still feel it there. That's why I know he is still alive," she answered. "With Lucius, I felt him trying to enter my mind. It was invasive, and I stopped him. When…I first saw you, and I felt you enter my mind, it was different."

"How was it different?" Snape replied.

Sirana thought for a second, then answered, "You asked," she said simply.

His expression softened at that. "Can you communicate with your grandfather through your connection with him?"

"Not really. I just feel it there, and I know he's alright. I think when I have the nightmares, though, he is there, his connection… I don't know how I know that," she said as if in deep thought. Perhaps that is why he could only see parts of that memory instead of all of it—as if some of it was seen through her eyes, and some from another's.

"Today, we will begin our lessons with Legilimency and Occlumency. In simple terms, Legilimency is the ability to enter another's mind and Occlumency is the ability to shield one's mind from another. My last student failed." He still felt the sting of that failure. "Perhaps you will prove to be more proficient."

"I will do my best," she replied in a serious tone.

"I am going to try to enter your mind, and I want you to stop me," Severus said.

He stepped several strides away from her, and turned to look directly at her, wielding his wand. He started slowly, feeling familiarity at this level, then abruptly tried to slip into her mind. Just as it had been at Lucius's when he'd first seen her, his mind was met with a wall of stone and fire. The wall was strong and unmovable, and the fire made even the attempt to get closer very unpleasant. He backed out, never having experienced defenses of this nature. There were others who had resisted him, but they were well-trained, and their method was expected. This was not either, but the power was undeniable.

"Legilimens!" he said, this time bringing his full force against her mind. He heard her gasp lightly, then the flames from the wall blazed even hotter, forcing him out violently. He unconsciously took a step back.

He stepped forward, "Again!" he almost shouted. This time, he caught her off guard. He'd stopped just before entering and softly 'asked.' Her wall fell, and he slipped in past her defense before she could realize and recover. He made her pay for the error. Not in a way that he would have with an enemy, but in the way that he wanted her to learn from the mistake so that a real enemy could not so easily take advantage of that weakness. When he left her mind, she stood with her head held in proud defiance, but he saw the tears in her eyes, too stubborn to fall. He wanted to stop, to give her a chance to gather herself, but he could not spare her for the graveness of the lesson.

"Again!" he commanded, and this time her wall would not fall.

Chapter 30

Pertrificus Totalus

Sirana was on her fifteenth book of the day. Severus had discovered after a few days that her unique talent of reading and retention allowed her to read through two or three times what he had originally estimated. She still found time to work out, but she made it quick before getting back to her studies. She felt driven. Severus had proved to be a tough teacher. When they were in his study, he was all business. Sometimes, when she left the room after a tough day of instruction, she had to take a break from him as well. She couldn't go too far, so she would just say she needed to lay down for a bit and go to the bedroom for an hour or so of privacy. Otherwise, she may have found a way to use magic to poison him or rid him of his lovely head. She tried to never let him know he got to her sometimes. She knew she got under his skin too. His expressions were very subtle, but also very telling. She felt like she was in magic bootcamp, and she wasn't always sure if she was meeting his expectations. She had decided it didn't matter, that she would do her best with or without feedback from him. She wasn't a child—and she didn't expect to be treated like one—but sometimes, she wished he was a little less stern. She was beginning to really miss him today, though. It had been several days since he had even been home. He had left enough for her to do, so she focused on that. She could still feel their connection, but she would really have liked to see him.

Sirana heard the door. She was already in bed, and it was dark. She knew it was almost the middle of the night, and he would most likely be exhausted, so she pretended she was sleeping in case he wanted to wait until morning to greet her.

She was a little surprised to hear Severus when he opened the door to the bedroom, "Sirana, come join me out here. I would like to talk."

She was happy to do so. She hadn't fallen asleep yet anyway, and she looked forward to spending a little time with him. She donned her robe and went into the living room, her bare feet padding across the cool floor. There was only a single lantern lit, so it was still a little dark. When she saw Severus, she started to go to him to give him a proper hello. But, there was something that seemed off, and she hesitated. She could see him look her up and down, and a smile touched his lips.

"Is everything okay, Severus?" Sirana said. "You seem tired."

She didn't want to say that he seemed more than tired. He seemed cold and distant. Even though he was not usually a man of many words, and even though he was a hard taskmaster at times, he was never cold and distant. It was unnerving. She tried to reach out to his mind, and she suddenly felt a cold panic rising through her. It wasn't that the link was not there, she could still feel it, but it was not with the person who stood in front of her. She was silent as she screamed through the link, hoping to send a message to Severus, wherever he was, that she was in danger. She felt an answer, however faint, and it was a mix of dread, desperation, and rage, but most of all, she felt him reaching out to help fortify her, like a tower of strength and courage.

She looked at the man, aware that there were spells that could change a person's appearance. If this man was a wizard, she knew what magic she had learned so far would not be an adequate match, but she would still fight if she needed to.

"Yes, everything is alright," the man answered. "In fact, things are especially well. I hope you are also well?"

Sirana didn't want to give anything away, even her closeness to Severus.

"As well as can be expected," she answered vaguely.

He stepped towards her, and she unintentionally flinched. She saw a smile on his face. "Don't worry," he said in mock concern. "I will take it easier on you—this time."

She thought that he had assumed she flinched because she thought it was really Severus standing in front of her, and perhaps that the sight of Severus would make her flinch with fear. He stepped closer to her, and she had the feeling in her gut that she recognized that walk, that arrogant tilt of his head, the shifty, side-eyed glare. Lucius! She felt her stomach tighten. He got close enough to touch her, and he reached out to put his hand gently on her face, then ran it back roughly into her hair, pulling her face to his. She reacted reflexively, swinging her arm up and over to break the hold he had on her, then swung back using her reverse momentum to crash the butt of her hand into his nose. She stepped forward, using her feet and legs to tie his up while pushing him back and down. She fell with him, and she used her momentum to bring her whole body forward, landing with her knee on his neck. She wrapped his neck with her legs, trying to squeeze the life out of him, but he was strong. He was able to pull his wand from inside his jacket and she felt herself thrown back from him in a burst of pain and light.

Severus lay paralyzed by the full body-bind curse on the floor in the small living room of his house in Cokeworth. He would never excuse himself for being caught off guard by Lucius. He didn't think the wizard would do something so bold to a fellow Death Eater. While he lay there paralyzed, but still able to see and hear, Lucius had laid out his plan to him, too arrogant to consider that it might fail. Lucius retrieved clothes from Severus's closet and dressed in them.

He stopped to look at himself, "Severus, it would kill me to have to wear this day in and day out...But I must admit, I don't look too horrid in it," Lucius said in a lively mood. He wanted to let Severus begin to see the plan unfold before he confirmed it.

He retrieved a small vial hidden in his own clothes, which he had placed in a rucksack. He sauntered over to Severus, plucking a single long black hair from his head. He knew Severus would be getting the idea by now, and proceeded to tell him the rest.

"You see, I have an inkling that you have grown too attached to your...*hostage*. I believe I will be doing you, as well as the Dark Lord, a favor by removing the distraction. I can hold her for you until our mission is at an end, and if she still...lives, you are most welcome to have her back. I always knew you had a soft spot for beautiful women—like Lily, like...Narcissa—but they were clever enough to avoid you. I would hate to think that this woman—the one that *couldn't* get away—might be your downfall."

Severus could see Lucius's intent. He would hold Sirana as a hostage against him, a contingency plan if events were to turn in an unexpected direction. Severus was sure that Voldemort didn't know of this, but he tried to think of a way out, whether he did or didn't. Lucius completed the Polyjuice Potion, which would have already taken at least a month to brew, by adding Severus's hair. When he transformed into Severus's image, he smiled menacingly, but with Severus's mouth. "What do you think? It is always a bit disturbing to see one's likeness donned by another, or so I've been told. You see, I am going to walk right into Hogwarts, save the young woman from your cage, then bring her back here to make love to her while wearing your skin. If you try to oppose me at any time, now or in the future, I will kill her in a most unpleasant manner."

Lucius's threat had a desperate sound to it, and he wondered what drove him to this. Perhaps he hadn't been seeing eye to eye with the Dark Lord after all. Severus was careful not to let any of his emotions pass into the connection he had with Sirana.

There was nothing she could do. With the spells he'd put on his rooms, she was in the safest place she could be. He wished he had talked to Dumbledore before and perhaps arranged for extra protection for her, but he hadn't wanted to take the risk of anyone else besides Albus knowing of her presence there. He cursed himself. If Lucius was able to break through the protection around his rooms, she would be completely vulnerable.

Chapter 31

Obliviate

S everus had felt Sirana in his mind. He tried to project his will to her, knowing she most likely didn't have a fighting chance against Lucius, who was a formidable wizard. He didn't think he could bear seeing Lucius hurt Sirana, especially not while in his own image. He counted the seconds, trying to devise a plan that didn't end the way Lucius had described. Lucius and he had been friends of sorts, going back to the time they spent as fellow students at Hogwarts. Lucius must be outside of his mind to try this. Every Death Eater knew of Severus's reputation, and none wanted to risk being his enemy. Severus knew deep in his soul that Sirana was his price, and perhaps Lucius had guessed that as well.

Sirana woke up with a pounding headache. At least she thought she was awake. She'd had dreamed she was awake over and over, but the dreams had turned into nightmares. She waited, and the pain in her head and body was evidence enough for her to know that she was truly awake this time. She was so thirsty. Her tongue was stuck to the roof of her mouth. She tried to move, to think, to remember—*anything*.

She heard something and she held completely still.

"I know you can hear me," she heard Severus's voice, and the memories suddenly flooded in—this man was not Severus! "Don't worry. I am simply liberating you from your prison. I must say I regret ever allowing Severus to make off with you in the first place. I should have known he would not have the stomach for such unpleasantries," he said, and Sirana knew now without doubt that this man was Lucius. Sirana was stunned. She felt herself being gathered up, and then, she fell to the floor again, recognizing the feeling of having just Apparated. She looked around, her senses coming back to her. She was in a small, dark room, surrounded by books—and Severus's body lay on the floor. She tried to move to him, but she was dragged up by her hair. Lucius pulled her to him roughly, licking her neck and face in a show of dominance.

He looked at Severus. "She is finally going to see what it is like to be with a real man. Maybe you can watch and learn from my example."

He threw her to the floor. She landed hard on her knees, her face planting into the hard floor. He pinned her to the floor, holding her down while he worked to undo his trousers then tore at her gown. She fought, whipping her head back to headbutt him in the nose. She broke free and spun away from him. He still looked like Severus, except his face was a bloody mess, and his hair and eyes were wild. She was close to where Severus lay. She looked at him, and they locked eyes.

He's alive! she screamed in her own mind. She had read of spells that could freeze, paralyze, or petrify someone, and she guessed it was something of that nature holding him immobile.

She knew she had to move quickly as Lucius was regaining his senses and was reaching again for his wand. She spoke the counter curse to free Severus, then launched herself at Lucius. She sent a spinning back kick to catch him off guard, hoping to also catch his wand hand with her heel. His grip was too tight to knock the wand from his hand, but she did succeed in delaying him from aiming his wand at her or Severus.

Severus wanted more than anything to protect Sirana from Lucius—to move, to speak a curse, to use his wand...he realized he was still holding his wand. Lucius had left him with it— he was an arrogant fool. Severus realized he had no chance of using it while under the Petrificus Totalus curse, but it was a risk he would not have taken himself against another opponent. It boded well, he thought. He watched in complete horror as Severus attacked Sirana, totally helpless under the curse. She fought him tooth and nail, and he was impressed how well she'd fared against him so far. If she could get Lucius's wand away from him, or if she could even get his own wand, that may tip the scale. He had not begun instructing her in wand magic, as he had known it to bring about bad habits to those who relied on it too heavily. Suddenly, he felt her words scream into his mind, 'He's alive!' He then heard the counter curse coming from her mouth. He didn't have the time to consider how she could possibly know the counter curse, as it only took moments for it to work to release him. It was as if he was moving in water, though—every movement felt slow and difficult. When he saw Lucius draw his wand, he was sure he would be too late.

The rest was a flurry of action. Sirana spun and kicked at the same time, ruining Lucius's aim. He aimed his own wand, only making it to his knees at this point. Sirana smartly ducked under with her momentum from the kick, and Severus used the opening.

"Stupefy!" he yelled hoarsely. Lucius flew back against the wall, falling in a heap, his wand sliding away from him. Severus lurched forward, taking Sirana in his arms.

"I'm sorry," was all he could say as he held her to him.

"It's alright...I'm alright," she said in ragged breaths. Severus pulled her away from him, holding her face in his hands, looking her over. Her cheek was red and swollen, probably from where she had hit the floor. Her lip was swollen as well, and he wondered how long they'd fought before they made it here.

He looked at Lucius, who was in far worse shape, and was beginning to morph back into his original self. Severus gave Sirana one more look before breaking away and going over to him.

"This may actually work in our favor," Severus said before using his own curse against Lucius to paralyze him. "We need to get him back into his own clothes. I have a spell that I can use to remove his memory. If he has not yet told...anyone of importance...of your existence, that may give you your freedom."

Severus had not yet told her of Voldemort. He had only hinted at the threats that they could possibly face. He thought it riskier to put the name into her head where it could more easily be found. When they finished redressing Lucius, Severus found some more appropriate clothes for Sirana as well.

He Apparated the three of them to Knockturn Alley. He knew of a place that was dark and hidden. He'd Apparated there before on business. He placed Lucius's wand back in his jacket, knowing it would raise more suspicion if he were to find it missing. He drew out his own wand, releasing him from the paralyzing curse, only to immediately stupefy him again, then spoke in a low voice as to not risk anyone overhearing, "Obliviate!" He erased any memory of Sirana from Lucius's mind along with any memories of plans that he had to come to this abduction. Lucius would hopefully awaken with a bad headache and think that he'd been ambushed and mugged. It would have to do.

He Apparated with Sirana back into Hogwarts. He was one of the few who were able to do so, due to his work as a double agent for Dumbledore, and he only did so when the occasion required it. As soon as they arrived, he quickly put protective spells back on his rooms, adding a couple more for good measure. Then, he returned to Sirana. He thought he'd lost her to Lucius. Lucius had underestimated her. Severus himself had underestimated her. He had a lot of questions for her. But for now, he settled on holding her and kissing her without words.

Chapter 32

Neighbors

Severus and Sirana spent the rest of the night laying together in their bed, talking softly, holding each other. Severus worked on Sirana's bruises, and she looked almost new, except for the tiredness in her eyes. Severus knew it was time to talk with Albus Dumbledore again. As the Headmaster of Hogwarts, he would have access to options that Severus would not. Albus always seemed to be a few moves ahead of the game, and perhaps he could offer a path that was not outside of the playing field. This time, he would bring Sirana with him.

They arranged the time for their meeting when the students would be in their beds. Severus and Sirana arrived to find Albus already in his nightrobes and bedcap. He greeted them warmly, and Albus took Sirana's hand in his, kissing it, then lingered to hold it for another moment, looking up at Severus with an approving smile. Severus had the unsettling feeling he was bringing home his fiancé to meet the parents, and he was relieved that Professor McGonagall was not present as well.

"Sit, please. Let me pour you some drinks," Dumbledore said. "I've been saving a bottle of wine for a special occasion."

Severus had told Sirana very little about Albus Dumbledore. He thought that it would be better to meet in person before having any impression already made. From the smile on her face, he thought she was quite taken with him already.

Once they had their drinks in hand and were seated comfortably, Albus said, "I've received word from your grandfather, Professor Cadogen. He wants you to know how happy and relieved he is to find that you are well, and to let you know that he has settled nicely in the States with your parents."

Sirana's goblet of wine hit the floor. She felt fortunate that it was a metal goblet, but she jumped up, apologizing for making such a mess. Dumbledore assured her calmly that it was alright, using his wand to remove any trace of wine on the floor. He insisted on pouring her another drink.

When they had all resettled into their chairs, he continued, "Perhaps I should have started off a little slower, but I find that it is often better to get right to the meat of the matter."

Sirana was shaking a little as she drank her wine, "You're fine, Headmaster. It's my fault for being so clumsy. I have so many questions about my grandfather and about what happened."

Dumbledore answered kindly, "First, I would like for you to call me Albus while we are outside of our school duties, and I would be happy to clear up your questions—that is, if I know the answers. There are some events that have transpired that have not yet come to light."

Chapter 33

Kane

S irana and Severus sat enthralled in the story of Professor
Kane Cadogen and his role in the First Wizardly War.
He had been one of the first members of the Order of the
Phoenix. During a key battle, his wife, Katherine, Sirana's
grandmother, was killed, leaving Professor Cadogen alone
to raise his only child, Sirana's mother. He was forced into
hiding with her after the war, as he was a high-level target for
the Death Eaters.

"There is more, Severus," Albus said, adopting a grave tone.
"When Professor Cadogen went into hiding, he was still an
active member of the Order of the Phoenix. He provided key
intel as well as protection for those who needed it." Severus had
been listening intently, wanting to learn more about Sirana and
how she came here, but Albus was now speaking to him, as if
it concerned him directly. "Severus, when the Potters went into
hiding at Godric's Hollow, Professor Cadogen was tasked with
looking after them—discreetly of course. He lived in the house
next door, along with his granddaughter—Sirana."

Severus was stunned. His mind tried to work over the details
of that night. He stole a glance at Sirana. The dates just didn't
fit—the math just didn't add up.

"I don't see how that would be possible. Sirana has told me that she moved to be with her grandfather after her husband passed. But she would have been just a child if she were there when that happened—when they were killed," Severus said, trying to make it work in his mind.

"Sirana, how old are you?" he asked, realizing he'd never asked her the question before.

"I'm thirty-two," she answered, not understanding the dilemma.

"How old were you when you moved in with your grandfather?" he asked next.

"Thirty-one. Why?" she replied.

Severus looked at Dumbledore. "So if she is thirty-two now, how did she move in with her grandfather at the time when… the *Potters*…lived next door?"

"That is the question that I still do not have the answer to," Albus answered. "However, according to her grandfather, she has been missing for fifteen years."

Severus continued, thinking of the night Lily died, "Sirana has visions in her dreams, that I myself have seen in her mind, of her grandfather, and of herself, running towards the house. After that, she doesn't remember how she came to be here."

Albus looked at Sirana, who was quietly listening to the two of them. "What do you remember of your neighbors and of the last night at your grandfather's?"

Sirana began slowly, "My grandfather and I were friends with the neighbors. Their names were Leia and Jacob Powell. They had a little boy, Henry. Leia was very nice to me, and I used to help her watch the baby sometimes. They stayed to themselves a lot though, but they were always friendly with us. That night, I remember I heard something. The door, it was squeaky, and I went to check. That's when I saw my grandfather running towards the neighbors. I ran after him. He looked wild, fear and rage in his eyes. The neighbor's house was flashing upstairs, and I was afraid for them…for them and for my grandfather."

She stopped, and Severus noticed tears in her eyes. She continued softly, "That's it. I fell, I saw a light…it surrounded me. That's the last thing I remember before I was here. Well, not here. I was lost, I didn't know where I was or even who I was. I just kept going. Things didn't become clearer until I was with Lucius, and then, everything was so outside the realm of possibility, I thought I was crazy…or maybe in a coma, living out a dream in my head. I'm still not sure *where* I am, but I decided that since I knew *who* I was, I was just going to build on that and see where it led. Now, I'm not even sure of who I really am."

Albus offered one more telling question. "Sirana, what year is it now?"

She looked at him oddly, and Severus did as well.

"1981," she answered.

Severus looked at Sirana, then back at Albus, finally asking, "Where has she been for the last fifteen years? Where has her memory went for that time? Not to mention she does not look older than thirty-two, and much younger in my opinion."

"Thank you," Sirana said, smiling in the face of a somber mood.

"She did say that she felt transformed when she arrived here. And she was…well…renewed." Severus stumbled on the words and was grateful that Albus didn't inquire further.

Albus took a drink of his wine and continued, "After Sirana's arrival here, I was curious. One does not simply fall out of the sky. Her name was familiar to me, and I made some inquiries. I knew that Professor Cadogen's granddaughter had disappeared after the Potters were killed, and her name was Sirana as well, but I too was unable to reconcile the two to be the same person."

"The Potters?" Sirana asked, trying to keep up with the story.

"Yes, Sirana," Albus explained. "Your neighbors were in hiding, and they had changed their name to the Powells. Lily, James, and Harry. They were killed that night from your dreams, except for the boy…The boy lived."

"I'm sorry to hear that his parents died," she said, then asked, finally catching on a little more, "What year is it now?"

Severus looked at her, hoping she would take the answer well, then leaned forward to grab her goblet of wine and placed it on the table. She saw his thought process and smiled up at him before he answered, "1996."

Severus thought she took the news better than he had expected, perhaps better than he himself. His mind was drawn back to that night. The grief, the hopelessness—he didn't want to live after Lily had died. Sirana had somehow been tied to that event. She had known Lily. It was too much to process, too much pain to relive. He felt like the scab was pulled off of the wound that had finally started to heal. He stood up and walked away.

"What does this mean? Why?" he asked no one in an anguished cry.

Albus came to him, standing beside him, and placed a hand on his shoulder. "I do not know why, or how...but I do know that matters of substance usually find their way into the light."

Chapter 34

Courage

Sirana's emotions were torn. She was relieved to hear news of her grandfather, as it made her feel more grounded in reality, but she was dismayed to hear of the circumstances surrounding her neighbors' death. There was so much to absorb. Some sort of magic had taken her from her grandfather's side and delivered her here, to a different time.

Severus seemed distraught. He must have been close with her neighbors. She hoped he didn't blame her—or her grandfather—for their death...A part of her wished her grandfather would have told her the truth about him being a wizard, and even that he would have taught her magic. Maybe she could have done more. She retrieved her wine and sat, waiting for them to talk privately. What had happened to her was not nearly as grievous as the emotions Severus was experiencing at the news. She wished she could comfort him in a way that would strip him of his pain. She had felt it in him before, buried deep within him, a love lost. He was a passionate man, and he felt deeply. She was no stranger to pain, and she knew the courage that he must hold to fearlessly love again. She held that in her thoughts, looking at what it meant to her. Yes, she knew he loved her. He had not said the words, but she had felt it, and she too loved him with a courage that would not relent, that would transcend even death.

Albus and Severus made it back over to apologize to Sirana for their absence. Albus spoke to them, his tone more hopeful, "I am making arrangements for your grandfather to come for a visit. I believe there may be answers that he may hold for you, Sirana. It may be a month or two before he can make it. He has had some health issues, but he assures me he is feeling much better. I have the feeling that he is making preparations so that he doesn't have to return. He has been away too long, and now, he has ties to which to return, and possibly remain."

Sirana was elated. "That would be wonderful. I have so much to tell him," she said, tears forming again in her eyes.

Severus could see that they were joyful tears this time. He stepped over to where she was sitting to place a hand on her shoulder and bent down to kiss her on her head. He could feel the connection with her, and it was unbreakable. Severus had surprised himself at how deeply these events had affected him. It brought so much from the past to the forefront—the heartbreak, the shame, the desperation, the grief. It all seemed to fade when he was with her. He looked at her now, and he knew that whatever was revealed about the past, his life with her filled any void.

Dumbledore looked fondly at the two of them. "Before you go, Severus, we have to find our new resident a place at Hogwarts. I can arrange for the rooms adjoining yours to be for her, as to allow close quarters without the appearance as such to our students and teachers. However, we need to assign her a position so that she may earn her keep." Albus smiled at that, then continued, "What would you recommend that would be suitable?"

Severus thought only momentarily before offering, "Sirana was a Physical Education teacher before. I have since been made aware that she might provide invaluable instruction to students in the art of hand-to-hand combat. Perhaps she could work with Madam Hooch as an assistant?"

Professor Dumbledore perked up at that, "It seems as if our path has been laid out before us. That is, if Sirana agrees."

"That would be wonderful," Sirana said. "I don't know how ever to thank you."

"You have done more already than I could ever repay you for," Albus said tenderly, taking her hand in his once again. He leaned in and said quietly, "You are as lovely as I remember your grandmother. She and your grandfather were dear friends of mine. I see their fire and courage in you—and eyes of blue flame. Whatever life you make here at Hogwarts, we will all be the better for it."

That was the last time Severus spoke with Albus Dumbledore before hearing the news that the Headmaster had escaped the attempt by Professor Umbridge and the Ministry to have him dispatched to Azkaban to await trial for conspiracy. The student organization, dubbed 'Dumbledore's Army,' was led by Harry Potter, and the Ministry had accused Professor Dumbledore of amassing an army to seize control of the Ministry. Severus felt the sharp sting of failure at having been unable to protect the knowledge of the student's secret organization. In Dumbledore's absence, Professor Umbridge had assumed the role of Headmaster, and Severus feared the possible threat to the school this could pose, as well as to his own mission. He knew he must not allow this complication to distract him from his focus, and he planned to continue his lessons with Potter regardless of the trials facing the school.

This evening, however, had not went as Severus had planned. He didn't know what had set him to attack the boy by throwing insults about his father. Actually, he *did* know. He had said that the boy was weak, like his father, but he knew differently. He also knew that he must use all that was in his arsenal to give the boy a fighting chance. When Harry had turned to attack his own thoughts, Severus revealed his own weaknesses, but those were of the past. Even though he would never be rid of the past, he was no longer weak, and he was able to keep Sirana from being revealed in his thoughts. Harry was as prepared as he could ready him for, and it was becoming dangerous for both of them to continue. He tried to tell himself that was the only reason he had abruptly ended the lessons with Potter, and yet, he still felt the sting of shame and regret. He knew he must maintain a balance of appearances versus outcomes. He also knew that neither Lucius nor Voldemort must learn of Sirana, and if they did, he must be prepared to explain, or at worst—he couldn't consider that yet. He must not fail...he *cannot* fail.

Every day at Hogwarts with Umbridge as Headmaster brought new levels of shockingly ridiculous decrees and equally absurd punishments for the students. Severus was no longer supplying Headmaster Umbridge with genuine Veritaserum, although she had already used the truth serum to force Cho, the amicable Ravenclaw girl, to divulge her knowledge of the student's secret meetings. Professor Snape wasn't usually inclined to involve himself in the sophomoric politics of the students at Hogwarts, but it had not gone unnoticed to him that the once popular student was being shunned by the other students because of the unfortunate circumstances of her betrayal, to which they were unaware. Severus had wondered at the girl's unwillingness to defend her actions with the truth that she had been coerced by the use of the forbidden potion.

Severus set off to begin his mission for Lord Voldemort, tasked with ensuring Lucius Malfoy did not fail to obtain the prophecy from the Ministry of Magic, which would be used in an attempt to thwart the prophecies' ill omen. Before he was able to make his leave from Hogwarts, he was called by Argus Filch to Headmaster Umbridge's office for a supposedly urgent matter. There would still be time if he hurried. He wasn't overly surprised to find Professor Umbridge up to her usual imperious measures to interrogate the students, but he was a bit astonished that she would be so brash as to not even attempt to conceal her abhorrently outrageous torment of the students. Severus entered the Headmaster's office to find Harry Potter in the hot seat. Headmaster Umbridge had summoned Severus to supply her yet again with more Veritaserum. He used the opportunity to not only inform her that there was no more to be found, but that she had used the last of the supply on Cho. He found some satisfaction in seeing the realization of that knowledge cross the faces of those who had questioned the girl's loyalty. He was dismayed with the revelation of Harry Potter's cryptic words,

"He's got Padfood at the place where it's hidden," which were obscure enough to confuddle Umbridge. Severus replied, "No idea," as if oblivious to the meaning of the riddle, knowing that he must now hasten his departure to share the intelligence with the Order of the Phoenix. Once again, he must find a way to navigate his clandestine commitments to the Dark Lord along with his loyalty to Dumbledore and his students.

Severus sat in his study, alone, brooding over the circumstances that had resulted in the ending of Headmaster Umbridge's rein, bringing about the rightful reinstatement of Headmaster Dumbledore. The death of Sirius Black weighed on him, and despite his turbulent relationship with the wizard, he mourned his loss and even what that loss would mean to Harry Potter. Even with the return of Albus and the protection his presence bestows, Severus's foreboding that Hogwarts and the Ministry would not long survive unscathed drove him to the solitude of his somber thoughts. When he heard the light tap on the door, he was mercifully brought from his thoughts by the welcomed reminder of the unexpected and mysterious gift that was Sirana. He took a deep breath, and as he slowly exhaled, he felt his mind settle into a more comfortable state…determination.

Chapter 35

Adjoining

True to his word, Professor Dumbledore had the adjacent rooms to Severus's prepared for Sirana. Severus heard the buzz around from the students that they were getting a new teacher, and that she would be staying at Slytherin house. Severus created a hidden doorway between the rooms so they could travel between the two freely.

"You don't intend to move over there, do you?" He asked Sirana bluntly. He was quite content sharing his bed, and the rest of his rooms, with her.

"Not unless you ask me to," Sirana said, smiling. "Although I plan to make good use of the space. I can do my workouts over there. And…" She stepped up to him and put her arms around his neck, playing with the back of his hair. "…when you get under my skin during our magic classes, I will have a place to retreat to, and I can lock the door."

Severus grabbed her around the waist and pulled her into him. "Ah, maybe I will finally get some respite from your insufferable whining."

Sirana laughed loudly at that. "Watch it, now. You're just lucky that the bed is so much warmer with you in it, otherwise my new bed might be more comfortable. And I wouldn't have to share the blanket."

At that, Severus leaned down, picked her up, and hoisted her over his shoulder. "We will see about that," he said, carrying her into her new rooms.

She screamed playfully as he dumped her on her new bed. "Aaaaahh, Severus!"

Severus began removing his jacket and shirt. "I will do you the service of assessing the comfort of your bed. However, I would recommend that you remove your clothing, because if there are any left on you when I join you, they may require mending when I'm done assisting you in disrobing."

Both of her eyebrows raised at that, and she didn't attempt to call his bluff. He withdrew his wand and set silencing spells on the room to provide privacy.

"I would not want the students to hear anything, otherwise they may think that I am killing their new teacher," he said, almost smiling down at her.

"You're killing me alright," Sirana replied, but Severus could see that she acknowledged that he wasn't wrong.

She lay there in her glorious nudeness. He stood and just enjoyed looking at her, noticing appreciatively that she was looking at his nudeness in the same manner. He climbed into the bed on his hands and knees and kissed her body top to bottom. She stretched contentedly under him like a newly awakened kitten, then rolled onto her stomach. He kissed her body again thoroughly, stopping at the nape of her neck to brush her hair aside and kiss her ears and neck.

"Mmmm…that's nice," she said softly. He reached his hand back down between her thighs and let his fingers dip into her. She was already warm and wet. He heard her gasp and moan lowly. It had been at least a fortnight since they'd had the opportunity to be with each other, and he didn't plan on putting it off another minute. He raised up on his knees behind her and pulled her by her hips up to him. She looked back at him a bit surprised, but he could see the same immediate need in her eyes as well. He rubbed just his tip in her at first to help ease his entry, then he pushed himself into her deeply while pulling her towards him by her hips. From her hoarse cry, he could tell that she hadn't expected the magnitude of sensation that this position allowed. He closed his eyes a moment, taking pleasure in the feeling of being buried deep inside her. He began slowly, moving in long strokes, only gradually picking up the tempo. He drove into her until she screamed his name, caught up in her orgasm. He could feel her warmly gush over him and he leaned down to kiss her adoringly on her back. He rolled her over and kissed her eyes and nose and lips. She reached her hands to his face, looking lovingly in his eyes. She pulled him down to kiss him deeply and wrapped her legs around him, inviting him to find his own release. He didn't break their kiss as he reached down to guide himself into her. He made love to her slowly, his eyes closed, experiencing this moment together with her for all that it is. When he spilled into her, he felt as if he spilled his heart into her as well.

Chapter 36

The Dark Lord

Sirana was very excited to get started in her new role as the new Combat Instructor. There wasn't much time left in the school year, but Dumbledore had said that a professor named Umbridge had left unexpectedly, and they weren't going to replace her until the next year, so a new teacher would be a welcome distraction. She didn't ask why, but she got the impression that the students really didn't like the former Professor. She had already met Madam Hooch, and they hit it off nicely. Madam Hooch had helped her acquire the appropriate teaching wardrobe and supplies. She had more fun than she thought she would picking out her teaching attire. She chose tight breeches that lace up the front, soft soled boots, and a tunic that looked like it was something out of a pirate movie. She felt like she looked a bit like a swashbuckler when she was done. *It's a bit romantic,* she thought, *like I'm in a movie.* She had a stock of wasters for sword fighting, some pugil sticks, along with some mu ren zhuangs to use as practice dummies. She was going to meet her students soon—real witches and wizards in training— and she wanted to impress on them the importance of being able to defend themselves with more than just magic. By the midday meal, she was sure of one truth—children are children, whether they are magical or not. It had been a bit of controlled chaos at first, but within the hour, they had already started getting the hang of the drills. She was quite proud of them. She entered the Grand Hall, looking around for where to sit. Luckily, Madam Hooch caught up with her and took her over to sit next to her. She caught a glimpse of Severus. He looked regal, sitting at the large banquet table with the other professors. Dumbledore introduced her as the new teacher, Sirana *sensei*. She had been a martial arts teacher with a black belt back in the States, and had always enjoyed being called Sensei, so it seemed like an appropriate title for her new position. Severus caught her eye, and she thought he was looking at her with pride, and she felt flattered. The kids all applauded loudly. They made her feel pretty special too. After she finished her meal, several of the professors came to introduce themselves. She got to go home afterwards since she only had to teach morning classes, and she left for the day feeling welcomed.

When Severus came home later, he found her in the bathtub, soaking in a steaming bath.

"Has it been a month already?" Severus asked. "I've lost track. Rough day?" He sat on the edge of the tub.

"I've been keeping up my exercises, but I still feel like I'm going to be sore tomorrow. I went all out," she replied, smiling.

"I've heard that you've made quite the impression already, with the students and professors. It seems you've filled a niche that we didn't even know was needed," Severus said.

"Well, that makes me feel good. I guess it makes sense. Not all students are interested in Quidditch, so this gives them a chance to participate in something athletic that isn't necessarily a team sport."

Severus removed his jacket, asking, "Have you charmed the water yet?"

"No," she answered. "I was hoping you would come home in time to do that."

Severus charmed the water, then removed the rest of his clothes and joined her in the bath. He sat at the other end of the tub from her, stretching out his legs in the hot water.

"Turn around. Let me wash your back," he suggested, and she complied. They took turns washing each other's backs, then lay soaking in the tub together until the water started to cool.

They moved to the sitting room after the bath. Sirana started the record player and turned it down low. She brought them a tray of bread and wine and settled in her chair.

"I would like to talk to you about some things I've been thinking about. My neighbors…I know you must have been close to them. I can't help but feel like I failed them somehow… failed you," Sirana said, looking down at her glass.

Severus thought about that night, along with everything that came before and after.

"Sirana, you mustn't harbor any feelings of regret or responsibility. There were a lot of circumstances leading up to that night, and the events that were set in motion before then have still not completely been resolved," he said solemnly. He was quiet for a minute, thinking of how best to start. "Lily," he started, then stopped again, closing his eyes for a moment before continuing, "Lily was my childhood friend when I had none. When we came to Hogwarts, we drifted apart. She meant more to me than I ever let her know. I am now tasked with protecting her son, who is presently a student here at Hogwarts."

Sirana was silent for a while, then said, "I'm sorry. I know she was special. I used to help her watch her boy on occasion. We were friends of sorts. She was always so sweet to me. She always seemed a little sad, but she loved her son more than anything. Why do you have to protect him? Is he in danger?"

Severus thought about it. It was time to tell her everything. Sirana meant the world to him, and he did not want to make the same mistakes he'd made in the past of not letting the person that mattered the most to him not know of his feelings. It was never easy for him to open up completely.

He put his head back against the back of his chair, looking up at the ceiling. Suddenly, he felt a warmth come over him, like the warmth of a cozy fireplace. Once again, he felt the familiarity he had felt before. He wondered if it was the connection he had with Sirana. He felt comforted, and it bolstered his courage. He sat up and asked Sirana to sit on his lap—she seemed too far away.

"From before the First Wizarding War, there was a powerful wizard. He used to be a student here at Hogwarts.

He was powerful, but that wasn't enough for him. He didn't want to suffer the same fate as every other living being in this world—he wanted to live forever. Whether his desire for immortality was due to his fear of death or his desire for omnipotent power, I still do not know. This desire corrupted him, and he became malevolent, vicious…evil. His great power attracted others who wished to share in it." He reached to touch her face, brushing a stray strand of hair away from her cheek, continuing with deep regret in his voice. "After Lily drifted away from me, starting her own life with James, I felt lost…maybe angry at the cards I'd been dealt. I joined his ranks, and she never looked at me the same way again. I fear now that if you were to know the person I was, the things I have done, that you would no longer look at me the same way either."

Sirana looked at him at that, deep into his eyes. "I have seen into you, Severus. Maybe I haven't seen all of what happened in your past, but I know the person you are now. I know you more than I've known anyone before in my life. Whoever you were in your past, it is still a part of you—a part of what has made you who you are. You don't have to worry about me…my feelings for you are constant."

Severus reached up and brushed a tear that had fallen on her cheek. He pulled her to him and kissed her tenderly, and she felt his love for her. He continued, "He killed her—them. There was a prophecy that foretold of his death. The prophecy pointed to Harry, Lily's son. He went to kill Harry, and Harry was the only one to survive the attack. Lily sacrificed herself—and Lily and

James, and the Dark Lord all died…and yet, the Dark Lord was reborn, and he lives still."

Sirana felt a chill in the room that Severus must have felt as well since he wrapped his arms around her tightly, as if to protect her from the cold. She wrapped her arms around him tightly, as she vowed to protect him as well.

Chapter 37

Foul Mood

Sirana finished out the rest of the week of teaching her combat classes in good form. She had started teaching so late in the school year, so she wanted to accomplish as much as possible in the remainder. Severus told her that the students would go home during the summer break, and that he would as well. She would stay at Hogwarts for the summer, and she could use the time to better prepare for the next year. She would miss him dearly, but he assured her that they would find time together.

She was hoping that Severus could continue his magic lessons with her. She had so much left to learn. Severus had been distracted recently. There was a sense of a growing threat around Hogwarts that she didn't fully understand yet, although she knew it had something to do with the Dark Lord that Severus had told her about. She tried to keep her own students focused on more positive things—and learning combat skills could work to boost their confidence to better deal with the stress and fear they faced. She really didn't know what to do to help Severus. He would come home late many nights, and was often broody. He was never short with her though—other than sometimes during their magic lessons, and she could handle that. She would be there for him when he was ready to divulge.

Severus entered as Sirana was finishing up the homework he'd assigned her for her magic lessons. She usually tried to finish early so she could work ahead on other aspects of magic that she had interest in. She had learned how to break the paralyzing curse Severus was under that way. Now, he seemed in a bit of bad temper as he greeted her. He looked over her progress, saying sourly, "If you think that my lesson plan isn't adequate for you, perhaps you should look for another teacher."

She stepped back as if he'd struck her. "You never told me that I was limited to learning only what you teach me. I'm always sure to finish what you've assigned before I pursue subjects of my own interests. Not to mention what I've picked up in my free time has come in handy on at least on one occasion," Sirana said defiantly. She wasn't much of a cusser, otherwise she would tell him what he could go do with himself.

Before she said something they might both regret, she turned on her heel and went into her own rooms. She stopped short of locking the door, since she was never the kind to be spiteful. She did, however, feel like she could spit fire. She tried not to take what he'd said to heart. Some things said weren't worth dwelling on unless they actually came to fruition. For now, she would let it be.

She worked on preparing her lesson plan for next week, finding something else to focus on. She suddenly heard banging and crashing that sounded like objects being thrown around Severus's room and realized that the silencing spells did not block sound between their adjoining rooms. Unless she heard screaming or a cry for help, she'd be damned if she was going to go check to see what it was. Perhaps since she'd left, he'd resorted to taking his temper tantrum out on inanimate objects instead of her. She hadn't eaten dinner, but she didn't have an appetite. She poured herself a glass of wine instead and donned her bedclothes. Maybe some light reading before bed would soothe her spirit.

Severus could kick himself. He was such an idiot. The events of the week had set him on edge, and he had taken it out on the last person who deserved it. As soon as the words had left his mouth, he'd regretted them. He was glad to see that she hadn't withered or cried. That would have done him in. It was bad enough as it was. He poured himself a few glasses of brandy and sulked a bit before getting so angry with himself that he took it out on his room. He was one to preach about controlling one's emotions. He ran his hand through his long black hair. He needed to focus. Things seemed out of his control, and his dread of what was happening with Voldemort threatened to get the best of him. He would not let the darkness extinguish the only light in his bleak world. He used a spell to set his room right and headed to see if it was too late to make amends.

He knocked softly on the door without testing to see if she had locked him out.

"Come in," he heard, and the tightness in his stomach eased a little. She was in her bed with a glass of wine and a book. He entered and stood in the doorway, not yet sure of his welcome.

"I said you could come in. You don't need to hover on the periphery," she said shortly. He took that to mean she was open to reconciliation. He walked in slowly and moved to sit on the edge of her bed. He leaned towards her slightly, and she put her book down and finally looked at him.

"Is it too late to retract my earlier statement? If so, I will be forced to apologize for it," he said evenly, testing the waters. He was pleased to see a smile turn up the corners of her lovely lips.

"Can I get a written retraction? Otherwise, an apology might be more suitable for mending the injury," she replied. He knew she was partly joking, but he accepted his penance willingly.

He rose to go to her desk and began writing. She patiently waited, and he thought she was probably curious to see her request put into written word. He returned to sit on her bed and handed her the letter. She read the letter before looking up at him, and he noticed her eyes were misty.

"Severus," she said softly, "This is beautiful. Thank you."

He smiled tenderly, "I mean every word. A friend once said that words can be powerful weapons, and I swear that I will try to never use them to harm you again."

Sirana folded the letter he'd written her and put it in the drawer of her nightstand. "It is forgotten, then. And yes, I think you are more than an adequate teacher. I will do as you say if you wish me to follow stricter study parameters, because you have never been unfair to me. But I would like you to consider that the more capable I am, the more valuable in the future I could be. As far as I'm concerned, this is my home now, and I will defend it with my life," she said with a conviction that he could see mirrored in her eyes. He let his mental connection with her deepen until she could see his complete trust in her, as well as his admiration for a passion that he too shared.

"Have you eaten?" he asked. "It's not too late in the evening to break bread."

She smiled and rose to put on her robe. "It's never too late, Severus," she said, taking his arm.

Chapter 38

Cypress Wood & Unicorn Hair

"What are your plans for the day?" Severus asked Sirana. It was Saturday morning, and Sirana was looking forward to the weekend.

"Madam Hooch and I are going to go to a place called Hogsmeade for lunch. She said there are some interesting shops and a cozy little pub. Would you like to join us?" she asked.

"Heavens, no. But thank you for the invitation," Severus replied. "I would like to take you somewhere when you return."

"Looks like I will have a busy day, then. I can't say that I'm not happy to get out and about. Everyone here has been so nice to me," she said happily.

"If you have no plans tomorrow, I would like to take you to meet someone. Since you will be staying here for the summer, I would like for you to meet some of the others that remain here as well," Severus replied, drinking his morning tea.

"That would be nice. I've already met Professor Trelawney, although briefly. She said she would like to talk to me more one day. She said something about my aura," Sirana said. "She stared at me for the longest time. It was a bit unsettling."

Severus looked serious for a moment, as if thinking about something unpleasant, then he stood, coming over to her, "I think you will enjoy meeting the person I have in mind. I have asked him to keep an eye on you when I'm gone. His name is Hagrid. I think you might enjoy his good nature."

"Then it looks like I will have a full weekend. I was hoping we could have some time to work on some magic lessons. I've been looking forward to try a couple of the spells I've been working on," Sirana said, standing to leave.

Severus leaned down to give her a kiss goodbye. He traced the side of her face with his finger. "Is that all you are looking forward to working on with me this weekend?" he said suggestively.

She blushed. He smiled at her, and she knew he saw her cheeks flush.

"Wonderful," she replied, trailing her finger down his chest, "Now Madam Hooch will think I'm daft, walking around with a silly smile on my face all afternoon."

Severus snatched her finger from his chest and brought it to his mouth to kiss it. "We could always postpone our plans for a couple hours," he said, now tracing his lips with her finger. "But I think the anticipation will do you good."

She felt a little weak in the knees suddenly, and she had to laugh at herself a little. "Just remember, Severus, what's good for the goose is good for the gander," she said smiling sweetly up to him.

"Touché," Severus replied, raising one eyebrow as if that bit of irony had just crossed his mind.

Sirana had a splendid time in Hogsmeade. Madam Hooch was the perfect guide. Their last stop was at the Hog's Head, and they each had a pint of butter beer. Their conversation turned to the subject of men, and Madam Hooch informed her that there were a few at Hogwarts that had made inquiries of Sirana's status.

"Well, I'm flattered for sure," Sirana laughed. "But I have someone in my mind at the moment."

Madam Hooch smiled knowingly. "Yes, I figured. I've seen you looking at him. I will keep it our secret. I can't pretend to understand it, but love is a strange and wondrous bird."

Sirana smiled back conspiratorially. "Yes, yes, it is."

When Sirana made it back, Severus wasn't home. She found a note on the table with a map. He was called away for business, so he wanted her to go to meet Hagrid today instead of Sunday. She was supposed to meet with him in half an hour.

She followed the map to find a hut towards the edge of the Forbidden Forest. When she knocked, the largest man she'd ever seen answered the door.

"Well, hello, miss! Come on in," the man said, stepping aside to welcome her in. "I'm Hagrid. I'm the Professor of Care of Magical Creatures. It's lovely ter meet yeh."

Sirana liked him immediately. He reminded her a bit of her husband who had passed. Her husband was a big man, although not nearly as giant as Hagrid.

"It's a pleasure to meet you as well. I'm Sirana. Severus—I mean, Professor Snape wanted to introduce us since we would both be spending the summer here," she said, shaking the giant's enormous hand.

"Yes, Professor Snape didn't want us ter miss the chance ter meet before summer break. I'm ter keep an eye on yeh during the summer. He said if yeh had some extra time, yeh might even be able ter help me with the animals," he replied with a hopeful tone.

"You say you care for magical creatures!?" Sirana asked, wide-eyed.

"Erm, well, yes," Hagrid replied, as if suddenly proud of his title since she seemed impressed with it.

"That's wonderful! I would love to help out when I get a chance," she offered, excited at the opportunity.

They agreed to meet the following week to get started, and Sirana made her way back to Hogwarts, feeling a bit more optimistic about the summer break. She loved animals after all, and magical creatures sounded intriguing.

It was early in the evening when Sirana made it back. Severus was waiting for her.

"If we leave now, we can still keep our appointment," he said. They Disapparated from the room.

"Do you think you can teach me that sometime?" she asked him when they arrived in Diagon Alley.

"Yes, I can, although Apparating in and out of Hogwarts is not permitted—or possible—except for a rare few who have express permission from the Headmaster."

He led her through the back alley since he thought it best not to be seen together by too many people. They arrived at Ollivander's wand shop, and he escorted her in.

"Ah, welcome. I was beginning to fear that you wouldn't make it," Mr. Ollivander said.

Suddenly, he stopped and looked at Sirana, then came around the counter to get an even closer look at her. "Sirana Cadogen...I haven't seen you since you were a young lass."

Severus looked at her and saw she was confused. "I'm sorry, I don't remember meeting you before," she said.

"That's odd," Mr. Ollivander replied. "You and your grandfather, Professor Cadogen, came here, quite some years ago. I haven't seen him since..." he looked a little confused as he thought about it. "You've already been chosen by your wand. Made from cypress wood...yes...and unicorn hair. Don't tell me that you've misplaced it?"

Severus didn't want to risk more questions, and quickly replied, "No, she just received word that it had been found. I had considered a temporary wand might be suitable, but I think we may wait until it is returned. Thank you for your assistance." Since Ollivander would assume she would already know how to use a wand, he didn't want him to hand her one to try out and her give away that she had no idea what to do with it. He quickly ushered her out the door and told her he'd explain when they had more privacy.

When they were back at Hogwarts, Sirana went and sat in her chair, a little tired from the events of the day. Severus poured them both a drink and joined her.

"What was all of that about?" she asked.

"I was going to ask you that same question. Do you remember getting a wand with your grandfather?" Severus asked.

"No, I don't remember a wand or meeting Mr. Ollivander," she replied.

"There is a chance he erased that memory. Perhaps he was trying to protect you, " Severus said as if thinking out loud. "He will be here within the month. I will ask Albus to inquire of your grandfather if he knows of your wand, and if he has possession of it, ask him to bring it to you. I was hoping to begin your instruction to wand magic, but it looks like that may be delayed. If your grandfather is not in possession of your wand, I can acquire a substitute for you, but it will be inferior to having your own."

He wanted to begin teaching her wand magic before he left for summer. He knew he wouldn't get to see her as often, and he didn't want to leave her defenseless. He thought they would work on more wandless defenses after he spoke with Albus. But now...

He thought of the rest of the plans he had for the day. It had been a long day, and she looked as tired as he felt. He didn't want the opportunity to go to waste, and he thought of a remedy. He went to retrieve the rest of the elf-made wine, and after pouring them both a drink, he turned the record player on low.

"Are you trying to seduce me, Severus?" Sirana asked in mock innocence.

"Perhaps," he answered slowly in his velvety voice, handing her the glass. "Would you like to dance?" he asked, offering her his hand.

"Why, of course I would," she answered.

Chapter 39

Reward

Sirana loved dancing, especially with Severus. He had a way about him that made the whole world disappear when they danced. Their dance was casual and light, drinking their wine, talking softly, laughing. She was enthralled with this man. From the look in his eyes, she could tell he found her equally captivating. There was also an air of danger that always emanated from Severus, but she never felt threatened by it nor did she feel that she had any control of it. Something was driving this man to some unknown fate, bound by a promise. She often felt it there, hidden in his mind, encircled by a ring of regret. Now, as they danced, she felt none of that in him, she felt only a sense of love and contentment—and the flames of desire for her. Her own flames burned hotly, and as he lowered his head to kiss her, she felt the intensity of their flames heighten, feeding off of each other's fire.

Severus felt the fire in her mind, and it was matched by his own. He didn't want to think of any of the troubles weighing on his mind. He had her with him here, now, and the rest could wait.

"Are you going to carry me off again like a war prize, or are you going to let me walk to your bed on my own accord this time?"

Severus couldn't help but laugh. She had a wit about her that only added to her charm.

"You should feel fortunate that I haven't yet dragged you in by your hair," he said playfully. He bowed and motioned with his arm. "As you wish."

She drank the last sip of her wine, then took his glass and finished the last drink of his as well, setting them down before accepting his invitation into his bedroom. He couldn't shed the feeling that this time with her was precious—that their time together would be limited in the future. He pushed that thought from his mind, determined to live in the present and relish their moments together.

He relieved her of her blouse and moved to her breeches, untying the laces slowly.

"These are nice," he said. "Is this your retribution for my multitude of buttons?"

She laughed. "Perhaps. If I have to work for my reward, it's only fair that you have to work for yours."

Severus smiled. "If this is considered work, I think I would be tempted to change my profession."

"Well, you definitely have a calling for it," Sirana said, as she started on his buttons

"As do you, my dear," he said as he looked down to see she had made quick work of his buttons and was starting on the clasp of his trousers. He groaned lowly as she reached into his pants. She grasped him firmly, moving closer to him as she stroked him sensually. He was caught off guard when she lowered herself in front of him, licking his tip with her tongue. His breath caught, and his hips jerked forward involuntarily. She looked up at him with an impish smile, then moved seductively to take him deeply in her mouth. He was transfixed. She was a provocative, tantalizing, and exciting lover, all while embodying an essence of sweet innocence. He reached down his hand and brushed her hair back, then wrapped his hand in it. Severus knew he could take no more of this sweet madness, and he brought her up to him and on to the bed. He knew he didn't have much left in him, so he entered her swiftly, slowly moving in and out of her to try to prolong their lovemaking. She was exquisitely warm and wet, and she moved under him, meeting his force with her own.

His climax was swiftly approaching, and he could no longer hold it back. His release was agonizingly intense, and he cried out hoarsely. When he recovered sufficiently, he kissed her impassionedly, then moved his hand down to stroke her gently. He saw her initial surprise at his intention, then she closed her eyes and allowed him to bring her to her climax. Afterwards, she snuggled up next to him, and he pulled her to him, then moved to lay on his back, pulling her to lay on top of him with her head on his chest. They fell asleep, feeling the closeness of their bodies and minds, and slept in each other's arms until morning.

Chapter 40

Sweet Sorrow

The day had arrived—the end of the school year. Sirana was sad as she said her goodbyes to her students and fellow teachers at the year-end feast. What she dreaded most was Severus leaving Hogwarts for the summer. She felt it in the pit of her stomach. She was beginning to understand more of the threat facing Hogwarts, and that Severus was ineradicably involved in a manner that was intricately complicated. Severus was leaving for his own home in Cokeworth at Spinner's End for the summer as usual so as to not arouse the suspicion of the Dark Lord. It complicated things even more since Voldemort had ordered Wormtail to stay there as well to provide assistance, although Severus had said that he was more likely there to spy for the Dark Lord. Sirana was deeply worried for Severus. She knew he was a powerful wizard in his own right, but she couldn't shake the dread that he was in danger.

Severus waited for Sirana to return home from the feast. He knew she would probably linger longer with goodbyes than him since she was quite popular already among the students and staff. He could almost imagine if he had made different choices how things could have been different for himself. But he was aware of the nature of things, and without his life as it had been, who would have taken his place to help balance against the forces of evil? He thought he would have to face his trials alone and had felt a deep sorrow at times that he would sacrifice himself for those who thought he was the enemy. That thought had not deterred him from his steadfast loyalty to them. Sirana had not altered his course; however, her presence in his life had changed the plot. He was no longer the poor broken soul—unloved, tragic. He was given a new role to play, and he knew that if he were to fall to his cause, he may be unsung, but he would not be ungrieved.

His introspection was gratefully interrupted by Sirana's return. He could see that her eyes were red and puffy, as if she'd been crying for some time. He rose from his chair, dreading the thought of saying goodbye, even though he knew it wasn't for forever. He reminded himself that his departure would have been empty without her, and for the first time, he understood how parting could actually be a sweet sorrow. He walked to her without words and took her in his arms, holding her head against him. His heart was touched deeply as she sobbed into his chest. He had seen her heart, but it was a rare occasion for her to show any vulnerability, and he loved her even more for showing it to him now.

As her crying subsided, he produced a handkerchief from his jacket. She wiped her eyes and nose, then finally looked up to him, brushing her hair away from her face as if to gather herself. "I'm sorry. Thank you," she said, her voice wavering.

He took her face in his hands and leaned down to kiss her tear-streaked cheeks.

"It's alright. It's going to be alright," he said comfortingly.

She smiled a little at that. "I know, I know. It's just…I didn't expect all of this…to fall in love with this school, the students, the teachers…you."

Severus felt his heart ache with love for her. "Sirana, I love you. No matter what happens, that will be eternal." He kissed her tenderly, then deeply. Not wanting their time together to end, they held each other until it was time for him to leave.

"It's not for forever," he said, then Disapparated from the room.

Sirana wasn't one to wallow, but the cry she had had helped washed away some of the sadness. She put on a record and worked on her itinerary for the summer. Tomorrow, she would visit Trelawney as promised. The next day, she would go see Hagrid. Severus had left her an abundance of homework to work on. She would make good use of the summer to grow stronger in her magical abilities. She was also looking forward to seeing her grandfather as his arrival was drawing closer. Later, when she snuggled into Severus's bed, she touched their connection lightly. She couldn't deepen their link from this distance, but she could tell that his mind had touched the ever-present thread that bound them at the same moment, and she fell into a warm and blissful sleep.

Chapter 41

Trelawney & Hagrid

Sirana was really not looking forward to her meeting with Professor Trelawney today. She seemed nice enough, but Sirana was always a bit suspicious of Divination.

Maybe suspicious is the wrong word, she thought. If clairvoyance was indeed a possibility, she did not feel comfortable with the idea of a prediction or prophecy hanging over her head. She preferred the mystery of not knowing what the future held.

Professor Trelawney met her in her classroom, then led her up the narrow stairs to the small room where she lived and worked. She looked around at all of the eclectic items in Professor Trelawney's room. Trelawney stared at her wide-eyed for a few uncomfortable moments, before finally offering her a seat.

"Professor Trelawney, I appreciate you inviting me to meet with you, but I need to tell you first that I am not interested in seeing any of my future before it happens. I prefer my path be fluid," Sirana said as politely as possible.

"Oh, dear," Trelawney said. "Our life is like a history book—already written, just waiting to be read. We are already dead…"

Sirana thought about that, and answered, "If my life is already written, I would like to be the one to read it as it happens, not before."

Trelawney fidgeted as if she wanted to ask a question but was afraid of not getting the answer she wanted. Finally, her curiosity won out over her trepidation and she asked, "Would you allow me to take a peek at a few of your pages if I promise not to tell you what they reveal? Please, have some tea with me."

Sirana thought about the offer. She liked Professor Trelawney. She didn't feel any threat from the eccentric lady. She finally acquiesced. "Alright, but please, promise that you will also not share it with others if it is something dreadful."

Professor Trelawney agreed and prepared their tea. Sirana did as Trelawney instructed, then as she handed the cup for her to read, she couldn't stop herself from looking.

Trelawney saw her and asked, "What do you see my dear?"

Sirana answered, not seeing any harm as long as Trelawney kept her promise, "I see a fawn."

Trelawney looked for herself, and Sirana wondered what more she could see than she had herself. Trelawney gasped, looking up at Sirana and then reached out as if to caress her aura. Sirana noticed a tear fall down her cheek and couldn't help but wonder what would be so sad as to make her cry. But then, she saw Trelawney smile serenely and felt as if the tear was one of happiness instead.

"Thank you, dear. Thank you for that. We may be bound by our books, but it's the chapters between the beginning and end that make up our stories."

Sirana felt at peace with that and thanked Professor Trelawney.

"Please, call me Sybill," the Professor continued. "I don't know if you were aware of the tribulations of the school year before your arrival, but I am happy to have been reinstated, and I will be here all summer if you need anything—even if it's just company."

They both reached out to grasp each other's hands, feeling closer from the experience, and Sirana offered the same invitation to her before leaving.

Sirana woke up early the next day to get ready to go see Hagrid. She hoped their first day together would go as well as her meeting with Professor Trelawney. Hagrid was already outside, waiting for her. He was carrying a leather satchel and a huge walking stick. When she approached, he handed her a walking stick that was more suitable for her height.

"We'll 'ave a bit o' a hike today inter the forest," Hagrid said, taking off straight away towards the forest. He continued talking as she followed him closely. "Dawn is the best time ter see 'em. Not everyone can see 'em, mind yeh, but we won' know if yeh can 'til yeh do."

She had no idea what he was talking about, but Severus was right—she enjoyed the good-natured way about Hagrid, and she was enjoying his company already. She felt like she was going on an adventure, and he was her giant guide. She had to take three steps to each one of his, but because of his size, he didn't move that swiftly, so it worked out nicely. He liked to talk it seemed, and she liked to listen, so that made for an enjoyable hike.

As they approached a small clearing, she noticed that Hagrid slowed his pace, breathing and walking more quietly, as if to not startle whatever he thought was ahead. Sirana gasped as she saw the creatures slowly appear from behind the trees and brush.

"They smell the meat I 'ave in me bag," Hagrid whispered loudly. "Clever creatures really...Can yeh see 'em, then?"

"Yes, I can. They're beautiful!" Sirana exclaimed breathlessly.

Hagrid raised his eyebrows at that. "Most people don' share yer opinion. I was hoping yeh wouldn' be scared of 'em. They're magnificent creatures in my opinion."

"I can see that. Can we touch them, or are they wild?" Sirana asked hopefully.

"Touch 'em! Ride 'em! This herd o' Thestrals are tame," Hagrid explained proudly. He pulled out a few pieces of raw meat and tossed them to the Thestrals closest to them. "If they take to yeh, maybe yeh can ride 'em one day. Of course, *I* don't ride too often, 'cause of me size. I'm too heavy fer most of 'em. Except fer Tenebrus. He's grown ter be pretty strong. He bravely offers ter give me a ride, but I don' like ter take 'm up on his offer too often since I know it's probably a strain fer 'em," Hagrid said affectionately.

Hagrid handed Sirana a piece of the meat, motioning her to hold it out to Tenebrus. The large Thestral walked up to her and gently took the meat from her hand, then tossed it up in the air and caught it in his mouth. Sirana clapped. Hagrid said, "Show off!" to Tenebrus. The Thestral then walked up close to Sirana, sniffing her up and down, then laid his head on her shoulder. Sirana's mouth dropped open in awe, and she petted the Thestral on the muzzle.

"Well, he seems ter 'ave taken a liking to yeh," Hagrid said, with a bit of surprise in his voice. "Maybe next week, he'll let yeh ride 'm."

"Really?! That would be wonderful!" Sirana exclaimed. "Thank you so much for bringing me here, Hagrid. It's magical."

"Yer welcome. Thank yeh fer comin' with me. If yer up fer it, there's a few more magical creatures I'd like ter show yeh over the summer. Yeh can learn and help at the same time," Hagrid suggested hopefully.

"I'm up for it for sure," Sirana answered, and she had a much more optimistic feeling about the summer break.

Chapter 42

Unbreakable

S everus hadn't been sleeping well. He missed sharing his bed with Sirana. There was so much he wanted to tell her. Today was not what he would have considered a good day. He had met with Narcissa and her sister Bellatrix. He was sure it would have gone much better if Bellatrix had not wormed her way into the meeting. Severus was fond of Narcissa, as she was of him. Before her marriage to Lucius, Narcissa had come to him several times when she and Lucius would argue and take a break from their relationship. He had provided her comfort—among other things. Even though they never mentioned it again after she was married, they never had ill feelings towards each other, and they had not expected anything more from each other than what they received. She had looked at him with tears in her eyes, wanting protection for her son, Draco. The Dark Lord had recruited Draco as his assassin, and since Lucius had been imprisoned in Azkaban, she needed someone to watch out for her only son. He would have done so voluntarily, as Narcissa and he had an understanding of each other, but Bellatrix had pushed the issue, calling him a coward, and asked him to make the Unbreakable Vow. Now, he felt the dread beginning to seep back in, and he wanted nothing more than to see Sirana. He knew she wouldn't be able to stop the inevitabilities to come, but she was his reminder that he still had a soul to offer—that his sacrifices weren't meaningless.

He remembered what Dumbledore said—"The time comes swiftly for each of us to give perhaps our last pound of flesh." He had hoped that the time would not have come so quickly, but he could see the signs, and he felt the weight of it all settled on his shoulders. It had been almost a month since he'd seen Sirana. So much was happening that he couldn't risk seeing her and alerting the Dark Lord of his feelings for her. He had kept in contact with Dumbledore, so he knew she was doing well. After making the Unbreakable Vow, he knew it would reinforce the Dark Lord's trust of him, and he could move more freely for a while.

He sat in his chair for a while, trying to clear his mind before going to see Sirana. He didn't want her to feel any of the sorrow and pain inside him. Once he finally felt satisfied that his emotions were under control, he gathered a few items he wanted to bring with him, then Apparated into his room at Hogwarts.

Severus found that Sirana had not as yet arrived home for the evening. He had checked her rooms and his. He was careful not to let his mental connection with her give away his arrival. He wanted it to be a surprise. He had brought a bottle of elf-made wine for them to share. He hoped it would soften the sting of the time he had spent away. He hadn't gone a day without thinking of her, and he could feel a twinge of nervous anticipation building in him.

He went into his study to pour himself a glass of brandy. Maybe that would take the edge off. He noticed that Sirana had completed all of the work he'd left for her. He would have to set out more for her this time. He sat in his study. The living area was too empty without her. He swore at himself for being so emotional and went into his bedroom instead. He was a little surprised that it appeared she had been sleeping in his bed instead of her own. He didn't mind in the least though, and he thought he could smell a faint trace of her soap and wine. It was still early in the evening, and he wondered what she'd been doing with her time. He heard the faint click of a door coming from her rooms. He had left the door open between them so that she would suspect someone was there and come to check.

He went back into his living area to wait for her to find him. The brandy hadn't helped, and his stomach was almost up in his throat. He saw her peek her head around the corner, then she screamed, "Severus!"

He was frozen for a moment, not sure if she was screaming in anger or joy, until she ran to him and threw her arms around his neck. He squeezed her tight and swung her around, her feet lifting from the floor. They kissed as if they were starving for each other. Finally, they broke apart, holding each other's faces, staring into each other's eyes. Severus had noticed that her hair was wet and that she was completely soaked to the bone.

Sirana saw his confusion and offered, "Ah. I've been out all day in the rain with Hagrid. We've been riding Thestrals. I finally talked him into riding with me today. It was so much fun."

She looks so happy, Severus thought, with a bit of guilt for coming to her in such a solemn mood.

Her smile faded a little, and she asked, "How have you been, Severus? I've missed you so much. I tried not to be sad about it, but some days, it was almost too much to bear."

Severus stroked her cheek with his fingers. "I too have missed you dearly. I wished I could have come sooner, but I couldn't risk it. I'm sad to say I can't stay long. Just until tomorrow."

"Oh no," Sirana exclaimed. "My grandfather is expected to arrive the day after tomorrow. I was hoping you could meet him. But it's alright. I'm sure the opportunity will present itself again some time. I'm just happy to have you back now." She looked at him more closely, then asked, "Are you really alright, Severus? You look tired. Have you been sleeping?"

It was Severus who avoided a direct answer this time. "I will be fine. I brought you home a gift. First, you can go get changed out of your wet clothes."

He went and retrieved the elf-made wine and poured them each a glass while she went to her bedroom to change. He couldn't help but make his way into her rooms. Surely, she would forgive him for the intrusion. He leaned against the doorway to her bedroom as she finished removing her undergarments, her back to him. She took a brush from her side table and brushed her long hair. He felt like a cat watching a bird, and he let his mind enter hers to show her what he was thinking. He saw her pause and set her brush down. She turned around in her full glory and walked towards him. He noticed his mouth had dropped open and he quickly shut it. She stepped up to him slowly and gently took one of the wine glasses from his hand.

"Elf-made wine…for you," he managed to croak out. He was bewitched. He knew she was beautiful from the start, but he had almost forgotten the powerful alluring force that drew him to her. He felt it now in spades.

"Thank you, Severus. It's my favorite," she said, taking a drink. "I'm sorry. I don't have a gift for you."

Severus raised an eyebrow to that, his mouth turning up in a grin. "Actually, my dear, you have presented me with the perfect gift, and you were kind enough to unwrap it for me already."

He drank the last of the wine in his glass, then dropped it to the floor.

Chapter 43

Mesmerized

Sirana had felt his thoughts enter her mind before she turned around. It was a sweet reminder of how surprisingly passionate this fierce man was. It emboldened her to walk over to him, feeling the intensity of his desire for her deepen with every step. When he dropped his wine glass on the floor, she saw the look in his eyes, which was smoldering, and she was startled by the ferocity of it.

He stepped closer to her, not quite touching. She drew in a quick breath when he slowly reached out to her. He drew his hand back, and clasped his hands behind his back. Before she could wonder why, he leaned forward and kissed her neck. He moved slowly down her collarbone with his lips and tongue, kissing a tantalizingly slow trail across her chest and down into her cleavage. He kissed and licked at each nipple until she was quivering, her breaths coming in gasps.

Suddenly, he dropped to his knees and moved his mouth to her stomach, kissing and sucking at her skin. It was all she could do to stand there, watching this stunningly sensual man as he made his way down her body, touching her with only his mouth, and her own empty wine glass fell to the floor. He kissed across her, from one hip to the other, then back to her middle.

It was like slow torture, and she was mesmerized by it. He sat back on his heels, then brought his hands to grab her hips, and moved her to stand over him. His mouth delved into her and she gasped. She could feel how wet she was as he plundered her with his tongue until she instinctively wrapped her hands into his hair, saying his name in an impassioned plea, "Severus... Severus..." He replaced his mouth with his fingers, driving them up into her, looking up into her eyes with the need to see her in his. She was close, she could feel it, and her body shuddered uncontrollably now. As if he could sense she was close to her climax, he stood and moved her against the door frame. Severus pressed his body against hers and kissed her roughly. He quickly undid his trousers, pulling himself out, then reached down to lift her up, pulling her legs around him, and set her down on him. Sirana gasped loudly from the intensity of the sensation as he slid deeply into her. She reached back and grasped onto the doorframe as he lifted her up and pulled her down onto him over and over, driving into her with a fierceness that brought her quickly back to her climax. She cried out at each thrust until she made it through her orgasm. She could tell he was close to his as well as his eyes closed, his head leaned forward, the muscles in his arms and body contracted tight, and he drove into her hard until he let out his own guttural cry. Sirana thought it was the most beautifully erotic experience ever in her lifetime.

Severus leaned into her, still holding her on him, taking in long, hard breaths. He finally lowered her and took her face in his hands, kissing her tenderly. Smiling, he looked down into her eyes, and she smiled shyly back up to him.

"You're lucky you're a wizard, or I would be tempted to tie you to your bed and not ever let you leave again," Sirana said.

He laughed at that. "Be careful of putting thoughts in my head, or you may suffer the same fate when I return," he threatened playfully.

They enjoyed each other's company the rest of the evening, not talking about the world outside them. That could wait until tomorrow. Tonight was for them and them alone.

Chapter 44

Payment

Sirana came in to join Severus at the table for breakfast.

"I brought you something else I thought you might like. I don't know if you've heard already," Severus said.

She sat and looked on the table in front of her. It was a newspaper. Lucius was going to Azkaban.

"What is Azkaban?" Sirana asked.

"Prison. For his crimes as a Death Eater for the Dark Lord. I thought it might make you feel more at ease for the duration. I wouldn't expect it be long-lived though, if the Dark Lord wants him out," Severus said dryly.

Sirana felt so much more at ease with Severus within her sight. She had been so worried about him. She knew he was embroiled in something bigger than she could fathom. As it was, he seemed distracted, as if something was weighing on him heavily.

She looked over at him, asking softly, "Can you share it with me? What's on your mind?"

Severus stood, walking to stand in the middle of the room, standing with his eyes closed. He finally turned to her, reaching his hand out to her for her to join him.

She went to him, and he took her in his arms. "Sirana, I haven't been fair to you. I wanted to safeguard you from any of it. I felt that if I could keep you detached from that part of my life, it would be easier for me to endure." He stood quietly for a moment, holding her against him, stroking her hair. He stepped back, holding her by her shoulders. "When I first met you at Malfoy Manor, I felt your strength. I felt that I needed to ally myself with you. And yet, I could not bring myself to involve you in anything that might put you in danger." He walked away in frustration, then spun back to look at her. "Tomorrow, your grandfather will arrive. He is bringing your wand. Professor Dumbledore wishes to begin your instruction since I will be away. He believes that you will be an asset in defending Hogwarts. I've informed him of how far you've made it under my tutelage, and even of your self-directed learning. I cannot stop this now, nor do I wish to. I've seen you thrive at everything you attempt, and I will not hold you back any longer." At that, he walked into his study.

Severus was not prepared for the barrage of emotions hitting him. He needed a moment to gather himself. He could not tell Sirana about the Unbreakable Vow. He didn't want to hold anything back from her, and he felt regret for not being honest with her about such a serious matter. That was a burden he would have to carry on his own. He began preparing her lessons for his departure. Even though Dumbledore would take over her wand instruction, there were things he wanted her to learn from him.

Unfortunately, she had no hands-on practice with potions, but he made certain she had a rudimentary knowledge. It was still several weeks until the new school year began. He didn't want to imagine spending so much time away from her again, but it was unavoidable.

Severus did not want to think about what was really weighing on his mind concerning Sirana. He always knew he couldn't keep her to himself alone. He always knew she had a strength in her that others would see too. And he always knew she was meant for more than either of them could foresee. He turned to see Sirana standing in the doorway to his study.

"Severus," Sirana said softly. "What if—what if I was sent here for a reason? And just as you, what if I have a role to play in this battle of good and evil? If I didn't think it were so, I would be content to live as I have. My life here with you has been fulfilling. I would give anything for it to stay as it is. But you and I both know that it can't. I have seen and heard—and felt—the darkness coming. I am not a Seer, like Professor Trelawney, but I can see this. And from the look in your eyes, I know you do too."

Severus turned away and slammed both his hands down on his desk.

"And what would you have me do?" he cried angrily, leaning with his hands flat on his desk, his head down, unable to meet her eyes. "I too would give anything...and yet, I am forced to give everything! I was willing to sacrifice myself—my very soul. I fear that the universe has deemed my sacrifice unworthy, that it will demand a payment that I am unwilling to pay, and that no matter what I do to stop it, the payment will still be collected."

He straightened, then turned towards her, fire in his eyes. "*That* is what haunts my sleep. *That*…is why I choose to remain awake at night—because the night is not merciful." He walked to take her face in his hand. "You are not my possession to give, or to keep, but I cannot bear to lose you. I have seen what our lives could be together, what *I* could be. And to have that ripped away now…"

Sirana pulled him down gently to her, embracing him, pouring all of her love into him, feeling it returned in their link. She whispered to him, "Our love is eternal, Severus. It is more than either of us. And it will not end with either of us. That is what is in my dreams."

She felt his burden lighten, and a feeling of light and warmth entered their link, emanating to soothe both of their spirits.

Chapter 45

Reuniting

Sirana's grandfather was to arrive today. She waited in Dumbledore's office for their return. Dumbledore had spoken to her before he left to bring her grandfather. She felt at ease with Professor Dumbledore. He was good natured like her grandfather, but his eyes held a sadness, whereas her grandfather's held a fire. She often heard that her own eyes were like his—eyes of blue flame. Professor Dumbledore wanted to prepare her for the fact that her grandfather would be older than she remembered, as more than a decade had passed since she'd seen him.

She was used to the idea that her previous life wasn't completely as it seemed. Part of her regretted that she'd missed out on so many years of knowing that she had magical abilities. She could have attended Hogwarts if things had been different. She wondered what house she would have been sorted into.

She heard and felt the air in the room change. She stood to see Professor Dumbledore with her grandfather by his side.

"Sirana!" her grandfather called, holding his arms out to her.

Sirana ran to him, and he wrapped his robe around her as he did when she was a child. She wept in his arms.

"Sirana, I have missed you. We have so much to talk about," her grandfather said, unwrapping her and holding her face in his hands. "I still see my beautiful Katherine when I look at you. I have often regretted not telling you how much I adore you, Sirana. After all these years, I hope that you know how much you are loved." Sirana saw that her grandfather's eyes were misty now.

She smiled up at him. "Grandfather, you never needed to worry about that. I felt your love always. I always thought we were so much alike. I never felt that we needed to put into words what was here all the time," Sirana said, holding her hand on her heart.

"So, you felt it too then?" her grandfather asked. "The feeling that you and I were tied, as if by a string. It's how I knew you hadn't died that night—because it never went away. It faded, like you were sleeping—for fifteen years—then, it was like you'd returned. I didn't know what it meant. And then, the Professor contacted me. It was like a miracle. A wonderful, magical miracle," her grandfather reached out and put his hand on her shoulder. "I do not understand the magic that has returned you to us, but I know that it is—I've had dreams—momentous."

She looked at Professor Dumbledore. "Thank you, Professor Dumbledore—Albus—for bringing my grandfather to me."

Her grandfather turned to him as well. "Yes, thank you, Albus, for reuniting us."

Albus smiled, both at her and at Professor Cadogen. "You are both very welcome. Please, both of you, sit. We do have much to talk about."

Albus poured them all drinks, and they spent at least an hour catching up on all that had transpired.

"What about my parents? Do they know I'm still alive?" Sirana asked.

"Yes, I told them that you had been found, and that you had been in a coma all these years. They are awaiting your recovery, and I assured them you had the best of care," her grandfather answered. He continued as if he'd just remembered, "Oh, by the way, here is your wand." He drew it out from inside his robes, handing it to her.

She accepted it, holding it gingerly. "I'm sorry for the circumstances that led me to have to hide it from you—both it and the memory of it. Those were dark times," he said, and his eyes held the haunting memories for a moment.

"It is a fine wand," Albus remarked. "I believe it will be well-suited for you. We will begin your instruction tomorrow afternoon. Until then, I would recommend you try not to use it. Your magical abilities are already quite powerful, and your wand will make them doubly so."

Sirana tucked the wand in her sleeve. "Yes, sir," she replied. "I look forward to it."

Albus shifted in his chair, looking more serious now. "There is another matter," he said, looking at them both. "The night you disappeared. The night the Potters died. What do you remember of that night, Kane?" he asked her grandfather.

"I'm sorry. I don't think I can offer you what you are looking for. My memory of the night is…hidden. I assume that whatever magic was at work that night also dulled my memory of it," he said sadly.

"Would it be too much to ask of you to draw out your memory for the Pensieve?" Albus asked. "Perhaps it may more easily be seen through another's mind's eye."

Sirana had read of all of this, but she hadn't imagined seeing it firsthand.

"Yes, Albus. I will do whatever is needed to help," her grandfather said, drawing out his own wand.

He held the wand to his temple, drawing out what looked to be threads of silver light. Albus held a vial, and helped her grandfather direct the memory into it. Albus retrieved the Pensieve, poured the memory into it, then submerged his face into the liquid of the Pensieve. After he was done looking at the memory, he stood, looking wide-eyed at them both.

At that moment, Severus strode into the room, meeting eyes with her only briefly. "Is it there, Albus? What did you see?" he asked brusquely.

Sirana was surprised to see Severus again so soon. She wondered why he had not told her he was coming. He hadn't greeted her—or anyone else for that matter—when he walked in either. She had seen Severus's awkward nature before, even around her at times, so she simply attributed it to his single-minded focus.

Albus politely corrected his misstep. "Severus," Albus said. "I was hoping you could make it. First, let me make introductions. This is Professor Kane Cadogen, Sirana's grandfather. Kane, this is Professor Severus Snape."

Severus turned to him. "Pleasure to make your acquaintance. Sirana has spoken fondly of you," Severus said, and Sirana smiled at his words.

"It's wonderful to meet you, too," Her grandfather replied. "Sirana has spoken fondly of you as well." He said the last part with the mildest hint of a smile, and Sirana blushed as Severus looked nonplussed.

Gratefully, Albus spoke quickly, "I'm sorry to say that the memory did not hold more than what Sirana has told us previously. It seems her presence here may remain a mystery."

Severus stepped forward. "There is something I would like you to consider, Albus. Since Sirana now has her wand in her possession…" He paused to look at Sirana, raising his eyebrow as if asking for her confirmation, and she nodded in affirmation. He continued, "She may be able to extract her own memory from the night in question. I could not see far enough into her mind when I tried, and I did not wish to cause injury by pushing farther, so this may help to better reveal what we are looking for."

Sirana thought about that and felt her heart swell knowing that he could have forced himself into her mind but didn't. She truly trusted him, and she would try to provide them with the memory for the Pensieve if she could. She looked at Albus and nodded her silent agreement.

"I will show her how," her grandfather said before Severus or Albus had the chance. "Please, allow us a moment."

Chapter 46

Lily's Gift

Severus and Albus stepped away while Sirana and her grandfather spoke.

Albus poured Severus a drink.

"Severus," Albus spoke solemnly. "I wish for you to be the one to see the memory if Sirana is able to provide it. I believe it to hold something that you are looking for."

Severus looked at him for a moment. "I will if you wish it of me."

Severus knew why he was hesitant to see what happened that night. It was the night Lily died. He did not want such a vivid reminder of the worst day of his life. He had loved Lily, and even though he loved Sirana as deeply as he could ever love anyone, his love for Lily was not diminished by this.

Sirana said just loud enough for them to hear, "I'm ready."

Severus and Albus returned to her side. Severus held the vial for her as she drew out the memory. He held her hand steady as she deposited it into the vial. He looked into her eyes and squeezed her hand reassuringly before striding to the Pensieve. Severus poured the vial into it, and lowered his head slowly, feeling the cool liquid on his face. The scene he recognized from Sirana's mind appeared before him now. Sirana's grandfather was running towards the house where Lily and her family were living. Flashes of light were coming from the window. Her grandfather was raising his wand. He was struck by a flash of light and he fell. Sirana dropped down beside him. She heard a scream. She got up to run towards the house. A flash of light hit her. She dropped to her knees. She felt herself dying. She saw a bluish light approach slowly. It was a doe. It walked up to her. She reached out. She saw Lily's face emerge, as if from the doe.

Lily didn't speak, but Sirana saw through Lily's mind's eye. "…Severus was holding her…crying…she knew she was dying… she was at peace that her sacrifice had spared the life of her son… Harry, she will always love you…James, not enough time for them…Severus, friendship lost, but never gone…regret for the past…love…always…she could not leave him to meet his fate alone…she must hold on to perform one last piece of magic…a gift…" The Patronus, which Lily had cast to protect them from Voldemort, was dying too, as a Patronus cannot continue when the one who casts them dies. Lily sent her Patronus to Sirana, her dear friend, who was dying. "Sirana…too soon…Sirana could be for Severus what she could not…" Sirana heard the unspoken request. "A new chance at life…a gift…" Sirana accepted the gift as she fell, dying. The doe lay beside her, and they both vanished into the night.

Severus rose from the Pensieve and fell to his knees, his hands covering his face. He hadn't really cried since he was a child, except for when Lily died, and yet, his body was now wracked with his sobs. He felt an arm around his shoulder, and another. His mind finally started to clear, and he was able to suppress his sobs, although his tears continued to fall.

Severus removed his hands from his face and placed them on his thighs, as if to hold himself up. He took a deep, ragged breath, then wiped his face with his hand. He moved to stand, and he felt the arms helping him up. They led him to a chair.

"Please, I'm alright. Thank you," he managed to say. He couldn't meet anyone's eyes yet. The images were still so vivid and the emotions so raw.

He felt a glass being placed in his hand and he took a long drink. Finally, he opened his eyes. Sirana was kneeling next to his chair, her hand on his, and Albus was standing on the other side in front of him, his hand on his shoulder.

"Severus," Albus was the first to speak. "Are you alright?"

Severus nodded, handing his glass back to him. He then turned to look at Sirana, taking her face in his hands, letting his mind enter hers. He wanted to share the memory with her before it had the chance to fade. She leaned in and their foreheads touched.

When he finally pulled away, her eyes were filled with tears, and they ran freely down her cheeks.

"It seems as if we have finally solved your mystery, Sirana," Severus said, his voice deep with emotion. He turned to address Albus and Kane, "In her final hour, Lily cast her Patronus, a doe, as defense against the Dark Lord. In one last act of extraordinary magic, Lily sent her Patronus to Sirana, who was dying. Lily's Patronus merged with Sirana, not only saving her life, but sending her into another realm, awaiting the proper time for Sirana to reemerge. Sirana was made whole, renewed. I now know from the feelings of…familiarity…that Lily's magic lives on in Sirana as well, as if her Patronus coalesced with Sirana into a singular entity."

"She loved you, Severus," Sirana said through her tears. "She didn't want me to die because of her. She wanted me to be there for you when she couldn't, and you for me. She wanted something more for each of us, and she gave us each a gift." Sirana broke down into sobs, and Severus pulled her to him as they shared their tears and their love for each other.

Chapter 47

Gattitude

S everus had said his goodbyes again to Sirana, and it was even harder than before. He couldn't stay much longer, which he regretted, because he knew they both needed each other right now. Severus needed time for himself too, to process everything. He felt ravaged, but he also felt as if some of the regret he had been carrying with him for so long was eased. His grief and anguish were replaced by love and gratitude. It was critical that he talk with Dumbledore though, so Sirana had taken her grandfather to help him get settled in. Her grandfather was going to be staying at Hogwarts for the remainder of the summer, and Severus knew Sirana would be happy about that.

"How could you know what I would see in the Pensieve, Albus? Have you taken to practicing Divination?" Severus asked, knowing Dumbledore did not have much confidence in it.

"No," Albus answered, smiling at the irony. "It is not a gift that I possess. Sybill came to me. She saw a vision in Sirana's tea leaves. Sirana asked Trelawney not to share her vision with her and to promise not to share the vision with anyone if it was grim. However, it was not." Albus explained, pausing as if finding the words. "It was a fawn, Severus. Sybill saw the rebirth. In her vision, Lily's sacrifice saved Sirana, providing a new path for her, and a new life. You have seen it now for yourself. Lily did die, and at the end, she sent her Patronus to her, and it is now a part of Sirana. Severus…Lily's sacrifice was tragic…and beautiful."

Severus turned away from him, the emotions still too close. Albus continued, "While all that passes is inescapable, our choices are not decided by fate, and our death mustn't always be grievous."

Severus knew Albus spoke of more than Lily's death. Albus had asked of him the inconceivable, and despite Albus's attempt at solace, he grieved his choices even now.

"How will she forgive me, Albus, if I won't even be able to forgive myself?" Severus pleaded.

"Severus, when you see yourself in her mind, what do you see?" Albus asked.

Severus remembered when he'd entered her mind. It seemed so long ago. She saw him as light, and warmth, a wall of stone and a blade of steel. And herself, encased in shining armor—his champion. He felt Albus ask to enter his mind at the question, and, surprising even himself, he allowed it.

Albus opened his eyes, the vision gone now. "Perhaps, Severus, you should ask instead, with her at your side, how anything could possibly come between you—or stand against you."

Severus thought about Albus's words. He could no longer doubt his own resolve, or his commitment to his course, and his devotion to Sirana was reinforced by steadfast courage.

Sirana was happy her grandfather was going to be here for the rest of the summer. Albus said that a place was being prepared for him to move to, and that it was close enough for her to easily visit. She had settled her grandfather into his temporary accommodations, which were cozy but comfortable, and she was now finally back home. She was so tired. She went to bed early. She lay there thinking about today. Seeing the profound sorrow of Severus was heartbreaking. She also knew it was not only sadness, because she had felt it too—it was immense gratitude and love, so powerful that it worked to heal a lifetime of bitterness and regret.

Sirana also felt their own love reinforced, as the last vestiges of remorse were stripped from Severus, and he was totally free to open his heart completely. She thought of Severus and reached out to him in her mind. She felt the bond that was precious and impregnable, and she knew that she would not take for granted this gift that was given to her.

Chapter 48

Slughorn

Albus proved to be a tough taskmaster in his own right. He was milder in his demeanor than Severus, but he did not relent in his determined objective. He was also quicker to offer praise than Severus, and she felt her confidence growing along with her skills. Albus was also very artful at providing her updates about Severus's wellbeing without her having to make inquiries, for which she was thankful. She had a few surprises for Severus when he returned. She hoped that it wouldn't be long now.

Even with his absence weighing on her, she had a splendid summer. Sirana learned so much and had so many new and exciting experiences. Today, she was going to finish her final lesson with Madam Hooch. She never imagined how much fun it was to fly. Since she had a knack for athletics, it seemed that flying came naturally to her. Madam Hooch said that she wished she'd had the opportunity to coach her for Quidditch. She was flattered. She wondered what Severus would think about it. She knew all of this was probably old hat to him, so she hoped she wouldn't bore him to death with her excitement.

Madam Hooch ran her through the course. They were flying side by side, and they were both smiling and laughing with the exhilaration of the maneuvers. When they finally landed and dismounted from their brooms, Madam Hooch put her arm around Sirana's shoulders and told her that she was welcome to fly with her any time. She looked over her shoulder, and smiled at Sirana. "I'm sorry, I have to go. But you're welcome to stay and play if you like."

Sirana thanked her, wondering a bit at her quick exit, until she turned around and saw him—Severus. He stood at the edge of the practice field. Her heart jumped up in her throat and she took off running to him. Their embrace brought joyful tears from each of them.

"I told you it wasn't for forever," he whispered in her ear.

She smiled, "It sure felt like it."

"All this time, I thought you were brilliant, and yet, you ran off and left your broom when you could have more easily flown over here," Severus said, poking fun.

Sirana laughed at that. "It would be boring if I was brilliant all the time."

"Boring is one thing you are definitely not, Sirana," Severus replied, kissing her soundly. "Now, go get your broom before anyone catches us snogging right here in the open."

When they got back to their rooms, Severus kissed her more passionately than he'd dared outside. He finally let her up for air, then went to prepare them a drink.

"Tell me everything," he said as he worked. "I want to hear all that I've missed."

He brought their drinks, and she took his arm as he led her to the sitting area. She started to sit in her chair, but he stopped her. "Please. I've been too far away from you for far too long." He sat in his chair, holding the drinks out as if to give her room to sit on his lap. She sat, and he handed the drink to her, then wrapped his free arm around her waist, letting out a long, contented sigh. "I see you've already mastered flying. How is your wand instruction with Albus coming along?" Severus asked.

Severus enjoyed just listening to her voice, feeling her close to him as she sat in his lap and chattered like a little bird about her summer. He wished he could stay in this moment, but he remembered that he'd reluctantly agreed to meet with Professor Slughorn for dinner. "I hope you don't mind. But the new Professor asked us to dinner, and I accepted. I was hoping to have the whole evening to ourselves, but I will make sure we don't linger. I plan on having our dessert here when we return," he said as he stroked her hair. He was satisfied to see her smile and blush. He understood. They had been spending too much time apart, and even though there was no doubt of their love, it seemed like they needed to reacquaint themselves. Having dinner with the Professor would afford them that opportunity. He thought it might kill him though. He wanted nothing more than to carry her off into his bedroom. He smiled as he remembered what he'd said about dragging her in by her hair. From the look in her eyes, he knew that would not be necessary.

Professor Slughorn's place was nice, and she could tell from his furniture and decor that he enjoyed entertaining guests. He was a friendly man who liked conversation. He seemed to know a lot about everything.

"I'm so sorry I missed seeing your grandfather, Sirana. He and I go way back—to the First War. Your grandparents were quite the dancers. We would host the grandest parties. Do you dance as well?" he asked.

"Yes, I love dancing!" she said as she glanced sheepishly towards Severus, who looked like he wasn't planning on joining in on the conversation.

Professor Slughorn eyed them both. "I've heard that you two were friends, so I thought it would be nice to meet you both together before classes resume. I've found that the more guests there are, the livelier the conversation. Wouldn't you agree, Professor Snape?"

"I do believe that would depend on the guests," Severus replied, glancing at Sirana.

Slughorn seemed elated at that. "Oh yes, you are exactly right."

Sirana got the distinct impression that Slughorn was a bit of a socialite. He seemed to enjoy being in the know, to see and be seen, and maybe even a bit of a matchmaker the way he was looking at her and Severus. He had tried several times to broach the subject of Harry Potter with Severus, but Severus didn't seem very interested in the subject. He finally gave up and talked about their new teaching positions instead. "So, since I am moving to your old position as Potions Professor, are you looking forward to your new position as the Defense Against the Dark Arts Professor?"

Severus simply answered with a "Yes."

Sirana was a little surprised, "I must be out of the loop. I didn't know you were changing subjects. That sounds exciting."

Once again, Severus replied with a "Yes."

Slughorn must have gotten the hint that it was about time to wrap up dinner. "Can I interest you in some dessert?" he asked.

"No, thank you," Severus answered quickly. "I'm sorry, but I have already made other plans for dessert."

Sirana blushed up to her ears. Slughorn seemed to take great pleasure in this exchange. "Yes, yes of course. I thoroughly enjoyed having you both for dinner. Sirana, give my best to your grandfather. Perhaps if I have the opportunity to host a party, we can see about having a dance."

"That would be lovely," Sirana answered, looking at Severus, who had no response.

They thanked him for his hospitality, and as soon as they left, Severus let out a breath. "I thought that would never end."

Sirana laughed. She had enjoyed Slughorn's light-natured company, but she was also feeling the need to be alone with Severus.

Chapter 49

Daring

When they made it around the corner, Severus grabbed her arm, and they Apparated directly to his bedroom.

Sirana smiled. "I thought you Apparated inside Hogwarts only if it was a pressing need?"

Severus stepped towards her with fire in his eyes. "I couldn't imagine a more urgent need than I have right now."

"Well, at least you didn't drag me in by my hair," Sirana said, smiling.

"That's still not off the table," Severus replied as he reached his hands into her hair, pulling her to him. His head lowered slowly, his long, black hair falling forward. Sirana could feel her insides turn into jelly. Their lips finally touched, and she heard a low moan come from Severus. She ran her hands up the sides of his jacket to his back. She was always surprised at how impressive Severus looked in his clothes. Of course, he was no less impressive when he was out of them, and she began removing them as quickly as she could. She noticed he hadn't started removing hers yet. He turned and sat on the bed.

"Let me watch you," he said. She smiled shyly, then seeing the look in his eyes, felt more daring. She started at her tunic, slowly unbuttoning it. She pulled it off of her shoulders, then started unlacing her pants, wiggling out of them. She turned the other way to pull off her panties, bending over to take them down to her ankles, and stepped out of them. When she turned back to him and started on her top again, he said, "Enough!"

He reached for her and pulled her to stand between his legs. He pulled her bra down and under her breasts, cupping her breasts in his hands and kissing them. The feel of his mouth on her, his gorgeous lips brushing against her skin, his warm breath caressing her softly…the intimacy of it all sent a shiver of excitement into her, and she breathed out a long sigh. Severus ran his hands down her body and behind her to grasp her hips, moving his hands to the bottom of her cheeks, kneading and massaging her, moving closer to her center. He had a way of awakening her senses, and she had never known it was possible to feel this deeply. She let her head fall back as he moved his hand to her front, slipping it between her legs, rubbing it in and out. She felt like all her nerves were on edge, and even his slightest touch made her quiver. She lowered her head and he pulled her down into a kiss, and she could feel his fevered passion that matched her own. He brought her down to him and pulled her back into the bed with him.

Sirana looked down into his face. He was such a beautiful man. Severus grabbed himself and guided her over him. She slowly lowered herself down onto him, and his fingers bit into her thighs as he groaned. She moved up and down on him, hearing his breathy moans. She gained more confidence as she moved, feeling some power in bringing him so much pleasure.

She also felt in control of her own pleasure, and she picked up her pace, gasping at the shockwaves hitting deep inside her. She felt herself getting closer…it was almost too much, and she slowed, struggling to reach the peak. Severus grabbed her hips, pulling up to her, and pulled her back and forth, grinding her on him. It pushed her over the edge, and she shuddered as the spasms of her orgasm wracked her body. His body was tense with effort now, and she knew he was close to his own climax. She pushed through her orgasm, starting to move again, sliding up and down on him. Severus groaned and bucked, and she could feel him erupt into her. Sirana fell on top of his chest, and he stroked her hair and back, softly saying her name.

Chapter 50

Embroiled

The day came for the students to start arriving. Sirana was excited to get the school year started. Everything seemed so much brighter when the students were here at Hogwarts. It was so big and empty and lifeless without them.

"Madam Hooch wants me to start teaching the older students as well this year. She said the younger students enjoyed the lessons so much that she thought the older students would too," Sirana said, happily preparing her schedule. "So, I will be teaching all day now."

Severus sat at the table, watching her as he finished his breakfast. "I have to attend to some business this evening. Draco Malfoy is arriving, and I've…promised his mother…that I will see to it he is safely settled," Severus said dryly.

"Lucius's son? I'm not one to choose favorite students, but he is definitely not my favorite. And it has nothing to do with my feelings about his father."

"He is…troubled," Severus offered.

"To put it lightly. And this year, I will have him in my class since I'm teaching the older students," Sirana said, exasperated.

"It seems I am in charge of his safety, since his father is... unavailable...so, I will ask that you not remove his head or any of his limbs in your combat lessons," Severus said wryly.

Sirana laughed. "Well, that still leaves a lot I can work with."

Severus looked like he had more on his mind, and he finally spoke, "It would seem that I have two wards under my protection, and they are both in the gravest of danger. I would not ask this if you if I didn't think you were capable. Harry Potter...if you could help watch over him, I would be able to focus more on Draco for the moment."

Sirana was surprised that he would ask for her help, but grateful that he did so. "Yes, of course."

She rose to go to him, and he wrapped his arm around her waist. "You may lack experience, but you are stronger than most of the witches and wizards here. I think it would be a waste not to utilize your assistance," Severus said, pulling her down for a kiss.

"Thank you, Severus. Coming from you, that means the world to me." Sirana meant it—Severus didn't offer compliments freely. She probably knew more about what was going on than Severus even knew she did. During her wand training, Albus had not been as tight-lipped about the threats facing them as Severus had. Albus seemed worried some days, and though he didn't want to seem to burden her with his own pain, he shared a lot about the Dark Lord and his history so that she could be better prepared. It seemed that Harry Potter and his friends were deeply embroiled in the fray, as was Draco Malfoy, and she was going to keep her eyes out for each of them. She wished she could keep an eye on Severus too, because she knew he was in deep, but it was almost impossible since he worked as a double agent for the Dark Lord.

"What do you think about me working with Professor Slughorn to practice potions, since you're so busy with everything?" she asked.

If she didn't know better, it almost looked like Severus rolled his eyes. "I will make time," he said bluntly.

"Good," she said. She had heard enough to know that Severus was by far a superior Potions Master. Plus, she would rather spend time with Severus than anyone else.

"Bring me your wand," Severus said.

She found that keeping it up her sleeve as many others did didn't feel natural. She had sewn in a thin sleeve on the right thigh of her pants and kept it there instead. She passed it over to Severus, who he raised an eyebrow when he saw where she'd drawn it from.

"I used to keep a dagger strapped to my ankle," she explained. "When I wasn't teaching, of course. I miss it. I didn't think to ask my grandfather to bring it with him. So, reaching to my side for my wand feels more natural."

He looked her wand over. "Nice weight. Have you read the meaning of a cypress wood wand and a unicorn hair core?"

She shook her head. "No. What does it mean? Do you think it is fitting?" Sirana asked, hoping her wand suited her nature.

"I assure you; it is more than fitting. Cypress wands denote nobility, which is also associated with courage and self-sacrifice. Unicorn hair is consistent and will assure your wand's loyalty to you. Ollivander does not choose the wand for you, the wand chooses you. And I know it chose wisely…as did I," Severus said, standing. He stepped to her, then slid her wand into her sleeve, running his hand around her waist.

"Yes, yes you did…as did I," Sirana said smiling, and they kissed to their agreement.

Chapter 51

Transgression

Sirana was growing more worried for Severus. She'd started reading the newspaper every chance she got. Things were looking grim. She wished that Hogwarts could remain untouched by all of that. It was a wonderful place. She could tell Severus tried to leave his worries at the door, but she could see his stress. Classes went better once Draco decided he didn't have much choice except to play nicely. She could even see changes in Draco, as if he'd aged with worry.

She received notice that Albus wanted to speak with her as soon as she received the message. She felt like she'd swallowed a stone and her stomach ached with worry. She enjoyed seeing Albus, but she couldn't shake the bad feeling.

When she arrived, he was standing, waiting for her in his office. "Sirana, I'm sorry. I have some bad news. I wish I could give you more notice, but your grandfather needs you. I can't tell you much more, because time is pressing. Please, can you leave now? Don't worry, I will let Severus know where you've gone." Albus's tone was gravely serious.

"Yes, of course. I'm ready when you are," she answered, knowing he wouldn't ask if the situation didn't require it.

He offered her his arm and they Disapparated from Hogwarts. The first thing she noticed was that Apparating with Albus felt completely different than with Severus, and she staggered a little when they arrived. Her grandfather approached them immediately, looking a little panicked.

"Thank you for coming so soon. I really didn't expect for you to arrive in time. Sirana, I'm so sorry. I didn't want to bring you in to this, but Albus thought you would be our best option."

"Of course, grandfather. You know I would do anything for you," Sirana replied earnestly.

"Come, now," Albus said hurriedly. "We must go immediately."

Her grandfather grabbed his satchel, they both grabbed Albus's arm, and they Disapparated.

They were in London. She recognized it from when she'd visited as a child. Albus said his goodbyes to them, assuring her that her grandfather would fill her in with the details. They were outside of a large line of brick buildings, and she followed her grandfather inside up the stairs to the third floor. There was a small, dark apartment and he hurriedly ushered her in. He drew his wand and set protective spells before he collapsed in a chair.

"This will do us for now. We will have to keep on the move. The Order of the Phoenix is being watched, and they've found out that I've returned. I was hoping they'd forgotten about me since it's been so long, thinking I was dead, but there are members of the Dark Lord's rank who still have a vendetta against me," He explained. "I wouldn't have brought you into this; in fact, Albus and I still do not see eye to eye on it. You see, I never really left the Order, although I've been very careful over the years to remain under the radar. It has helped me get more accomplished being closer to the Ministry since my return, but I can no longer operate alone. The Ministry is a major target, and it is becoming increasingly difficult to protect members of the Order from harm."

Sirana was surprised. Her grandfather had never hinted at this, which may be why he was able get by so long being undercover.

"What are you saying, grandfather? Am I here to care for you, protect you, or to work with you?" Sirana asked.

Her grandfather finally smiled, looking more like himself. "My dear, it looks like we are going to be comrades-in-arms," he stood, placing a hand on her shoulder. "That's if you are willing. Albus had assured me you are more than able—and I have no doubt he is right."

Sirana placed her arm on his shoulder as well. "I am willing, and ready." She'd just wished she'd gotten a chance to say goodbye to Severus.

Severus had been summoned to Albus's office as well. He had hoped to get home early to spend time with Sirana, as they'd both been so busy lately, but he knew she would understand. He'd planned on breaking out a bottle of elf-made wine, as he knew that always put her in a pleasant mood. Albus's mood however seemed somber.

"Severus, thank you for coming. I'm afraid I have some news that you may find displeasing. Here, please have a seat and I will pour us a drink."

Severus remained standing. "If it is bad news, I think I'd prefer to hear it standing."

"As you wish, Severus," Albus said, pouring himself a drink. He sat in his chair, then continued, "Sirana has left to be with her grandfather. I don't think I need to tell you that the circumstances were dire. Her grandfather needed assistance, and Sirana was the best choice for the job."

Severus couldn't stand to look at him this moment and walked angrily to the other side of the room.

"Severus," he heard Albus say gently. "It was necessary. She isn't as fragile as you might think. I would not have asked her if I hadn't believed she was ready."

Severus finally turned and walked back towards Albus, his voice sounding anguished. "You didn't ask me, or tell me, or even give me the chance to see her before she left."

"I'm sorry, Severus. There was no time. I had just received word. I couldn't even give her notice to pack," Albus said regretfully. "I told her that I would inform you. I knew you would be angry with me, but there was no other choice I could make."

Severus finally sat, leaning over to put his head in his hands. Albus came over and put a hand on Severus's shoulder. "I know that you care deeply for her, but I cannot spare her for the severity of our plight. She is stronger than you might think. She will not fail."

Severus stood to face Dumbledore. "I know how strong she is. I have seen her strength, with my own eyes and mind. I have no doubt of her abilities or her commitment. I cannot help but think you are throwing her to the wolves. If anything happens to her…I don't know if I could…live with myself."

"Or forgive me?" Albus added.

Severus walked to Albus's desk, bending to place his hands on it. "Why must the price always be so high, Albus? I would not place the blame on you, as I have said myself that holding her back would be unjust. I will place my confidence in her, as she has in me—and also in you," Severus said dejectedly, standing to face him once more.

"Thank you, Severus. I realize that I have asked more of you than is equitable, and I would not do so if I thought you were incapable. I do believe, however, that the time will come before the end when our sacrifices prove their worth," Albus said, offering a glimpse of hope that the outcome may still be worth their efforts.

He knew that Albus's own sacrifices were given without wavering, and he felt some shame for his own hesitation. "Please, Albus, it is I who must ask for forgiveness. I would ask that you keep me informed of her well-being," Severus replied.

Albus placed his hand on Severus's arm, saying gently, "Forgiveness is not needed where there is no transgression. And I will be sure to keep you informed. Also, it isn't for forever. She wanted me to tell you that."

Chapter 52

Remus & Tonks

Sirana once again found herself in a new bed. She was grateful to have a bed, considering some of the places they'd hidden out in lately were lacking even that. She was also grateful for her grandfather's company. They talked a lot, and he was full of exciting and harrowing stories that he probably had wanted to tell her for years but couldn't. He also imparted a wealth of magical knowledge, and one night he admitted regretfully that he'd wished he hadn't promised her mother not to tell her about magic.

"I understand, grandfather. It's alright. Things have a way of working out. I'm happy that I had a chance to live my other life before this one. After the death of my husband, I could never have imagined my life having so much meaning again. Handel would be so proud to see me now. He would have wanted this for me—the Order, teaching, Severus…," she said earnestly.

"About Severus…I've known of him for a long time. I know that he is working as a spy for Dumbledore, and that he is in as dangerous of situation as we are—maybe more so. If anything happens, anything, trust him," her grandfather said seriously.

"I do, grandfather. More than anything," she said with sadness in her voice.

"I know what this has cost you, Sirana. I know that you love him, and I know he loves you too. Your grandmother and I never allowed the trials we faced to lessen our love for each other. In the end, it was the only thing that mattered, the only thing that made it all worthwhile. He will be there for you when you return. Just don't let the darkness of the times take away the light you've found with each other," her grandfather spoke with experience from his past, and possibly even a foreboding of the future.

"I promise grandfather. I will honor your words…for you, for grandmother, and for Severus," she said, tears falling now.

"Tomorrow, we're meeting with some members of the Order. I think it will cheer you up. Plus, I think we're both due for a bath and a comfortable bed," he said with a reassuring smile.

Sirana was happy to see friendly faces again, people she could trust. It felt comforting, and she felt her body and mind relax as they hadn't since she'd left Hogwarts. Remus was welcoming and Nymphadora was a doll. She made her feel completely at home, offering her a bath and some of her own clothes to change into and to take with her. She didn't take too long because she knew her grandfather was looking forward to a bath as well. She was thankful Severus had taught her the charm for the bath.

When she'd dried and dressed, she joined her hosts in their living room. They offered her food and wine, and she partook gratefully.

"We've heard a lot about you," Remus said. "It's good to finally meet you. You've come a long way in a short time, it seems. Who can we thank for bringing you up to speed? Dumbledore?"

Remus was charming in his own way, and Sirana smiled at the compliment. "Dumbledore, yes, and my grandfather, but mainly Severus—Professor Snape. Do you know him?"

Remus and Nymphadora, who said everyone called her Tonks, looked at each other.

"Yes, we know him. We go back a while," Remus said vaguely. The conversation was cut short when a large man barged in the door.

"It wouldn't hurt to knock, Mad-Eye!" Remus barked.

Everyone stood to greet him, and he looked Sirana over, his glass eye moving up and down.

"Pleasure, miss. I heard you were coming. Is your grandfather not with you?" he said, sitting to join in on the meal.

"Yes, he's bathing at the moment. It's been a long road," Sirana explained.

Mad-Eye looked towards the back room. "Ah, understandable. We know of your escapades. You've been busy. We're lucky to have you both."

Her grandfather emerged from the back room and him and Mad Eye embraced joyfully, clapping each other on the back.

"It's been a long time, Kane. I didn't think I would see you again, although I've seen the fruits of your labor everywhere over the years," Mad-Eye said.

"Yes. And you as well, Moody. I'm happy to see you made it through—*almost* unharmed," her grandfather replied, looking at Mad-Eye's multiple war wounds.

"Ah, well, I'm told the ladies love the scars," Mad-Eye laughed. He then glanced over at Sirana, speaking to her grandfather. "I see your granddaughter has got your eyes, and your Katherine's good looks," he said directly. Sirana smiled at the compliment, as well as his amusing lack of tact.

Remus broke into the conversation at the right moment. "She also inherited her grandfather's magic abilities. She's proved Albus right once again. She's been invaluable to our cause."

Sirana blushed. She wasn't used to having so much attention on her, although it felt nice. She look at Tonks. "I hate to leave the party. You are all wonderful hosts, but would it be possible for me to go to bed early? I'm tired to the bone."

Everyone said their goodnights to her, and Mad-Eye even kissed her hand, which surprised her considering his brusque nature. Tonks took her to settle in for the night.

"It looks like you have an admirer, Sirana," Tonks whispered to her.

Sirana smiled, a little embarrassed. "I'd wondered. He's quite the charmer. But someone has already taken my heart, and it's the hardest thing I've done to be away from him."

Tonks smiled sadly. "I understand completely. It's not been easy for us…but to find love in these times is something worth fighting for."

Chapter 53

Holiday

Severus wasn't looking forward to Slughorn's holiday party. He'd hoped Sirana would have returned by now, and he was going to take her as his guest, which would have announced them officially as a couple. He still had to go as a chaperone for the party, though, and he was not in good spirits.

When he arrived, Slughorn asked him about Sirana. "Have you heard word from Sirana? Are she and her grandfather doing well?"

Severus knew Dumbledore had told everyone that Sirana had left to care for her ailing grandfather, but he suspected Slughorn knew more of the truth than he could reveal. "Yes, I heard they are doing well," Severus said blankly.

"I was so hoping she could make it to my party," Slughorn replied. "She owes me a dance, and I was hoping to collect. But I'm glad to hear they are well. There's always next year."

Severus didn't feel up to conversation and excused himself. He didn't want to think about dancing with Sirana—it made him miss her even more. He was a patient man, but the time away from her had started to eat away at his composure. Not knowing how or where she was at any moment or when she would return was wearing him thin. Dumbledore had kept him updated as much as possible, but now, with Dumbledore away, he felt completely disconnected from Sirana.

Not completely, he thought. He could still feel their link, and he treasured it as his assurance of her safety. The events of the party did not help his mood, and when McLaggen vomited on his shoes, he decided his night wasn't going to get any better. It did afford him the opportunity to relay the message to Harry Potter, though, and he would hopefully not have to talk to him again for the duration of the Holiday break. When Draco was found lurking around the halls, it sent him over the edge. He'd escorted him from the party and chased him down to push him against the wall. He knew Draco was scared, and he wished he could knock some sense in to him. Draco was still a child, and Severus knew he wasn't ready for the task he was given. If Draco wasn't so bitter and weak like his father, he could convince him to let him take care of everything. As it was, he would have to wait until the time to keep his promise to Dumbledore. He hoped Dumbledore was right, and that saving this boy's soul would be worth both of their sacrifices.

He finally headed back home, and his mood had grown fouler as he got closer to his rooms. As he stood outside his door, his mind touched on something familiar. Surely not. He took a deep breath, feeling the need to collect himself before he entered. When he entered, he could smell the familiar scent of her soap, and he could hear the faint sounds of bath water sloshing. His heart almost burst. He went to retrieve the bottle of elf-made wine he hadn't had the chance to share with her the night she left. It seemed like so long ago. He poured them both a glass and headed in to finally see the person who had been haunting his thoughts and dreams since she'd left.

He stepped in slowly, letting his mind reach out to let his presence be known before she heard him. He felt her mind open, and he felt her unbridled love pour into him. He felt it in his soul, and it washed away all of the pain and despair. He closed his eyes, soaking it all in, sending out the same in return.

"Mmmm...Severus. Let me see you," he heard coming from Sirana. He came over to the bath. She was smiling, and he sat the glasses down, freeing his hands to stroke her face. He leaned down to kiss her, wrapping his hands into her hair. He didn't want the kiss to end. He'd longed for this moment, dreamt of it, and he was almost afraid if he let go, he would wake up alone again. He finally found the courage to break away, opening his eyes to find that she was definitely still there.

Sirana smiled up at him, as if understanding him completely. He kept his hand on her face, enjoying just looking at her.

"Hand me my towel, Severus. I've needed a hug from you for way too long," she said. He happily complied. He couldn't help but look at her, his heart skipping a beat. He handed her the towel, then frowned. She looked too thin. She also had random bruises and scrapes all over her. He drew out his wand and healed her the best he could for the moment. She held the towel out away from her while he tended to her. She turned, and he took care of the particularly nasty scrape on her back.

She turned back around and thanked him, then donned her robe since the chill of the room had raised goosebumps on her skin. He then stepped forward and hugged her. She purred inn response, contented to be wrapped up in his warmth.

"Please, come have some wine with me. It was meant for the night you left, and I've been looking forward to picking up where we left off every day since then," Severus said, picking up the wine and leading them into the living room, her hand on his arm.

He led her to his chair, and they sat in their familiarly favorite way, with her curled up on his lap. They sat in each other's arms for a while, sipping their wine, just enjoying being in each other's company.

Severus broke the silence. "You missed Slughorn's Christmas party today. I was hoping to take you and show you off on my arm. Slughorn was looking for the dance you owed him. I didn't tell him that he might have had to fight me for the chance."

Sirana laughed. "I'm sorry. I would have loved to go with you. I missed you more than you can possibly imagine."

"I can imagine more than you might realize. I haven't gone a moment without you on my mind. I'm proud of you for all you've done, but part of me was too selfish to want to risk you or even share you. Maybe that's why Albus didn't share his plans with me. Maybe he thought I would steal you and run off with you to never be seen again," Severus said, not completely jesting.

Sirana placed her hand on the side of his face. "If it wasn't for the consequences, I would have been tempted by your offer."

"You know, it's not too late," he said, a bit of sadness in his voice.

She kissed him gently. "We both know that's not really true...but it is a nice dream to dream."

Chapter 54

Unconstrained

Sirana's weariness was replaced by the warmth of Severus's body and mind seeping into her. It had all been worth it. All of it. She had made it through, and the relief was overwhelming. She burst into tears. She didn't want to do that. It had been such a long road, and she was so happy to be back home. Severus felt like home to her, and she had fought so hard to make it back to him. He held her tighter, and he didn't let her go until her tears subsided.

She finally looked at him. "I'm sorry. I didn't want to cry. I'm okay now. I'm just so relieved to be back home—with you."

Severus pulled out his handkerchief and let her wipe her face. "Please, don't be sorry for your tears. They are shed from love. I love you, Sirana. I don't have the words to tell you how much. But I do. More than anything," he spoke softly, stroking her hair.

She smiled at him; he had no idea how his words always touched her heart. She could see his eyes were glossy with their own tears.

Severus didn't let her know that his own tears had threatened to fall. His throat hurt from holding them back. He didn't want her to worry for him. He wanted to be there for her. She had made it through hell and back to be with him, and he would make sure she knew how grateful he was for her—how much he loved her. He kissed her, letting his mind touch hers, letting her know what his words couldn't express. He planned on using his body to do the same. She didn't even complain when he picked her up and carried her to their bedroom, but he could feel her smile under his kiss.

He laid her down on the bed. He watched her watching him as he took off his clothes. She smiled, her eyes smoky, as he unbuttoned his shirt, baring his chest. He still didn't know what she saw in him, but when he touched her mind out of curiosity, he was soundly shocked at her attraction to him, and to the reaction of her body to him. He felt her peek in his mind in turn, and he could see her blush at his unconstrained attraction and desire for her. He rid himself of his trousers and shorts, and his body undeniably attested to what was in his mind.

Sirana hadn't forgotten how attractive Severus was—she had thought about him every day she was away. But the vivid reality of him here in front of her was profoundly powerful. She felt like the room was charged with electricity, and as he climbed into the bed with her, she felt like it tingled all over her body. When he laid next to her, she felt the intensity of his heat touching her body, all of her senses tuned into him. He started slowly, stroking her face and hair, and she was grateful for his gentleness. He always seemed to know what she needed. He kissed her forehead and then her cheek, moving to her mouth. He kissed her tenderly, and she melted under his soft kisses.

He looked in her eyes as he moved to kiss her breasts, and she gasped as he took her nipple in his warm mouth, his hand moving to her other breast, kneading it softly, then matching the movement with his fingers on that nipple to his mouth on the other. She instinctively arched up to him, and he moaned his satisfaction at bringing her pleasure. He let his hand trail slowly down her body, resting on her mound. Severus massaged her slowly, and she couldn't help but squirm with the need for him to touch her more deeply. He let his fingers slip in, rubbing her more firmly, and she moaned his name.

Severus wanted nothing more than to bring her pleasure, and he relished in the way she responded to him. He heard her say his name, and he couldn't hold back from her any longer. He moved his mouth to hers, kissing her once more, then raised up to look at her as he moved over her with his body. Her eyes told it all, and as he guided himself to her, he saw her bite her lip in anticipation. He pushed into her, groaning his own pleasure as he slid all the way in, hearing her gasp hoarsely. Severus felt the rush of heat move through his whole body, and he moved in and out of her slowly, taking long strokes deep into her. He could feel her tighten on him, her whole body flushing with the heat building inside of her. He heard her say his name, "Severus...I'm so close...please..." He maintained his pace, slowly driving into her. Sirana's hands were on his back, her fingers grasping at him, and he could feel her moving closer and closer. She gasped suddenly, her whole body contracting, and he could feel her spasms as he moved in her. It was an exquisitely gratifying feeling, and he savored every moment of it. Severus could feel himself getting closer, and he lifted himself higher on his hands, thrusting his hips forward and up, grinding into her in long, slow strokes. His own climax hit slow and hard, and he let out a deep groan that caught in his throat, making him gasp at the prolonged intensity. He fell to her side, pulling her to him. Even with the chill of the room, they were both covered with a sheen of sweat, and he pulled the blanket over them. She snuggled into him, and they lay, talking and holding each other late into the night.

Chapter 55

Dead

Professor Dumbledore had returned from his travels, and the students were back from their Christmas break as well. Sirana's students and the other teachers had welcomed her back joyfully. If it wasn't for the threat of danger hanging over them, all would have been well. Even the weather seemed gloomy, and she could see all of it taking its toll on the students and teachers alike.

She had just heard that Hagrid's Acromantula friend was ill and was on her way to go see how Hagrid was doing. She hadn't seen him since before she left, and she missed her giant friend. He greeted her warmly with a hug that was surprisingly gentle considering his size. She'd arrived early in the evening and noticed that he was preparing dinner.

"Can I help? I miss cooking," Sirana said, hoping he would say yes.

"If yeh don' mind," he said gratefully. "I get tired o' cookin' fer meself sometimes. Yeh have ter eat with me though."

"Well then, why don't you sit, and I'll cook for us," she offered.

"I'm afraid I don' 'ave much ter work with, bu' yer welcome ter any o' it," he said, sitting at the table.

She worked as they talked, mostly listening as Hagrid told her about Aragog, and how he was worried about him. She personally didn't like spiders, but she didn't like to kill them either. If she found one, she usually just caught it and let it outside. She'd never met Aragog over her summer with Hagrid, but the way he described him, she was glad she hadn't. She roasted some meat and potatoes and added some herbs and onions. There really wasn't much more to work with, but she did what she could to make it appetizing. When it was done, he poured them both a pint and she brought the plates over. She gave him the largest share, because she wasn't really hungry, but she wanted to sit and eat with him, so she'd made herself a plate too.

He took a bite and smiled. "Mmmm…this is good! And yeh did this with jus' wha' I already had, eh?"

"Thank you. You're too kind, Hagrid," she said, happy that he liked it.

"I usually eat a' the school during the school week, bu' there's nothin' like a home-cooked meal," he said as he finished up.

"To that, we agree," she said. "Could I give the scraps to Fang?"

"O' course yeh can! He migh' complain the next time I cook though," he laughed, then said more seriously, "Promise me, Sirana. If yeh ever need anythin', yeh'll make sure ter let me know."

She answered with equal sincerity, "I promise, but only if you promise the same."

Hagrid promised. He then offered to escort her home.

"Thanks, I'll be fine. It's not dark yet," she said, and headed home, enjoying the walk.

Sirana knew Severus would be home any time, so she hurried back. She was grateful when she entered Hogwarts because darkness had fallen quickly once she had left Hagrid's. She stayed up as long as she could waiting for Severus to return home. She knew Severus wasn't always able to share his plans with her, so she finally decided to go to bed alone.

Severus lay in bed waiting for Sirana to wake up, thinking about their future. He had never really thought about the long term, because he knew better than to hope for that. Now, he wondered what would happen to Sirana once he upheld his promise to Dumbledore and followed through with the Unbreakable Vow. Maybe she would stay at Hogwarts. Maybe she would leave with her grandfather. He wanted to tell her everything, but he knew he couldn't. He knew she would feel betrayed in the end though, and that pained him.

When Sirana woke up, she stretched and smiled at Severus.

Would she still look at me the same way if she knew? he thought.

"What's wrong, Severus?" she asked, as if she could see his mind wrestling with a dilemma. "Do you want to talk about it?"

"I was just thinking about Draco," Severus replied, knowing that to be only part of what was on his mind.

Sirana moved to lay against him, absently trailing her fingertips over the hair on his chest.

"I've seen changes in him," Sirana contemplated. "It feels as if he is torn between being who his father wants him to be and finding his own path. I know you've promised to keep an eye on him, but it seems like he's already lost…and I don't know what it would take to bring him back."

Severus knew how insightful her words were. He wanted to tell her that Draco was at a turning point in his life—and that Severus himself was entrusted with his soul. He knew that wasn't possible, and although it might lighten his own burden, it would put a burden on her that she didn't deserve to carry. Moreover, she might try to interfere, and that would put her in danger. He felt that in his bones, so he chose to bury it for now. There would be plenty of time for pain and regret when it all came to pass, he was sure of that. For now, he would imagine that all was right with the world and that there could be a life for them together, unmarked by the painful choices of his past or his future.

Chapter 56

Lesson

"What are your plans for the day, Sirana?" he asked, stretching out as if he wasn't planning on getting out of bed just yet.

"I hadn't really thought about it. I was hoping we could spend some time today on lessons. We haven't as much time for that lately and I have some questions on some of the homework you left for me," Sirana answered. She wasn't really thinking about homework, or lessons, or anything besides the man in bed next to her. She moved her hand from his chest, down his center, and was abruptly stopped by the hardness of Severus laid up on his belly. She rubbed her hand over and down the length of it, coming to rest at the base.

"Good morning," she heard Severus say in a low, husky voice that had a tinge of humor in it. "Or should I say, good afternoon."

"Yes, a very good one," Sirana responded, grabbing him with her hand, then running her hand back up to his tip. He grunted, his stomach muscles tensing. She kissed his broad chest, and he stretched and put his hands behind his head.

"Perhaps we can stay in bed for just a little while longer?" Severus asked, the corners of his mouth curling up. "I suppose we can spare some time if we make up for it tonight," she quipped.

"Tonight as well? Merlin's beard, woman, you're insatiable!" Severus teased.

She laughed. "I think the blame is yours this time," she said, stroking him while they bantered with each other.

"I will accept full responsibility," he said as he suddenly grabbed her and rolled with her, putting her on her back. He reached down and pulled up her gown just enough to slip his hand under. She closed her eyes and purred as he rubbed her soft curls with the palm of his hand. He grabbed her more firmly, massaging her slowly, and she gasped when he finally made his entry with his fingers, moving them inside of her and then on the outside, driving her to want more of him.

Severus enjoyed taking his time with Sirana, leisurely exploring her, seeing her desire build. He felt his own desire growing as he stroked his fingers in and out of her, imagining how wonderful it would feel when he slid into her warm wetness. He knew if he continued much longer, she would meet her climax, and he stopped just before. He moved on top of her, her legs opening for him, and he moaned his pleasure when she grabbed him to guide him into her. When he slid deep into her, it felt as exquisite as he had imagined. Her eyes were already heavy with desire, her mouth open sensually. When she met his gaze, he knew she was already close to the edge. He moved slowly at first, enjoying her expressions, then began moving faster, pumping into her at an even pace. She cried out at every thrust, her hands digging into the pillow. When she called out his name, he pounded into her harder until she cried out with her orgasm. The feel of it touched off his own climax, and he gasped as his own powerful release hit him in waves.

They lay in bed together, talking about their plans for the rest of the day before finally getting up to get dressed. Sirana surprisingly felt a bit shy, since the nighttime usually served as a buffer between the intense intimacy they shared and facing him in the daylight. He must have felt it and came over to her and kissed her on her forehead.

"Don't worry…I won't hold you to your promise to me tonight—unless you insist," he teased.

"I never break my promises," she replied, then immediately realized what he was referring to, her mouth dropping open for a second to make a correction.

He smiled devilishly. "Mmm…Looks like we have a deal."

Since it was the weekend, Severus was hoping to make use of the potions room while Professor Slughorn and the students were gone. Some of the more complex potions needed more than he had available in his study at home. Sirana was adept at the potions he'd introduced to her so far, but he wanted to make one with her that he'd been thinking about since the Weasley boy had been poisoned. He knew the antidote needed to be broad, considering all the poisons one might use, and he had written the recipe for the potion himself from a previous version that he felt he could more adequately develop.

It was interesting being in the classroom with Sirana. He wasn't new to teaching her because he had been working with her for quite some time in his study. It seemed awkward at first, but he quickly slipped into his Professor role.

"Professor Snape, is it alright if I take notes while you talk?" Sirana asked.

"Yes, please do, as long as you can keep up while doing so. This is the ingredient list. I would like you to gather each of these in the appropriate quantity and bring them to me," Severus said directly. He wondered how long it would take her to figure out the organizational system of the room and find everything on the list. She took a minute to find the first ingredient, but she picked up quickly and retrieved the rest in good time. It would take the rest of the day to brew this potion, so he had brought a bundle with some dinner and wine.

During their dinner, Severus decided to broach the subject. "Sirana, if anything were to happen to me, what would you do?"

He saw her think for a moment, her brow furrowed.

"I know it is important to plan for the future sometimes, Severus, but often, what we plan for doesn't even happen the way we might think. I don't have any intention of returning to the States. I've found a home here. Yes, I want it to be with you, more than anything, but if that isn't possible, I still care about this place and the people," she said thoughtfully. That had answered as much as he could ask, and he kissed her before returning to their professor–student roles.

When the potion was ready, he portioned them into several small vials. He instructed Sirana on how to recognize a poison victim and how to administer the antidote. Sirana had been capable and helpful, and he was proud as usual that she was his student. If she were a student at Hogwarts, her education would be close to complete, but he didn't plan on discontinuing her teaching. There was always more to learn.

It was getting late and there was one more thing he needed to take care of.

"One more thing, Sirana. The deal we made earlier...your promise?" Severus said as he took off his teaching robe, laying it across the desk.

Sirana had enjoyed working with Severus—Professor Snape—in the classroom. She could tell he was an excellent teacher. Even though he was often impatient, blunt, and short-tempered, he was also engaging, proficient, and thought-provoking. She wondered if any of his students found him as compelling as she did. She was jolted out of her thoughts when she saw Severus take off his teaching robe, and what he said just registered in her brain.

"You're joking, right?" she said, laughing but her face flushing. Surely, he didn't mean for them to...right here, in the Potions classroom.

"I don't joke," he said, moving towards her. She took a couple steps back, feeling like prey being stalked, and laughed again, nervously this time.

"What if someone comes in," she asked, still thinking he was just teasing her. "We would both be in trouble."

Severus drew out his wand and locked the door.

"There. Anything else?" he asked, resuming his slow movement towards her.

"Are you sure we—"

Whatever her next words were going to be, no one would know, as they were drowned out by Severus's mouth as he caught up with her and kissed her. He swung her around and pushed her back up to the desk.

"We can consider this extracurricular study in advanced wand use," he said, as he used his wand to remove her clothes.

"Severus! You're incorrigible!" she said in surprise.

"It's Professor Snape until I dismiss you," he said. He seemed to be enjoying the wide-eyed look on her face as he picked her up and laid her back on the desk. She saw the look on his face, as if he was thoroughly delighted. She realized her own exhilaration from the game, her heart racing, and decided it might be fun to play along.

"I'd better get extra credit for this, or I'm going to lodge a formal complaint," she said, as he unbuttoned his trousers.

"That depends on how well you handle the lesson," he said as he began the instruction.

Chapter 57

Parting

There were days Sirana knew that a lot weighed on Severus's mind. Often, he would be gone for a day or two at a time. She read as much as possible, and met with Professor Dumbledore occasionally, trying to keep abreast of all the happenings outside of Hogwarts, especially with her grandfather and the Order. The signs of grim times were escalating, and she knew it would get worse before it got better. She had conducted her classes as usual, although she had started blending magic into her training, and she could see the students' improvements daily.

She had just finished lunch when she heard that something had happened to Draco. She ran towards the bathroom just in time to see Severus, soaked with water, carrying an unconscious Draco. She wished she didn't have another class after lunch, but Professor McGonagall had instructed the students to return to their classes after the incident. As soon as her last class was over, she returned home as quickly as she could.

"What happened? How's Draco?" Sirana asked, seeing the look on Severus's face.

"He will recover...no thanks to Potter," Severus said blankly. "I don't know if the whole truth will out, but it seems that Draco and Potter were in an altercation, and Harry Potter prevailed. I cannot believe that Potter was aware of the malefic magnitude of the curse before he cast it, which was reckless and impetuous. I know he is Lily's son, but I could see nothing but his father when I looked at him. If I hadn't been there to administer the counter-curse…" Severus looked lost in thought.

Sirana prepared them a drink for them both.

"Severus, will you teach me the counter-curse? What if someone were to use it again and only I was there?" Sirana said, handing him his drink.

He took the drink, then stood, raising his glass to hers. "I will. I will teach you both the curse and counter-curse," he paused as he touched his glass to hers and they both drank. "However, this will be our last lesson together."

Sirana was confused. "What do you mean? Surely my lessons aren't complete."

Severus turned, stepping away from her. He didn't want to say what needed to be said.

"Sirana…You must leave. Tonight. I have made arrangements for your safe travel to be with your grandfather. I've spoken with Albus, and he knows where your grandfather is. He is with members of the Order, and you will be safer there with him than here," he said, finally turning towards her. She looked stunned, and he dreaded the pain he knew he must inflict on her for her safety, and possibly, his own. He knew what Dumbledore had said about her strength, and he knew how much she would need that strength now. He also knew he could not allow himself to be weak.

Severus saw her shock turn to anger, and he steeled himself against his own emotions.

"Severus, you know me. I don't pack up and run at the first sign of danger. I plan on staying and fighting when the time comes," she said, and he could see her blue eyes burning with the flames of anger and sadness.

He stepped towards her, taking her hands in his, bringing them up to his chest. He didn't want to see her leave angry, as it was as painful for him as it was her, but he knew it may be inevitable.

"Sirana, the time has come already. I need you to fight. I need your strength, but not here. There are things I must do, and if you are here, you become my weakness." Even as he said the words, knowing the painful truth behind them, he cursed his own path, and all that made it necessary to walk it.

"Come with me. There are things we must prepare for," he urged her gently but resolutely.

He could almost see her inner turmoil. He could see something else as well—courage. She wasn't frightened, but she wanted to make the right choice. He knew from his own experience that there wasn't always a right choice. He also knew that he wouldn't force the choice upon her. She pulled away from him, turning away, and he could see she was torn.

"Why must it be tonight, Severus? And how long would I need to stay away?" she asked, and he knew then that she would trust him.

"Tonight is the only night Albus can assure the location of your grandfather. The members of the Order your grandfather is with have been moving more frequently. Albus said they asked for your help, but that's not the reason I am asking you to go. Sirana, I cannot tell you everything, but I don't know when the time for you to return will be. I also cannot promise you this time that it won't be for forever," he said, unsure of his own future.

At that, she turned back to him, and he saw the tears in her eyes. Severus knew the pain she felt, because he felt it as well.

"I can promise that I will do everything in my power to see that you return to me—if you still wish to," he said, moving to her, wrapping her up in his arms.

"I will always wish to, Severus. I am trusting you, and I want you to trust me too when I promise you that it will not be for forever," she said, looking up at him, and they kissed as if neither could trust if that would be true.

Chapter 58

Counting the Minutes

Severus took the time to teach her the curse and counter-curse, as well as some others that might make the difference in a battle. He helped her pack, putting together some important potions and books for her to take. He knew he would regret her leaving tonight, but he did not want to regret this night together with her. He wanted to make love with her before she left, but he was afraid sadness would overtake their mood. He turned on the record player and offered her his hand. She smiled despite her sadness. It was their favorite song, The First Ever I Saw Your Face, and they danced with an awareness that comes from counting the minutes.

'The first time ever I saw your face

I thought the sun rose in your eyes

And the moon and the stars were the gifts you gave

To the dark and the endless skies, my love

To the dark and the endless skies

And the first time ever I kissed your mouth

I felt the earth move in my hand

Like the trembling heart of a captive bird

That was there at my command, my love

That was there at my command, my love

And the first time ever I lay with you

I felt your heart so close to mine

And I knew our joy would fill the earth

And last 'til the end of time my love

And it would last 'til the end of time

The first time ever I saw your face'

They listed to the soulful voice of Roberta Flack, swaying in tune with each other as much as the music. After the song ended, they remained in each other's embrace, holding on to the moment for all that it was.

"Sirana, we have some time left. Come to bed with me and let's imagine that we will wake up together in the morning," Severus said softly in her ear.

Sirana didn't get a chance to say goodbye when she'd left before to help the Order. At the time, it had broken her heart. She now knew Dumbledore had been merciful in giving her short notice. Each moment with Severus was like slow agony, knowing she may never get to see him again. She wiped all of that out of her mind while they danced. All of this was a gift, and no matter how long it lasted, she would appreciate every last minute of it. Just like life, the ending of it does not erase it. It is…They are…and even in death, they always would be… When he asked her to make love, she smiled. If it was going to be their last, they would make it worth remembering.

Severus was a bit nonplussed. Instead of leading him into the bedroom, she led him to the bath. He saw the smile in her eyes and caught on.

"Two birds, one stone?" she quipped. "Other than missing you when I was on the run, I missed taking a bath. It's very Muggle-y of me, I know."

Severus's mood lightened a bit at that. "I don't think Muggle-y is a word. Remember our first bath together? Before we knew you weren't really a Muggle?" Severus asked, drawing the bath.

"Of course I remember. How could I forget?" Sirana said, undressing.

She's brilliant, Severus thought. All of the dread was gone for a moment, and he felt lighthearted. He slipped into the warm bath with her.

Facing each other, wrapped in each other's arms, and this memory with her was even more glorious than the last—enough to last forever.

They met Hagrid at his hut. He was going to be flying her. Severus brushed Sirana's hair back with his hand, then lifted her satchel over her shoulder. She seemed to glow in the moonlight, and he suddenly felt melancholy. She smiled at him, and he felt the warm comfort wash over him, and in his gut, he knew she would be alright.

"I was wrong earlier...I can promise that it won't be for forever," Severus said as he kissed her, and their kiss held the promise of seeing each other again.

Severus walked slowly back to his rooms. He wasn't ready to face the silence yet, so he chose not to Apparate back. He thought of their evening together. He hoped it wouldn't be their last. Besides being a brilliant, beautiful, kind person, she was an amazing lover. It was like she was made especially for him, and he always felt like he couldn't get enough of her. She had playfully lured him to bathe with her, and it had been the remedy for their sadness. He thought of it while it was fresh in his mind—playing over the details as he walked. She had undressed herself, and as he started to do the same, she had stopped him. She had finally figured out how to work an ascot, and adeptly rid him of his, along with the rest of his clothes. He offered her his hand to step into the tub. She'd moved forward, expecting him to sit behind her like he had their first bath together, but this time, he sat in front of her, facing her, and pulled her legs over his and around his waist. He kissed her thoroughly, then pulled away and grabbed her soap. She smiled when he started on her shoulders, washing her. He reached his arms around her back, lathering it up with his hands. He washed the front of her next, and he could tell she enjoyed it as much as he did. When he finished with her legs and feet, he started moving back up to her middle. She took the soap from him, moving closer to him.

"My turn," she said, beginning to wash him in the same manner.

"I guess it depends on how you look at it," Severus said. "It could be considered my turn."

She smiled at that, making it to his front with the soap. She lathered up his chest, then the line of hair on his belly. He groaned as she washed his hardness with both of her hands. The feeling was exquisite, and he couldn't take much more of it, finally taking the soap from her.

"I believe that is clean enough," he said as he reached out and grabbed her hips, pulling her towards him. He slid his fingers in her. She was hot and slick, and he moved them in and out of her until she pleaded for him. He pulled her onto him, grabbing her hips to move her slowly on him, and they both moaned their pleasure, each enjoying the intimacy of being face to face. He could no longer withstand the constraints of their position and moved on top of her, pushing her to her end of the tub and lifting her hips up to enable himself to drive into her full bore. He felt himself getting closer to his climax, and he knew that he wouldn't last long enough this way to bring her to her orgasm, so he rolled them over so that she straddled him. He saw her knowing expression as she began moving on him, taking long, slow strokes. Her expression changed and her eyes closed, and she began rocking back and forth, grinding herself on him, and he knew she was close. He could feel her tighten and she whimpered with the struggle to keep her pace as her climax approached. Her eyes opened, and she met his as she pushed through her orgasm, gasping as she shuddered, and he could feel her pulsing on him. He sat up, then wrapped his arms around her, lifting her up and down on himself. She cried out as he felt her aftershocks hit her, and he burst into her, crying out hoarsely as his own climax hit hard. When they recovered from their passion, both of them breathing heavily, they suddenly started laughing. The sorrow of the day had washed away, and they were left with joy. Joy for each other, regardless of what the future might hold.

Severus made it back to his rooms, and when he entered, he could still smell her soap. He turned on the record player, listening to their song. He felt their link, the breathtaking strength of it, and his heart felt more contented than he could have imagined, especially knowing what was coming quickly for all of them.

Chapter 59

Two Silos

Sirana climbed out of the sidecar of Hagrid's flying motorbike when they landed. He came around the bike to her to say his farewells. "Take care o' yerself, Sirana. If yeh ever need me, I'll be there," Hagrid said, and she knew she would miss the giant and his easy natured company. They had grown to be close friends during the time they spent together over the summer, and she cherished his friendship.

"Thank you, Hagrid, I appreciate that. I'll miss you. Hopefully, I will see you again," Sirana said.

Hagrid pulled her into a hug. "I know yeh will, miss. Trust me."

Hagrid had delivered her to a small, old farmhouse in the middle of nowhere, and Sirana recognized it as one of the many hideouts she had seen while working with the Order. Her grandfather emerged from the house.

"Thank you for bringing her safely," he said to Hagrid.

"Yer welcome. Anytime," Hagrid replied, and left with a wave to her.

Sirana hugged her grandfather. He looked younger, but sadder.

"It's been hell without you, Sirana. We make a good team. I'm sorry you had to leave Hogwarts. I know you love it there, but we really do need you. Come, there's some people I'd like you to meet."

There were two ladies and three men staying in the house with her grandfather, and they all looked like they'd been on the run for a while. Her grandfather introduced her to them. She'd met two of them previously with her grandfather.

Everyone greeted her kindly, except one. A big, burly chap stood at the window with his wand drawn. He looked her way and said, "I hope bringing her here was worth it. If anyone saw them arrive, we'll have to be on the move again, and quickly."

"That's Grayson. He's as mean as he looks," her grandfather said, winking at her.

"Not all of us have the luxury of having a nursemaid, and if the young lady here is expecting to be coddled, she won't get it from me," he said gruffly.

That irked her more than she'd like to admit, and she started to tell him, but fortunately, one of the members she knew spoke up. "I've worked with Sirana before. You don't have to worry about coddling her. From what I've seen, you might need a nursemaid if you cross her."

Grayson huffed, then left the room. "Sorry about that," Finn, the man she'd worked with before, said. "His bark is worse than—well, actually, his bite is pretty bad too. He'll warm up to you," Finn smiled. "He is really one of our best members once you get used to him."

Finn's wife, Ava, who'd she also met before, chimed in. "We're happy to have you back. We've got lots to do, and we can surely use your help."

"Thank you. I will do whatever I can," Sirana said, and she meant it. This would be her team for the time being, and she wanted to make sure they all made it through.

They sat in front of the fireplace until late into the night, discussing strategies. They could only stay here tonight and then they would be back on the move. Grayson came back into the room to join them.

"So, when it comes time to kill Death Eaters, you will be up to the task?" he asked her. She knew that Severus had been a Death Eater, but as a spy now for Dumbledore. She had never had to kill before when she worked with her grandfather, but she knew she might have to, now that the war was brewing.

"Yes, I know what needs to be done, and I'm ready to do it," she said with conviction.

He looked at her hard, then nodded and left for bed.

"Let's all go to bed," Her grandfather said. "We're going to need our sleep."

"I'll take first watch," Sirana spoke up. "I'm not tired."

She stayed up until dawn. Finn relieved her so she could get a couple hours sleep. She felt her link with Severus, and she said a silent prayer that she would see him again before she drifted off to sleep.

It had been a week since Sirana had rejoined the Order. They were meeting with Mad-Eye that night. They were in a small apartment in a rough part of town. They didn't stand out among the rough-looking residents of the area. They didn't travel in public in more than groups of three so as to not bring attention to themselves.

Mad-Eye was alone, as he was usually known to be. He greeted her warmly when he arrived.

"Good to see you, again. Although I'm sorry for the circumstances," he said.

They all sat in the cramped apartment, and Sirana brought him a drink. Mad-Eye laid out a hand-drawn map on the small dining table.

"This is where we think they've been meeting. We can't go there when You-Know-Who is there, and we need to take out as many as we can. It's not going to be easy. You seven and four more will have to come in from their blind side, across the river. You will get only one chance, and then you get out. Understand?" Mad-Eye said.

He told them where to regroup afterwards and split them up so they wouldn't all be going to the same place. Sirana and her grandfather were with Finn, Ava, and Grayson.

"How soon?" Ava asked.

"Tomorrow night," Mad-Eye answered.

Finn reached to hold Ava's hand. Sirana noticed she looked scared.

Mad-Eye noticed too. "Are you all up for it? Now is your last chance if not. Our scouts say there's usually six of them, and we need the numbers on our side. We'll all be on brooms, and we need to be stealthy. I don't want to lose anyone."

Everyone said they were in, and even Ava sounded ready for the mission.

Sirana lay behind a small, rocky hill with her grandfather and Grayson. There was a dilapidated farmhouse with two silos. It looked like it had been abandoned for years. They saw the first of the Death Eaters start to arrive. Sirana had pretty good vision, and she saw something move towards the far side on the hill in a cluster of trees. When she pointed it out, her grandfather couldn't make it out, but Grayson saw it.

"It's probably their lookout," he said. He told Sirana that she was to target that Death Eater first, then swing around to help them. She felt encouraged that he trusted her to do that. They had worked together all week, and she'd proven herself to be a good flyer, and he must have noticed.

They waited for the signal from the other side of the ridge, and she felt her grandfather squeeze her hand in reassurance. When they saw the signal, she mounted her broom, and Grayson slapped her on the thigh. "Go get 'em," he whispered, and she took off, flying so close to the ground that she almost brushed the grass with her knees. They were only going to give her a twenty-second lead—enough time to engage—and then they were going to attack the main target at the silos.

As she drew closer, she saw the Death Eater, and broke hard to the left so that she could come up behind him. When she was close enough for good aim, she drew out her wand. She knew she only had one chance, or she would draw too much attention to herself if there was a firefight. She aimed her wand and sent the killing curse straight at the back of his head. She cursed inwardly, feeling the sharp sting of the raw awareness that she had killed another being. As the Death Eater cried out and died, Sirana vowed to herself that she would never allow herself to become callous to the pain from taking another life, regardless of the circumstances, and she felt no shame for the tears that fell in sorrow now, even for those who threatened to bring darkness to this world. She swung around to head to the silos and saw the other members of the Order closing in quickly. One of the Death Eaters must have heard the scream and was headed her way on a broom, his wand drawn. She peeled up hard, and the ball of fire barely missed her. She shot back down, flying fast, pulling up at the last second to come in behind her attacker. She fired her curse, and it missed her target, hitting his broom instead. He went rolling, tumbling down a rocky hill. She flew in to finish him off. He was laying in heap, and she aimed, but he rolled behind a large rock and her shot missed, sending a cloud of dirt and rocks into the air. The dust hit her eyes, and she veered off. She couldn't let him get away, and she wiped her eyes, frantically trying to clear them. She stayed low, knowing she would be an easy target in the open air, swinging around trees to come in from a better angle. Suddenly, she felt herself being yanked off her broom, and she landed hard. She tried to roll up so she could have a chance, but her attacker landed on top of her, knocking her wand away. It was almost dark, but she could see the Death Eater's mask only inches from her face. She fought, kicking and punching, knowing it was too late for her, but she wouldn't give up until she was dead. She didn't plan on being captured alive knowing what her fate would be at Voldemort's hands.

The Death Eater had trapped her legs with his, grabbing both of her wrists. He held them down above her head, and then removed his mask. She gasped. It was Severus!

He raised his finger to his mouth to quiet her. "Shhh…" he said. He looked around to make sure they were alone, then kissed her. She was never so happy and sad at the same time to see someone.

"Sirana, we don't have much time. I love you. Please, be careful. Please," he said, and kissed her again before putting his mask back on.

"I love you too, Severus, and I will," she said, as he let her up.

She retrieved her wand and ran for her broom. She looked at him once more before joining the fight. She saw a Death Eater bearing down on Mad-Eye and she broke hard to the right to get the angle she needed. She took the Death Eater out in one shot to the back.

"You take the left side!" he yelled, and she swung around left as he went to the right. They met in between the silos to take out the last two Death Eaters.

"That's it! Let's go!" Mad-Eye yelled. They all took off. She looked back towards the direction she'd seen Severus and she felt him in their link. Tears ran down her face when she saw the vision he sent to her of them standing together, clad in armor of love and courage.

Chapter 60

Thunder

Severus entered Malfoy Manor apprehensively. He knew the Dark Lord would find his report of the attack unsatisfactory. His scuffle with Sirana had at least provided him with proof of his participation in the skirmish. His broom was badly damaged, and he had cuts and scrapes from his fall.

Voldemort was tall and thin, his limbs looking impossibly long. Severus watched him as he moved toward him, the layers of his robe moving as if there was a breeze in the still room. The Dark Lord moved in a way that seemed unnatural, as if he hadn't quite grown accustomed to his reformed body. The image gave Severus the impression of a snake, slithering standing up across the floor. Severus looked into The Dark Lord's large, hollowed eyes, making a concerted effort not to cringe at his serpent-like appearance.

"My Lord, the attack was planned. They were waiting for us. Either we have an informant among us, or they had gained intelligence of our meeting site. If I hadn't been knocked off my broom and left for dead, I would have befallen the same fate as the rest," he explained as the Dark Lord stroked his snake, Nagini.

"This has been the fifth attack in as many weeks. If there was a spy among you, then they are dead now," the Dark Lord said as if his problem had been solved for him.

"Yes, my Lord. We must be more cautious in the future not to reveal our hand" Severus offered.

"It does not matter. It won't be long now, Severus," Voldemort said.

"I am prepared, my Lord," was all he could bring himself to say. He left the Manor, knowing his trial was impending.

When Severus returned to Hogwarts, the darkness settled over him. Seeing Sirana fighting so valiantly had filled him with loving pride. She was impressive, and he could see why they wanted her to fight with them. It also filled him with regret for what he had sworn to do. He had to meet with Albus tomorrow, and he would implore him to change his mind.

Severus left the astronomy tower, having just begged Albus to release him from his oath. Albus had been unmoved by his plea. When he passed Potter on the way back, he stopped, but couldn't bring himself to say anything to the boy. He returned to his room to prepare himself for what would come soon. He hadn't slept well since Sirana left, and he felt the weariness fall upon him. He turned on the record player, feeling somber and alone, and sat in his chair thinking of his time with her. He leaned his head back, letting his mind drift through memories of his life. Lily...He wondered if she would have forgiven him the weakness of his youth. Harry...his eyes held his mother's courage. Albus…he would sacrifice his own soul for this man. Sirana…she had renewed his spirit, and he now knew his own soul was worthy of his sacrifice. He felt her there, in his mind, and he touched upon their link. It steeled his courage. He heard the sound of thunder and felt the darkness creeping in. He left to face his fate.

Sirana made it back it to the rendezvous. It was a house that looked like several additions were added over the years, one on top of the other. It was the middle of the night, but there was a soft glow coming from one of the windows. She was the first to arrive. A tall, well-built man with ruddy red hair and a pleasant face came out to greet her.

"Come in, please. Did the others make it?" the man said, ushering her in the door.

"Yes, they should be right behind me," Sirana said.

He looked out the door, then closed it, turning to face her. "I'm Arthur Weasley. And you must be Sirana. I know your grandfather," he said.

"Nice to meet you," Sirana said.

They heard a noise outside. He went out and brought in the rest of the group that were supposed to meet here. He must have already known them, and he greeted them all jovially. A jolly woman with red hair came down the stairs and welcomed them to the kitchen.

"This is my wife, Molly. We've been waiting for your arrival. Molly, this is Sirana, Kane's granddaughter," Arthur said.

Molly had a kind, motherly face. She was short, only coming up to Arthur's chest. They were a lovely pair. She greeted Sirana kindly and brought them all drinks.

"How did it go? Did you lose anyone?" Arthur asked.

"It went well," Grayson replied. "Just as planned. Everyone made it. We were lucky this time."

Arthur breathed out a sigh of relief. "Good. Two more members will meet you here tomorrow night. We'll go over plans when they get here. For now, you can all get some sleep. Molly will show you to your rooms. Our children are in school, so we have extra beds."

Molly led Sirana's grandfather away first. He looked beyond tired, and Molly must have noticed it. She came back for Finn and Ava next. Ava had done splendidly in the battle, despite her initial trepidation. Sirana noticed no one usually spoke directly following a mission, like they needed the night to move past the unpleasantries before going over the details.

Arthur spoke while they waited for Molly. "Some of my children are students of yours, Sirana. They are quite fond of you. I'm sorry you had to leave. I know they were told you had to care for your grandfather. Are you planning to return next year to teach?"

"I hope so," she said. "I really enjoy it." Albus had invited her to stay as long as she wanted. It seemed like really far in the future, considering she was happy to even survive week to week.

She knew who their children were, not only by their last name, but by their hair color, which they all had in common.

"As far as I'm concerned, she can work with me as long as she wants," Grayson said. She felt flattered, especially since he wasn't one to dole out compliments.

When Molly came back to get her, Arthur asked her to take Grayson next. "Go ahead, Grayson. I need to talk with Sirana for a moment." He poured her another drink.

"It's been great having your grandfather back full-time. He's done so much for the Order," Arthur said. "I've noticed the last few times I've seen him that he's looking more and more tired. Have you considered talking to him about not taking on so dangerous of missions? I didn't feel it was my place to ask him myself."

"Yes, I have. I've noticed the same," Sirana smiled sadly. "He said he will stop when he is no longer capable. I don't think it will be much longer, though I think he wants to see it through this war."

Arthur nodded. "Well, he's still one of our best. And I hear you're following well in his footsteps."

Sirana blushed. She was glad that she didn't let all of the praise go to her head, or she would probably float away.

Molly came back and took her to her room. She said it was her youngest daughter's. For a moment, Sirana envied Molly for her large family. Their home was full of warmth and love, and she could only imagine how much more so it would be with all of the children in it. She knew that her life would probably never include her own children, but she was content with her lot in life regardless.

"Thank you, Molly," she said, and snuggled into the soft, warm bed.

The next day, she spent helping Molly prepare for the evening meal as the two new members were supposed to arrive. It was nice to cook again, and they worked well together. Arthur was an attentive husband and would come in to offer help and flirt with his wife regularly. Sirana enjoyed their good-natured company, but she couldn't help but miss Severus. Suddenly, what was left of the evening light coming through the windows darkened. Arthur and Grayson ran outside to look. When they came back in, their expressions were bleak. She felt darkness come over her as well, and she reached out through her link with Severus, finding it too was tinged with darkness.

Chapter 61

The Astronomy Tower

Severus made himself some dinner, but he barely ate. He poured himself a glass of brandy instead. As the night drew on, his mood darkened. He poured himself another drink and went to sit in his chair. He could hear his clock, and his own breathing, and the pops and cracks of the stone building as the temperature grew colder in the night. He suddenly felt alone. He reached out with his mind, trying to touch the link he and Sirana shared. It was there, and he could feel the connection between them, like a silvery thread. Now, it seemed tenuous, like it would snap if he pulled too hard. He felt dread settling in his gut. A wave of comfort suddenly washed over him as he felt Sirana reach out to him through their link, and he found comfort that she would be safe from the events that were on the brink tonight. He rose, slowly making his way from his chambers at Hogwarts, uncertain if he would ever return.

Severus had felt the darkness approaching as well, and he stood, gazing out at the sky. When Severus went to the Astronomy Tower later in the night, knowing that the Death Eaters had come to make sure Draco followed through for the Dark Lord, he saw Harry Potter below the scene. Severus wordlessly reassured him, asking for his silence, knowing that he wouldn't understand what was about to happen.

Severus then went up to face Dumbledore, and he knew it would be the hardest thing he's ever done.

"No," he said. He saw Draco, who had his wand trained on Dumbledore, struggling with the impossible choice before him. He saw Albus's face, which held the courage and wisdom of a man who had already made his choice. When Albus looked at him, he felt it to his soul, and he knew he would see this vision for the rest of his lifetime.

"Severus…Please," Albus said. Before he could change his mind, Severus sent the killing curse, and Albus fell from the tower to his death. He was numb. The time had finally come and passed. He had kept his promise to Albus Dumbledore, and now, Albus was gone forever. He closed down his brain and just moved, grabbing Draco, who was standing in shock. When Harry Potter attacked him outside of Hagrid's hut, he felt the culmination of his life come to a head, and he revealed to Potter that he was the Half-Blood Prince. Even that admission seemed distant, as his past paled next to all that had come to be. His path was forever changed, and he wasn't yet convinced that any of his soul remained.

Sirana noticed the mood at dinner. The two members of the Order they were expecting hadn't showed up yet. Molly finally told everyone to eat, and she would save their dinner for them if they came. It was late into the night when they finally showed. No one was asleep, as the mood of the house held a foreboding that hung like a fog over them. Sirana had seen them before, and she knew they were key members in providing intelligence for the Order. Their eyes were wide, and they seemed out of sorts. Arthur and Grayson talked to them in low tones before they joined the group. It was Arthur who broke the news—Dumbledore has been killed. Sirana covered her face with her hands, her tears running freely. She wasn't the only one devastated by the news, and she heard the sorrowful cries from around the room. Dumbledore was beloved by many, and the wizardly world felt lessened by the loss of such a powerful, respected wizard. Sirana had always felt as if Dumbledore was more than just the Headmaster of Hogwarts, and she had envisioned him as a Patriarch for the magical community. Now, she had no idea how they could possibly move past the unfathomable loss.

"They're not sure who did it. Severus's name was mentioned, along with Draco and Bellatrix. Hagrid's house was torched. No one else was harmed," Arthur said, looking at Molly, knowing she would be worried about their children.

One of the men spoke up. "Now, with Dumbledore gone, we believe that the Ministry of Magic is the next target—and the Ministry of Magic decides the fate of Hogwarts. We must not lose the Ministry to him."

Sirana had heard Severus's name and tried to focus on the rest of what was said. How was he involved with Dumbledore's death? She looked at her grandfather, and his eyes held fire for her. She remembered what he had said about trusting Severus, and it seemed so long ago. Had he known something even then? Had Severus? She couldn't bear not knowing, but she had no way to find out. They all decided to sleep on it and discuss their plans in the morning. She finally fell asleep, not knowing if she had the courage to face tomorrow.

Chapter 62

Forged

S everus entered Malfoy Manor to find an eerily familiar scene. A professor he'd known from Hogwarts was floating above the grand dining table, obviously under the Dark Lord's curse. He guessed that it was not unlike the one Lucius had used on Sirana the night he met her.

Voldemort sat at the head of the table, and every other chair except the one that was saved for him was filled with members of the Dark Lord's ranks. Severus saw no way he could save Professor Burbage's life, and he tried to show no emotion at her presence there. He knew what he had to do, and although Dumbledore was dead, Severus still had his counsel via his Dumbledore's portrait. His next meeting at the grand table was no more pleasant, since, as per Dumbledore's instructions, he had to give away the plans to move Harry Potter, thus securing his position at Voldemort's table. Severus had done everything he could to protect Harry Potter while posing as a Death Eater for Voldemort. He hated the mask and what he had to do keep up appearances for the Dark Lord. During the battle when Harry Potter was moved, he had killed Potter's owl to draw the other Death Eaters away. Mad-Eye had perished as well, although not by his own hand, and he mourned even his loss. Summer break had been long and lonely, and after Sirana's departure and Dumbledore's death, he felt almost completely isolated from the life he had known. Finally, he had accepted the position of Headmaster of Hogwarts, knowing it was the only way he could continue to provide protection to the students and staff. He would have a tough time ahead. Alecto and Amycus Carrow were Death Eaters who were appointed as professors at Hogwarts, and he knew they would be merciless. He would also no doubt be seen as a villain as well, and he would not have any true allies. He thought about Sirana—he felt her there in his mind, and he decided he was wrong. He still had one, the only one that mattered.

Sirana was heartbroken to hear that Mad-Eye had died in battle when Harry Potter was moved. She had worked with Mad-Eye many times over the last few months and had considered him a good friend. She had cried alone, not wanting to share her emotions with anyone. It seemed like a lifetime ago that she had cried on Severus's chest. There was no way she could have foreseen this future for herself. She hadn't heard from Severus since she had seen him at the Battle of the Two Silos. She had heard his name in connection with Dumbledore's death. She also knew he was going to be the new Headmaster of Hogwarts. There was no way she could return as a teacher with Voldemort in control of the Ministry, and therefore, Hogwarts. Her name was known to Voldemort and his Death Eaters because of her grandfather's role in the wars. Her name was starting to become more infamous in its own respect as well, and she knew she had a bounty on her own head. Her link with Severus remained, and she cherished it more than if it were forged from gold. She would find a way to help protect Hogwarts and its students, but for now, she was fighting from outside its walls. Whatever Severus's role in all of this was, she had chosen to simply trust him until she could no longer do so.

Chapter 63

Headmaster Snape

It had been over six months since Severus had seen Sirana. He heard mention of her occasionally, as her escapades with the Order were becoming well-known. Consequently, she had become a prime target for the Death Eaters. He wished he could send her a message to lay low for a while, but he knew her well enough to know she wouldn't hide from the dangers she faced. He also heard she was usually seen working with another member of the Order named Grayson, and he was high on the list of targets as well. He had met him once before the war and felt a twinge of jealousy that it was Grayson instead of himself spending time with her. He didn't want to imagine anything else between them, because he knew that he would drive himself mad envisioning her in love with another man. Since Severus was now the Headmaster of Hogwarts, he had moved into Dumbledore's room. His old rooms held too many memories of his time with Sirana anyway, and he found it distracting to go there, even to move his belongings. Nighttime was the worst, and some nights, it was almost too much for him when he thought of her. He had to use all of his self-control to quell his emotions. He would sometimes dream of her, and feel like she was really with him, her warm, soft body against him. His sleep would bring him the relief that he had not allowed himself while he was awake. He swore to himself that if he were to ever see her again, he would not ever let her go.

Sirana was sitting on the edge of her grandfather's bed. They were in one of at least a dozen hide-outs she could remember. Her grandfather looked so tired. His eyes still shone a brilliant blue though, and when he smiled at her, he looked like a man half his age.

"I'm sorry, Sirana," he said sadly. "I want to see this through with you, but it's wearing on me. I received word from Hagrid, and I will be joining him until I can recuperate. There are things I can do to help, but I would be risking others' safety to continue to try to fight with you. I really am sorry. I feel like I'm abandoning you after you have sacrificed so much."

"Grandfather. Please don't say that. You have given me so much. I will miss you, but I have so much worth fighting for now because of you, and that gives me life. If I were to die tomorrow, I would only have one regret, and that would be that I couldn't be there for Severus, as Lily wanted. I can't tell anyone how I feel about him except you," she said, knowing she would miss talking to her grandfather.

"I understand, Sirana, as my life has held so much for me. I still miss your grandmother, but she will be with me forever, and I believe I will rejoin her when I die. But now is not that time. Hagrid is coming to get me soon. I will keep in touch." He held her hand, and she felt their strength like a bond through their own link.

She was happy to see Hagrid again. She'd seen him occasionally since he was a member of the Order as well.

"Please take care of him Hagrid," she said as Hagrid hugged her goodbye.

"I will, miss. And yeh promise ter take care o' yerself too," he said.

She was sad to see them leave, and she sat on the hassock in front of the fireplace, just staring into the flames. Grayson came over to her with a glass of liquor, handing it to her.

"I'm not sure how old it is exactly, but I found a bottle of it. It tastes like brandy, and it has a bite."

She accepted it thankfully. She considered Grayson a friend. They'd found that they worked together very well, so they rarely were in a team without each other. He sat on the floor next to her, crossing his legs. She sipped the brandy slowly, and it reminded her of Severus. She closed her eyes for a moment, thinking about him. She missed him. She sometimes dreamed about him, and sometimes, the dreams were so vivid that she thought she'd actually been with him, so much so that it took a while to wake up and realize it was just a dream.

Grayson spoke and it brought her out of her thoughts. "Sirana, we've known each other for a while now. I've never heard you mention having anyone…special, in your life. Do you?"

Grayson was not a man of many words, and this was the first time she'd ever heard him speak in a gentle tone.

"Yes," Sirana replied. "There is someone in my heart. I haven't been able to see him because of the…circumstances…but I love him."

Grayson didn't speak for a few minutes. Finally, he said, "I don't want to make you uncomfortable. It seems the drink has loosened my words...but sometimes, I hear you at night while you sleep, and your dreams sound like you are...making love."

Sirana had felt the effects of the drink too, and she was glad that it had numbed her mind a bit from the embarrassment.

"I'm sorry, Grayson. I hope it didn't make you uncomfortable. It is embarrassing," she said, unconsciously turning her face away from him.

"Please, no, don't be embarrassed. I shouldn't have mentioned it. I just...Some nights, I wished I could come to you and be there for you...and we wouldn't have to even mention it in the daytime," he said it as if it took all of his will to say it.

Sirana looked at him then. "Grayson, I'm flattered more than you could know. If I wasn't in love with someone else, I—I wouldn't hesitate to take you up on your offer. But. I can't."

She didn't want to hurt her friend. She'd noticed before how he looked at her sometimes. She had noticed how attractive he was, but she only had a place in her heart, or her bed, for Severus.

"I hope we can still be friends though. I value your friendship, and I wouldn't want to lose that ever," she said sincerely.

Grayson took her hand in his, "I would never want to lose that either, Sirana. Your friendship means more to me than you can imagine."

They smiled at each other, and they sat enjoying each other's companionship until they fell asleep together in front of the fireplace, knowing that neither expected anything more.

Severus had recently found himself increasingly reliant on the counsel he received from Dumbledore's portrait in aiding the trio in finding and destroying the Horcruxes. He had sent the Sword of Gryffindor to Potter in the Forest of the Dean and lead him to it with his Patronus. He had trusted Dumbledore, and he would do all he could to carry out Dumbledore's wishes, even with the knowledge of how it must end. Until then, he did all he could to protect the students and the professors. He knew some of the students had started hiding out in the Room of Requirement, and he had kept the knowledge from the Carrows. He could not share his burden with anyone, because he knew that would make them complicit if the Dark Lord were to find out. He was a patient man. He would wait to see what the future held for Sirana. He hoped it was not another part of the epic tragedy that played out in his life. After losing Lily and Albus, and soon the boy, each with his own hand playing a part in their death, did he deserve mercy, or would he meet his fate grieving the loss of anyone he ever dared to love?

Sirana finally heard word from Severus. It came from her grandfather. He sent the letter through the Order, and she knew from her grandfather's message that it was sent with great peril. She opened the envelope, which looked like it had itself made it through hell to reach her. The note from her grandfather read in ornate cursive:

My dearest,

This comes to you at great risk, and as such, I hope that you find it to hold your heart. All my love.

She touched the paper with her grandfather's words, then opened the sealed letter. She felt hot tears run down her face, and she felt Grayson wrap his arm around her shoulder, holding her while she cried. The letter was from Severus, and it was the letter he had written her over a year ago as a retraction for the words that had hurt her. It was more than a poem, more than a love letter, and it was the most beautiful thing she had ever read. She felt a warmth come over her, like all of the love she'd ever felt in her life was received and returned through the link she had with Severus.

Sirana finally controlled her tears, and she smiled up at Grayson. "Thank you. I'll be okay," she said, and she saw his concern for her. She thought she saw a tinge of sadness too, but it was quickly gone, and he wiped her tears with his sleeve. She thought for a moment that she might have understood how Lily had felt years ago about Severus. In another life, there could have been more than friendship, even love, and she hoped one day that Grayson would find his own love.

Severus sat at his desk in the Headmaster's office. He was suddenly overcome with the warm familiarity he hadn't felt for so long. He could almost touch it for its magnitude, and he felt all the love he ever known in his life through his connection with Sirana. Somehow, he knew she had received his letter, and that their love still endured and would carry them both to the end.

Chapter 64

Lightening has Struck

The winter had been brutal, not because of the weather so much as from the battles. Sirana had seen several members of the Order fall to Death Eaters. Voldemort's army was growing, as if he was desperate to stop something he feared he couldn't win against. Now that spring was in sight, it felt as if some ending was drawing near. The Order must have felt the same, or maybe they knew more than they revealed, for they began organizing themselves as if for an all-out war.

Sirana, along with over a dozen members of the Order, were gathered at The Burrow. The Death Eaters had seemed to almost disappear in the past few weeks, and according to the leading members of the Order, this didn't bode well. They figured that Voldemort was amassing his army for an attack, and a final siege. She didn't completely understand, as she thought he was already in control of the Ministry and Hogwarts, but there was something about Harry Potter, Lily's boy, that was at the crux of everything that had transpired since that night in Godric's Hollow. It threatened the Dark Lord, and somehow, his quest for immortality was entwined with the fate of Harry Potter himself. Even her grandfather was present at the meeting with the Order, and they were preparing for any word or sign to make their stand.

As if on cue, she heard Arthur Weasley yell. He ran in to the middle of the group, turning up the radio. "Lightening has struck!" she heard, and the whole house erupted into chaotic action.

Grayson grabbed her by the shoulder of her jacket and pulled her aside. "Stick with me. We are going to Hogwarts to battle. They know as well as I that this will decide the war," Grayson told her, his eyes matching the fire of her own.

He started off to join the rest, but it was Sirana's turn to grab him by his shoulder, bringing them face to face again. "Grayson, I have to tell you. The man that I love…is Severus Snape, the Headmaster of Hogwarts," she said, looking in his eyes for his reaction.

Grayson said with a rare smile, "I know. I've known for a while. I am also one of the few who knows where his allegiances lie. Let me just say…he better deserve you."

With that, he grabbed her by the nape of her neck with his hand and planted a kiss on her before she could react. He smiled and winked at her. "I figure he owes me that for keeping your ass alive." He then slapped her shoulder as he had many times before they left for battle.

Severus hadn't wanted to injure Professor McGonagall when she stepped in between him and Potter. He took her fire, defending himself without retaliating. He heard her yell "Coward!" and the irony of it wasn't lost on him as he flew from the building. His role in this war was not complete, but there was one thing he would do for himself before he faced his own noble course. The Order had showed up to back up Harry Potter before he'd left, and he knew that by now the rest members of the Order would be on their way to defend Hogwarts. He wanted to see her one last time before the battle decided their fates. He reached out through their link, hoping she was growing near enough for her to see his thoughts. He felt her answer, like a whisper on the leaves in a forest. He would lead her to him, and she had agreed to follow.

Sirana flew with the group she left with from The Burrow. Others had gone ahead to enter from the secret passage at Aberforth's. Grayson and her grandfather flanked her. She felt Severus through their link, and knew she had to go. She flew closer to Grayson, and said within earshot, "I have to go on ahead. It's him. Tell my grandfather—he will understand. I'll be back."

He nodded, and she locked eyes with her grandfather before veering off so no one would see her, and took off fast towards Hogwarts. She was one of the fastest flyers among them, and she knew she could buy herself some time by flying solo and at full speed. She landed at the outskirts of the Forbidden Forest, feeling like her ribcage was going to burst with the pounding of her heart. She put her hands on her knees to try to catch her breath, and she finally felt some control coming back.

She heard him in the air, a low, whooshing sound, and saw him ahead, rematerializing at a run towards her. She ran towards him. They came together in a flurry of motion, his robes billowing and swirling as he embraced her, lifting her to him. She held his face in her hands as they kissed a kiss that may have made up for all of their longest nights without each other. They broke their kiss but embraced each other even tighter. Severus lowered himself to one knee, bringing her with him, as if to protect themselves from being seen, looking quickly around them and up into the sky.

He looked into her eyes. "Sirana," he said, his mind asking hers for permission to enter.

She opened her mind without hesitation, knowing that the moment did not have time for words. Their exchange of thoughts and emotions was powerful, and they both had tears running down their faces by the end.

"Severus," she said, as they embraced and kissed goodbye. She sprinted to her broom, and Severus watched her as she flew away.

Chapter 65

The Boathouse

It didn't take too long for Sirana to catch up with Grayson and her grandfather. They were in one of the towers of Hogwarts, along with several other members of the Order and a few of the older students. They all stood clustered together, looking at the black sky, which was suddenly lit up with streams of fire and light coming from Voldemort's forces. There was an almost pleasant stillness in the air, and her eyes grew wide at the deceptive beauty of the fiery sky. They watched in silence until the battle started growing nearer, and then the fear started to settle in her gut. The action started quickly, and there were several times amidst the battle that she'd found herself backed up against the others of their group. They were initially successful at warding off multiple attackers, but as the battle wore on, they became sorely outnumbered. She saw her grandfather waning fast, so she slowly worked her way towards the interior and parked him with other members who had made a makeshift triage for those who were injured. Her grandfather was an adept healer, and his assistance there would be greatly appreciated. It would also give him a chance to rest.

She motioned to Grayson for them to retrieve their brooms. They were both good flyers, and they would be more effective if they were on the move. She knew Hogwarts like the back of her hand, so she took the lead when they were inside the building, and he took the lead on the outside. They darted in and out, surprising many Death Eaters and warding off attacks when their members found themselves boxed in and outnumbered.

Severus stood waiting in the boathouse, having answered the call from Voldemort. He had spoken to the Dark Lord a hundred times, but this time was the first he felt true fear of him. He told Voldemort that the Elder Wand answered to him alone, knowing the Dark Lord suspected the lie for what it was. Even though the Dark Lord was in possession of the Elder Wand, he was not the wand's true master. Severus knew that even he was not the wand's master, despite being the one that killed Professor Dumbledore, as it was Draco Malfoy who used the Disarming Charm to take it from its previous master. The Dark Lord stared unblinking into his eyes, trying to find the truth, which Severus knew he must not reveal. He controlled his thoughts, feeling the Dark Lord trying to pierce his mind, and he adopted a casual pose as to not give anything away while waging a silent battle with the Dark Lord's mind. Only when the Dark Lord spoke of the Elder Wand's allegiances and Dumbledor's death at Severus's hand did Severus realize that the Dark Lord did not plan on allowing him to leave alive. He would not let his courage fail him in this final hour. He tried to keep any of this realization out of his link with Sirana. If she came for him, Voldemort would kill her too—or worse. He had also felt Harry Potter's presence nearby, and he was aware that he and his friends would be in danger if they tried to help. He was ready to face his ending alone. Knowing all of this, it still caught him by surprise when Voldemort slit his throat with the killing curse.

He wondered if anyone was ever truly prepared for death when it came. He had so much left to do—for Albus, for Potter, for Sirana. He had not fulfilled his last promise to Dumbledore, to tell the boy that he must die at Voldemort's hand in order to defeat him. As he fell, his mind did cry out for Sirana, and he cursed himself for his weakness. He knew he was dying, and yet the Dark Lord ordered Nagini to attack him as to ensure there was no chance of life for him. As Nagini struck him over and over, he did not cry out. He would not give into that weakness as it could put Potter in danger if he came to his aid. He also refused to give Voldemort the satisfaction of hearing his pain.

When Voldemort left, he knew he would surely die. When Potter came to him, his hope that he could fulfill his promise to Albus was renewed. He gave Potter the magical tears of his memories—"Take them." They would also reveal his true self to him, and he felt his spirit eased with that knowledge. "Look at me," he said to Potter, wanting to see Lily's eyes in his once more... a reminder of what he had made his sacrifices for...it hadn't been in vain. He saw Lily in his eyes, telling him so, and he once again felt the familiar warmth come and cover him like a blanket of enduring love. It was done. He could give into the darkness now. He thought about Sirana and the gift that Lily had given him that had restored his soul. He felt regret, not for loving her, but for not living for her.

Sirana felt Severus's cry and knew he had fallen to Voldemort. She screamed, and Grayson was able to grab her and help her land as the shock had made her lose control.

"What is it?" he asked, holding her shoulders.

"It's Severus. I have to go to him!" she said.

"Go, quickly, " Grayson said as he handed her her broom.

She flew as fast as she could towards him. He was still alive; she could tell by their link. Suddenly, she felt Voldemort in her mind, not talking directly to her, but to everyone at Hogwarts. She used all her will and experience from Severus's training to block him out. She could not lose her trail to Severus. She saw Harry and his friends leaving the building that she now knew Severus was in. She landed and ran as fast as she could to his side.

He was lying in a bloody heap against the glass windows, his limbs sprawled out amid his robes and cloak, left for dead. She grabbed his face, and she saw his throat and all of the blood. His eyes were closed, and he was starting to fade from her mind.

"Severus!" she cried aloud and in the link. She had to focus. If he were to have any chance at life, she would have to act quickly. She drew her wand, using Vulnera Sanentur, the counter-curse that Severus had taught her, to quell the bleeding. The bleeding stopped, but he had already lost so much blood. His face was white, and she could see that some of the wounds had been inflicted by Voldemort's snake. She drew her pack out of her jacket, hoping the general poison antidote that she had helped Severus brew would counteract any poison if it were present. She opened his mouth and poured it in, then held her mouth over his and blew in. She felt for his pulse, and it was there, but very weak. She pulled his head onto her lap and forced herself into his mind. He was still alive—he just didn't know it yet.

Chapter 66

Hope

Sirana didn't know what else she could do for Severus. She wished she knew more. She stayed in his mind, as if to hold on to the flicker of life she felt there. If he died, she would be with him in the end. Maybe that was what Lily had wanted for him…Maybe this was Sirana's reason to be here at this place and time—to see Severus to his end. "No!" she fought against that thought. She was grateful for everything, but she wanted more—more for herself, more for Severus. Maybe she was here because his soul was worth fighting for.

Severus! She called out to him in his mind. *Severus!!! Fight!!!*

Severus had shut down his mind, simply enduring, awaiting the inevitable end. He had no more concept of self, of place, or of the passage of time. Suddenly the pain his body intensified, taking forefront in his mind again, and he felt his consciousness returning, as if being pulled from an abyss of muddled memories. Was this just a part of his dying dreams? A specter of his mind's final death throes? He was vaguely aware of another presence through the mass of pain that was his body, and he fought against the darkness to reach the light he somehow knew awaited him.

Sirana felt hands on her shoulders. She didn't want to open her eyes. She was afraid if she left Severus's mind now, she might lose her tenuous hold. She heard a low voice, a whisper. It was familiar, but she could not spare any thought for it. She suddenly felt pain, and she gasped from the force of it. It emanated from her chest and neck. When she realized it was coming from Severus and not herself, she quickly reached out with her mind.

Severus?

Through the pain, she felt him answer, *Sirana!*

She felt the pain starting to ease, and then she felt him slip off into unconsciousness. It was as if he was no longer on the brink of death, though, and she felt relief coursing through her. She started becoming more aware of her own self as she gently moved out of his mind. She felt the hands still on her shoulders. She opened her eyes finally, and saw Severus's face, and some of the color had returned.

"Sirana," she heard, and she looked up to see her grandfather on his knees in front of her.

"Is he alive?" She realized that it was Grayson at her back with his hands on her shoulders from his voice.

"Yes," her grandfather answered. "We almost lost him, but I think he's going to be alright."

Sirana was starting to realize what happened. Her grandfather had come to help and had brought Severus back from the edge.

"Are you alright, Sirana?" Grayson asked her.

"Yes, thank you," she said and put her hand over his. She looked at her grandfather. "Thank you, thank you," she said, her voice catching. She hadn't cried. All her focus had been on trying to save Severus, and she felt the tears of panic and relief coming, and she couldn't stop them. She lowered her head onto Severus's chest, her body shaking, and she felt Grayson wrap his arm around her. She gathered herself and sat up, still cradling Severus in her arms. "We have to move him. Everyone here thinks he's the enemy. Where can we take him?" she asked.

"I know a place," Grayson said. "He will be safe there. We have to get him there though."

Sirana wasn't sure how they would move him. An idea shot in her head. "Please, grandfather, hold him for me. I'll be right back."

Her grandfather took her place, and she went to get her broom.

"Do you want me to go with you?" Grayson asked.

"No, please, stay here with them," she said, and took off flying.

She flew towards the Forbidden Forest. She had seen Thestrals in the air during the battle, and she hoped that they'd returned to the forest. She landed, dismounted from her broom, and called for Tenebrus. She didn't have much time. Thankfully, she heard him coming.

He greeted her as he always had and placed his muzzle on her shoulder. She whispered her urgency to him, and he lowered for her to mount him. They flew swiftly back, and landed next to the building, Tenebrus following her in as far as he could. She ran in to see the scene just as she had left it.

"Clever girl!" her grandfather said.

"Can he carry all of us?" Grayson asked.

"He is strong enough to carry Hagrid. So, he can surely carry us. We just have to lift Severus. Grandfather, are you coming with us?" Sirana asked.

"No. You go on. I will be of more use here helping with the wounded," he said, helping to lift Severus's unconscious body.

The three of them were able to hoist him atop the Thestral, and Grayson climbed on to help hold him. Sirana sat in front, and her grandfather handed them their brooms.

"Where will you go, Grayson?" he asked.

"To Andromeda's. Remus and Tonks knew about Severus. She will understand," Grayson said.

"Good idea, Grayson. Take care of Sirana," her grandfather said.

"I always do," Grayson said with a wink.

Sirana had been to Tonks' home before, as their house had served as a hideout for the Order. She whispered to Tenebrus, and they flew away quickly.

Chapter 67

Andromeda's

Tenebrus flew swiftly but steadily, as if he knew the precariousness of his cargo. Sirana knew where they were going. She had met Andromeda, Tonks' mother, a couple times before when she had hidden out at her home with the Order. She was as lovely as Tonks and was just as brave in her own right. Sirana had heard she had recently lost her husband, Ted Tonks, to Snatchers. She hoped Andromeda would welcome them, considering Severus Snape was with them. Maybe she knew of Severus's true allegiances as Grayson did. She didn't want to even think what they would do if she was unwilling to welcome them into her home.

When they landed, Grayson told her to hold onto Severus, and he ran towards the house. Several minutes passed before he returned, Andromeda following close behind. She helped them lift Severus down, and Sirana and Grayson were able to get their shoulders under Severus's arms to carry him in the house.

Andromeda led them into a bedroom, and they laid him on the bed. Sirana brushed his hair back from his face, which was still pale, but not as lifeless and white as it had been. Andromeda brought out a heavy quilt and covered him with it. Sirana leaned down to kiss him on his forehead, then told them she would be right back.

She went out to Tenebrus. She thanked him, patting him on his neck, and told him he could fly home. When she returned, Andromeda brought both her and Grayson something to drink. She was thankful. She was so thirsty, and her body was starting to shake with the exertion from the battle and its aftermath. She sat on the edge of the bed, feeling inadequate and unable to help Severus any further. She loosened the collar of his jacket and shirt, and Andromeda helped her to remove his robe and then his shoes, trying to at least make him as comfortable as possible. Sirana inspected his neck, seeing the wounds, which had been healed with her counter-curse. Andromeda brought back a basin with warm water and began washing the blood from his face and neck.

When they'd done as much as they could do, Andromeda spoke, "What happened?"

"The Dark Lord," Sirana answered. She knew some did not say the name "Voldemort" aloud. "He cursed him and had his snake, Nagini, attack him. He almost died. I used the counter-curse and antidote. He was still so close to death, and my grandfather came and brought him back," Sirana said.

"He seems stable for now. I will send for a Healer as soon as I can. It will have to be someone we can trust. I know of Severus's reputation since he took over at Hogwarts. There's not a lot of people who know the truth," Andromeda said.

"Andromeda, we need to talk." Grayson spoke up. Sirana noticed that Grayson's voice and expression were somber. She stayed at Severus's side when they went in the other room to talk. Suddenly, she heard Andromeda wail. Sirana went to the doorway to see if she was okay. Grayson was holding her as she sobbed, crying, "No, not my Dora!"

Grayson turned to Sirana. "I have some bad news. Remus and Tonks fell in battle." She too broke down in tears at the news, going to them, and he pulled her in as they all embraced, sharing their love and sorrow of lives lost too soon.

Later that evening, as Sirana set on the side of the bed, watching over Severus, Grayson entered the room. "Andromeda is sleeping now," he said, pulling up a chair to sit close by, his eyes looking haunted as he stared off at some fixed point in the room, "I saw them die, Sirana. Bellatrix killed Tonks. Bellatrix was Andromeda's sister, Tonks' aunt. Molly Weasley killed Bellatrix. Your grandfather came to get me after and led me to you. He said he heard you through his mind. When we found you and Severus, he said that you and Severus's minds were joined. I've heard of this magic, and I know it's a rare ability, but I've never seen it before." She could tell he was talking to help ease the pervasive sense of despair. They had lost so much today.

"What about Teddy, their son?" Sirana asked.

"He's with Andromeda, sleeping," Grayson answered. "She has made plans to care for him."

Sirana felt the overwhelming sadness of it all, but she knew Andromeda's pain was more than she could even fathom.

"You need to rest too, Grayson. I will be fine here. I need to stay with him," Sirana said.

"I will. You need to rest too though. Why don't you lay down? I'm sure Severus won't mind," Grayson said, leaving to be with Andromeda.

Grayson was right, —she was tired. She felt like she was starting to sway. She climbed into the other side of the bed, lying next to Severus. She touched his mind in their link and fell fast asleep.

Chapter 68

Madame Pomfrey

Sirana woke to the sound of dishes clanking. She could tell it was morning, and she could see the light around the curtains. She sat up in the bed and looked at Severus. He was breathing deeply. She reached out with her mind and could tell he was still unconscious. Severus's mouth was slightly open. She kissed his lips gently before rolling out of the bed. She was still wearing the clothes she had battled in, minus her jacket, and she hoped Andromeda had a change of clothes for her.

She went out to the living area. Grayson and Andromeda greeted her. They had made breakfast and were doing dishes together.

"Come on in. We have news," Grayson said.

They sat at the breakfast table, Teddy asleep in the bassinet next to them.

"The war has been won. Voldemort is dead," Grayson said.

It was such good news, but it was shadowed by the loss they all felt for their fallen friends and family.

"Your grandfather sent a message. He is bringing Madam Pomfrey today to see Severus," Andromeda said. "Don't worry, she will be discreet."

"Thank you so much…for taking us in. I know it's been so hard on you, and I'm so sorry for your loss. If there's anything I can do to help, please ask," Sirana said.

"Thank you, dear. I'm thankful to have you here. You are welcome to stay as long as you need. The dark times are past, and I dreamed last night of clear skies ahead," Andromeda said, smiling sweetly. Her eyes were still puffy from her tears, but her face held a peace that reassured Sirana that she would be alright. They ate together, talking about Tonks and Remus, and how much the baby looked like them both.

When they were done, Andromeda said she would clean up, and offered them a bath and a change of clothes. Their clothes were covered in blood and dirt, so she was happy to start the day out clean.

Her grandfather and Madam Pomfrey arrived early in the afternoon. Sirana took her to Severus, whose condition hadn't changed since they arrived. Everyone gathered around his bed, and Madam Pomfrey shooed them all out.

"One of you can stay. They rest of you can wait outside," she said.

Sirana stayed, hopeful that Madam Pomfrey could help. She knew she was a skilled Healer, and she trusted her to do all she could to help. She helped Sirana take off his jacket and shirt, which were stained with blood. Madam Pomfrey examined him thoroughly, then took a vial from her medical bag.

"Hold his head up," she instructed, and Sirana complied, grateful to be able to help.

Madam Pomfrey administered the medicine, then told Sirana, "Your grandfather told me of his injuries, and of the treatments he's received. You are very fortunate. Very fortunate. Without you and your grandfather, he would not have made it. He may be unconscious for a day or two. Any more than that and you must send for me again. If he awakens, he needs to remain in bed for at least a week. Just keep him comfortable. Your grandfather has told me of his true nature, and I can say that I am not surprised. I have known him for many years, and I am relieved to hear that he was not truly aligned with Voldemort. Even if he was, my responsibility to his health would not vary."

"Thank you. I really appreciate your help," Sirana said, grateful for the optimistic diagnosis.

When Madam Pomfrey left, Sirana stayed with Severus. It had been a year since they'd had more than a few stolen moments together. She missed him. Seeing him now tore at her heart. She was so thankful he was alive. Their life would undoubtedly change, and she couldn't envision what their future would be, but as long as they were together, she knew they would carve out their own path.

Sirana's grandfather came into the bedroom and put his arm around her shoulder. "We're going back to Hogwarts. There's still a lot of injuries to tend to. We won, Sirana. There's going to be a lot going on for a while, at Hogwarts and the Ministry. We have sustained losses that we will never forget, but we will rebuild. We must be vigilant to protect what we have regained, but I can see the hope in everyone," her grandfather said, and she heard the conviction in his voice and his message.

Sirana stayed with Severus the rest of the afternoon, caring for him the best she could.

Grayson came in to check on her. "So, this is the one, huh?" he asked.

She looked up at him and smiled. "Yes, he's the one," she said.

"Well then, he's a lucky one. I always thought you were fairly mad. I just figured that was why you were such a good flyer— and fighter," he chuckled.

"Oh yeah? So what's your excuse?" Sirana asked.

"Oh, I'm a bit mad too. I just hide it better," Grayson said, kissing her on the head before leaving. She'd never seen Grayson in such a good mood. Maybe the weight of the war lifting off of his shoulders had freed his spirit.

"If he kisses you ever again, I shall have his lips removed," she heard a low whisper.

She swung around in shock. "Severus? Severus!" she cried, looking to see his eyes open, but barely.

"Yes. Remember that, because it won't be long before you will be saying it with much more passion," Severus said, then closed his eyes again.

Sirana kissed his forehead, placing her hand on his cheek. "Severus, I love you. I'm happy to see that you've developed a sense of humor while you've been out," she said, amazed at how much she could love a man.

"I love you too, Sirana. Now, leave me be. I'm sure you've been doting over me like a mother hen. I need to sleep," he said, opening his eyes again for a moment. His lips turned up in a small smile, and he fell off to sleep.

Chapter 69

Harry & His Godson

Sirana went to tell Grayson and Andromeda that Severus had regained consciousness. When she went into the living room, Grayson was holding Teddy, feeding him while Andromeda sat next to them, smiling.

"You look like a natural, Grayson," Sirana said.

"I have two younger sisters—twins. My mother would let me help with them. She said I never dropped a baby, not even when the rocking chair I was sitting in broke...I held on to that baby," he said proudly. "They have their own children now, and I've done my fair share of babysitting."

She noticed how happy he looked. "Well, I have some good news. Severus woke up," Sirana said.

"Is he alright?" Grayson asked.

"Yes, he spoke. I think he's going to be just fine. He shooed me off and went back to sleep," she said, smiling.

"I'm so relieved for you, Sirana. I can see how much you care for him. I know he'll be fine with you taking care of him," Andromeda said.

"Oh, I'm sure that's going to be a battle in itself. Madam Pomfrey said he needs to stay in bed a week, and I don't think that's going to go over well," Sirana said, knowing she was going to have a fight on her hands. She would take it though, and she knew it would all be worth it to have him back.

"Harry Potter is coming tomorrow to see Teddy. He is Teddy's godfather. We will have to keep Severus's presence hidden. I don't think Harry would understand," Andromeda said.

"Maybe one day. I hope that eventually people will know the truth about him," Sirana said, thinking aloud. "But I'm not worried about that now. I haven't really thought about what happens now—where we will go or what we will do. My grandfather may still have the place that Albus gave him, so I'm not really worried about having a place to stay when he recovers. I just don't know what he will do. I can't see me going back to Hogwarts without Severus, especially now that Albus is gone."

"You don't have to worry about yourself, Sirana," Grayson said. "The Order will need you, now more than ever, to regain control of the Ministry and maintain order. I don't know about Severus though. You will have to cross that bridge when you come to it."

"Or build our own bridge," Sirana said, surprised that she had no worries for their future. They had stood against the gates of hell together, and she knew in her heart that they would find their way.

Andromeda was a good host, and the Order was lucky to have her on their side. Sirana noticed that Grayson hadn't mentioned how long he was going to stay, but Andromeda didn't seem to mind his company. Grayson helped her with the baby, as well as with the chores around the house. Her intuition told her that they were quickly growing fond of each other. She hoped that was the case, as Grayson had never seemed so happy and content since she'd known him.

Severus slept through the evening and into the night. At one point, he started to stir in his sleep, and he was talking. She woke up too late to really make out any of his words.

"Sirana," he said, more clearly now.

"Yes, Severus, I'm here. Is there anything I can get you?" she asked.

"A drink," he said. She took the water from the bedside table. She helped him take a drink and made him comfortable again.

"Stay with me," he said, and she sat next to him on the bed where he could see her. She stroked his face, speaking softly to him until he fell back asleep. She moved to the chair next to the bed, pulling her knees up under her chin, and sat with him until morning.

Later that day, Harry Potter came to visit his godson, and to pay his respects to Andromeda. Andromeda was feeding the baby, so Sirana met him at the door. He seemed surprised. "Welcome, Harry. Come on in," Sirana said.

Harry entered the living area, and Grayson stood to meet him.

"Harry, this is Grayson. He's a member of the Order of the Phoenix," Sirana said, and they shook hands.

"I knew your parents. It's good to finally meet you," Grayson said.

"Good to meet you," Harry said, then looked at Andromeda and the baby. "I'm sorry about Remus and Tonks, Dromeda. They were two of my favorite people. How's the baby?"

"Here, I'll help you," Grayson told Andromeda, picking up the baby from her lap.

"Here, Harry," Grayson said, holding the baby for Harry to take. "Here's your godson."

"He's so tiny," Harry replied, holding his arms in a cradle so that Grayson could place the baby there.

Grayson gently laid the baby in his arms, holding the baby's head. At that time, a voice came from the doorway. "Potter." Severus was standing in the doorway to the bedroom, shirtless, wearing only his boxers.

Harry's mouth dropped open, and Teddy almost slid from his arms. Grayson leaped forward and grabbed the baby, then handed him gently back to Andromeda.

"Well, she obviously didn't pick you for your timing," Grayson said to Severus in an admonishing tone.

"Professor Snape! It's not possible," Harry said, staring at Severus, still in shock.

Chapter 70

Reverence

Severus started to sway, his knees suddenly buckling. Grayson shot forward, catching him before he fell. Harry recovered from his shock at seeing who he thought was a dead man in time to help grab Severus. Together, they led him back to the bedroom, and he didn't protest as they laid him down in the bed. Sirana rushed in to pull up his blankets and get him tucked back in.

"Severus! You need to stay in bed. At least a few more days," Sirana said, not wanting to mention Madam Pomfrey in front of Harry.

Severus nodded, and she could tell he knew he wasn't ready yet to stand.

"The Pensieve," Severus said breathlessly. "Did you take them to the Pensieve?" he asked Harry.

Harry looked at Sirana, then back at Severus, as if this confirmed something in his thoughts. "Yes, Professor, I saw it all. I just don't understand how you can be alive. I saw Voldemort kill you. I saw you die."

Sirana saw Severus struggle to keep his eyes open, and he looked pale, like he was going to be sick. She grabbed the basin, setting it next to the bed, and placed a damp washcloth on his forehead.

"It's alright Severus. Go to sleep. We have plenty of time to talk when you feel better," Sirana said. He closed his eyes, a look of peace on his face, and he fell back asleep.

Grayson spoke up, "Looks like we have some things to go over. How about I pour us all a drink?"

Harry looked a little pale. Sirana sat next to him, and Grayson brought them all a drink.

Sirana spoke first. "Harry, I know you think Severus was on the wrong side of the war, but—"

Harry interrupted her. "Wait. What Professor Snape said about the Pensieve..." Harry took a deep breath and a drink before continuing, "When he was dying, he gave me his memories to take to the Pensieve. All this time, I had been wrong about him. He was protecting me. I look back at all of the times I should have known. He sacrificed his life for us. I treated him so unfairly," Harry's voice caught, as if he was holding back tears. "I saw him die, though. How is this possible?"

"There is something I want to share with you, Harry. I don't think Severus would mind," Sirana said. "Severus said you had the gift of Legilimency. Would you allow me?"

"Yes," he said, turning into to face her.

Sirana shared with him what Severus saw in the Pensieve from her mind—his mother, Lily, and how much she loved Harry; Sirana and her friendship with Lily and James; Sirana's grandfather trying to protect them; Severus's love and anguish; Lily's Patronus and her gift for Sirana; and finally, Severus, almost dying and fighting his way back from the brink. Sirana then felt the direction of the flow of memories change, and Harry was showing her his mind—the Resurrection Stone in the Forbidden Forest; his parents, James and Lily; his friend and teacher, Remus Lupin; his godfather, Sirius Black, all of whom were whispering "We are part of you"... There was one person absent—Severus Snape, and now the reason was apparent. The weight of it all touched them both, and tears were running on their faces when they broke the link.

Harry looked at Sirana, and she knew that his burden of regret for Severus was lifted.

"Now, you want to try holding your godson again?" Andromeda said, smiling.

"Yes," Harry said, sitting to hold him this time.

Harry spoke softly to Teddy, "I knew your mother and father. They were some of the bravest people I've ever known—and they loved you so much. I will tell you about them when it is time. I know what it's like to be an orphan. I will always be there for you, Teddy, and so will they—in here," Harry said and touched the baby's heart. There wasn't a dry eye in the room, and Sirana could swear she felt the spirit of Lily, James, Sirius, Remus, Tonks, and Albus all there with them.

Chapter 71

Nursemaid

Harry Potter's visit left a feeling of optimism in the house. Sirana felt like Teddy would have an extended family that would see him through. She felt the same way about herself. She had gained so many close friends, and she loved the feeling of being a valuable member of the extended group. She would have been more than willing to go hide out with Severus, but the possibility of them being able to reintegrate into the magical community gave her a new hope. She had some ideas of how she and Severus could find meaningful purpose, but she would wait until he had regained his strength before she proposed them to him. She was sure he would have some input regarding the path they would follow.

For now, she prepared some hot water in a basin to give him a sponge bath. Her mother had always called it a French bath, and she never realized the meaning until she was older. Her mother's humor was rare and subtle, unlike her own humor, which she considered a bit juvenile. She appreciated Severus's humor, which was also subtle but not so rare, and held a mastery of innuendo. She had enjoyed their banter, and she had missed his company the past year. She hoped they would be able to ease back into their relationship when he recovered, and that they wouldn't feel awkward together from their long time apart. She knew his feelings were still just as strong for her, if not more, from the link they shared before the battle.

She headed into the bedroom with her steaming basin of water. Severus was still in deep sleep after almost collapsing earlier. She placed towels around him and lightly soaped up a cloth, making sure it wasn't too hot. She waited until the last minute to pull the blanket off his chest so as to not give him a chill. She knew Severus would forgive her for enjoying this time with him. She loved caring for him, and for the closeness she felt to him. She washed his neck, being careful with his wounds, which were mostly healed but still raw and red. She worked down to his chest and arms, then his underarms. She'd always found it amusing that most of his hair was on his head, and besides his underarms and lower stomach, he wasn't a hairy man. There was something about his physique that she felt immensely attracted to, and she appreciated how it embodied a sensual masculinity, just as Severus himself did. She finished rinsing his upper body, then covered it again. She uncovered his bottom half and wetted the cloth again, pulling down his boxers. She jumped in surprise when she suddenly became aware that Severus was wide awake. She looked up to him, seeing his eyebrows raised in a mischievous expression.

"Continue," he said slowly, his mouth almost giving away a smile.

Chapter 72

Willingly So

"Severus!" she said, looking back at the bedroom door, which she hadn't thought to close all the way. She was sure she felt more embarrassed about the situation than Severus. He was obviously enjoying her predicament, and seeing her face grow hotter and redder by the moment.

"Where is my wand?" Severus asked.

"On the table. Why?" she asked, guessing the answer.

"Because we need privacy…for my bath," he said, matter-of-factly. She handed him his wand, not sure what else to do at the moment.

He used his wand to close the door and she heard it lock. He then set silencing spells on the room, looking at her as if he was waiting for her to comment.

"You would make a wonderful nurse," he said.

Sirana blushed, and she knew he was enjoying teasing her.

"Speaking of nurses, Madam Pomfrey said that you need your rest, and that you need to stay in bed for at least a week," Sirana argued, knowing she would not likely win this one.

"I don't plan on getting out of bed—at least, not tonight," he said. "You should probably finish my bath before the water gets cold." He pulled back the cover a little more.

Sirana finally smiled. "Well, I am happy to see that you seem to be recovering nicely."

She wetted the cloth again, then started washing each of his legs, starting at his ankles, working her way up to his thighs. She smiled, enjoying teasing him in turn, wondering how far his patience would go. She finally ran out of anything else to wash and moved his boxers down further. She dipped the cloth in the warm water, lathering him up with soap as he watched with his complete attention on her. She washed him thoroughly, and he let out a contented sigh, obviously enjoying her attention. She rinsed him off, dried him, and then pulled up his boxers, finding it a bit difficult to arrange everything adequately.

"Thank you, Sirana," Severus said in his alluring voice. "Come to me." He held out his hand to her.

She sat next to him on the bed, feeling that familiar feeling that she hadn't felt in way too long, and she knew it was going to be a long week. She would be patient though; she had waited for him this long, and she would wait longer to make sure he recovered adequately. After that, all bets were off.

"I dreamt about you, Sirana. The nights were long without you, and some nights, it seemed like you were there with me, in my bed," Severus said, holding her hand on his chest.

"I did too, Severus," she said, remembering what Grayson said about hearing her some nights, and her face grew warm with embarrassment.

Severus reached up to her, and gently pulled her down into a kiss. "Then, even our distance couldn't keep us apart," he said, his eyes slowly closing.

"Nothing will keep us apart again, Severus. You're stuck with me," Sirana said, kissing him on his forehead, then tucking the cover around his shoulders.

"Willingly so," Severus said before falling back to sleep.

Sirana took the basin back to the kitchen, washing it and drying it. Grayson sauntered over, a smile on his face.

"How is Severus? Is he feeling better after his bath?" he asked.

Sirana saw the glint in his eyes, and playfully smacked him with the towel. "He's doing fine. He's tired. But I'm afraid I'll have to tie him to the bed to get him to stay there a week," she said.

"Mmm...then I can see why he's so taken with you," Grayson teased.

"Ochs, you're as bad as he is!" she said, her cheeks blushing a bright pink.

He laughed at that. "Then I can see why you're so taken with him."

"You're one to talk. You seem to have an admirer as well," she teased back.

Grayson adopted a more serious tone, and he said in a low voice, "I don't know, Sirana. I know she's lost so much lately. I hope I'm not overstepping. I know it's probably too soon, but I can't help but feel drawn to her. You know as well as anyone that I'm not afraid of anything. But I'm scared to death I've already lost my heart to her."

"Oh, Grayson. Don't be afraid. Love is worth fighting for. I've seen how she looks at you. You will both be the luckiest people I know. You deserve her, and from what I've seen of her, she deserves you too," Sirana said, and she meant it. She wanted that for her dear friend—to find what she had found in her own life.

Chapter 73

The Order

Today was the fifth day since they'd arrived at Andromeda's. Sirana was surprised that she was able to keep Severus in bed—for the most part—for that long. Madam Pomfrey was right—he really needed the rest. He was still a little unsteady on his feet when he went got out of bed to use the loo. He was awake more of the day now though. Andromeda provided him with books from her library to stay busy.

Sirana brought him dinner, and she stayed with him while he ate.

"Some members of the order are coming here tomorrow," Sirana said. "Grayson said he's heard that there is still some activity within Voldemort's Army since his death. We need to make sure another doesn't try to take over."

Severus looked at his arm. His Dark Mark was starting to fade. "So, when you say 'we', does that mean you're staying with the Order?" Severus asked.

"Yes, I had planned to. Hopefully, not full-time. Especially once everything settles down. Grayson told me you were in the Order—before Albus died," she looked at him expectedly.

"Yes. Very few knew. And now, it seems that we have lost several of those to the war. Do they know I'm here? That I'm alive?" Severus asked.

"Yes, Harry has told them. It looks like he may become a member himself, along with several of his friends. He also told them about what he learned from the Pensieve. What if they ask you to stay in the Order?" Sirana asked, hopeful that he would.

"That remains to be seen. The Order has played a pivotal role since their inception. I will hear what they have to say," Severus said, finishing up his dinner, then laying back in the bed, obviously weakened.

Sirana moved away his tray, then sat on the bed next to him as he continued, "I have thought about our future, Sirana. I've had plenty of time to think the last few days. I don't plan on returning to Hogwarts. That is no longer part of my future, even if it were possible. There is something I've been considering, and I would like to discuss it with you after the meeting tomorrow. I still need to think through some details, though."

He had successfully piqued her curiosity. She wanted to ask him more, but she heard in his tone that he wasn't ready to discuss it further for the moment. She also saw the fatigue that settled over him. She tucked him in and kissed his cheek.

"I've thought about it too. It is a little scary starting over—again. But it's exciting too, especially with you by my side," she said.

He smiled sleepily. "Albus told me once, that with you at my side, nothing could possibly come between us—or stand against us. He was an extraordinary wizard," Severus said, and fell off to sleep.

The next day, they prepared for the meeting with several key members of the Order. Andromeda had washed up Severus's clothes, and Sirana helped Severus change into them. She would have to arrange to get the rest of his wardrobe from Hogwarts, along with the rest of his things. She didn't have to worry about all of that now though.

She looked at Severus. He looked striking in his clothes, although she was getting used to seeing him without them.

"I will never again take for granted the ability to dress myself," Severus said as she put on his shoes.

"Just think of it as practice for fifty years or so from now," Sirana said, smiling up at him. She would love to grow old with this man.

He must have been thinking the same thing. "Fifty years will not be long enough to spend with you. But I will be grateful for every single one," Severus said, giving her his hand to stand.

Sirana smoothed down his jacket. "I will ask you in fifty years, and you'd better have the same answer," she said.

He drew her close and kissed her with a passion that proved his strength was returning. "I hope you still have your humor in fifty years," he said.

"I hope you'll still kiss me like that in fifty years," she replied.

Sirana heard someone knock on the door, and they went out to the living area. Grayson answered the door and welcomed in the members of the Order. Arthur, Molly, and Bill Weasley were there, along with Hagrid. Sirana felt more at ease. She knew all of them well. Andromeda and Grayson brought everyone drinks after they were seated. Andromeda had already organized the seating area to accommodate everyone.

Arthur spoke first. "I think we all know each other, so we can skip introductions. I would like to remind everyone that the Order is just as important now as it's ever been. The Death Eaters are on the run, and we need to make sure none of them try to step up to take over Voldemort's army. We have agents, including myself, in the Ministry, and we need to help protect the integrity to suppress any further corruption. We will be gaining some new young members as well. My sons, George and Ron, Harry Potter, Hermione Granger, and Neville Longbottom."

"Grand," Severus said, and Sirana had to stifle a smile.

Arthur coughed, then continued, "We would like for you, Andromeda, to officially join us. You've been an asset to us all these years."

Sirana saw Grayson place his hand on Andromeda's, looking at her reassuringly.

"Yes. I will be busy with caring for Teddy, but Grayson said he would help, along with Harry Potter. But, yes, I will join you. My daughter would have been happy for me," she said, smiling at Grayson.

"I'll teach her everything I know," he said. He gave Sirana a quirk of a smile at that, and she knew they would have laughed at the innuendo if company wasn't present. He settled on winking at her, and Severus gave her a sideways glance.

"Severus," Arthur said more seriously, "Harry has brought to my attention the role you played in his life, as well as the other students', and the sacrifices you and Albus made at a great cost to both of you. If you are interested in staying with the Order, we would welcome you back." Arthur turned to speak to everyone in the room, continuing, "Of course, Sirana and Grayson are already members, and they are always welcome. With Voldemort's death, our purpose will change, but we do not plan to disband. The best way to fight the darkness is to be the light, and we will make sure the light has a place to live."

Severus thought about the proposition, knowing it would be important to Sirana. She had found a purpose and a talent with the Order, just as she had with teaching. Even though Severus had been somewhat of a lone wolf most of his life, he had a longing to join forces with others in an effort to do something worthwhile. He had sought that when he joined Voldemort's army, to his own detriment. In its stead, his position at Hogwarts and his association with Dumbledore and the Order had filled that need.

"I would like to accept your invitation. I also have a proposition to make, and it may work to fill a deficit that I have observed over the years. However, I wish to speak with Sirana before I make the proposal," Severus said, glancing at Sirana.

"I look forward to hearing it," Arthur said.

"As do I," Grayson said, and Sirana was pleased to see the look of mutual respect pass between Grayson and Severus. She heard a chorus of "Ayes" from others in the group, offering their mutual anticipation of his proposition. She offered her "Aye" as well, looking a Severus with a new awareness of the respect he must hold among the Order, especially now with the suspicion of his allegiance to Voldemort dispelled.

"Very well. It seems we are all on board then. We will send word if we need any immediate assistance. We will plan another meeting to prepare for our next mission. Kingsley is recovering from his battle injuries as well as a few others," he said, looking at Severus, who was growing paler by the minute. "Until then, if any of you need anything, just let us know."

"Now, where's the baby? I haven't had a chance to hold the baby yet," Molly said cheerfully.

As if on cue, the baby started crying from the other room.

"I'll go get him," Grayson said.

Chapter 74

Home

Sirana was happy to visit with Hagrid and everyone, but as soon as they left, Grayson hurried over to help her get Severus back into the bedroom. She was grateful he accepted their help, as he looked like he was about to collapse. She worried about him and wondered if they should summon Madam Pomfrey again. His condition had vastly improved over the last few days, but he was still weak.

"I will be fine," Severus assured her. "Madam Pomfrey gave me a week of bed rest, so that means I have another day of recovery."

"She said *at least* a week from what I remember, and I don't want you overdoing it," Sirana said, fussing over him.

"Tomorrow will be our last night here, and then we will go to my house in Cokeworth," he said directly.

"Is that right!?" Sirana asked.

"Yes, exactly," he replied, his eyes starting to close, and she heard the resoluteness of his words.

"We'll see how you feel. I suppose I can care for you just as well there as here," she relented. He smiled a little as he fell asleep, as if he'd won the point.

Sirana went out to speak with Grayson and Andromeda. The news that they were leaving so soon didn't seem to settle well with them.

"Don't worry. I will be sure to ask if I need any help, or if he doesn't improve," she said, appreciating their concern.

"He's a stubborn one," Grayson said smiling. "I can see why you two get on so well."

Sirana smiled, knowing this to be true. They were both stubborn in their loyalty to each other, and she would not want it any other way.

"Well, you two are welcome back any time. We will always have a place for you if you need it. I know good people when I see them," Andromeda said, and then looked over at Grayson.

Grayson put an arm around Andromeda's shoulder, then smiled at her adoringly before looking back at Sirana. "Just make sure he takes good care of you, Sirana. I've covered your ass for a year now, and I don't plan on giving up that job," Grayson said with a smile on his face. He seemed to have a smile on his face almost all the time now. It made him look younger, almost like a different person.

Sirana laughed. "I'll let him know that," she joked. "Maybe I will get my way more often."

"Oh, I don't think you have much to worry about there. I can see you have him wrapped around your little finger. Who would have thought?" he said.

"Yes, who would have thought?" she replied, looking at the happy couple in front of her.

True to Madam Pomfrey's word, Severus woke up on the day they were to leave looking like a new man. They gathered what little things they had there and said their goodbyes. She knew she would see her friends again, and soon. The Order was meeting within a week. It was still a little sad leaving them anyway. She had enjoyed the time with them and the baby. Sirana offered to babysit any time they needed it, and Andromeda said she would surely take her up on her offer. Sirana hugged both Andromeda and Grayson while Severus watched, and then they Disapparated together.

Sirana was a little nervous about going to Severus's home. She didn't know why. She'd been in dozens of different places over the last year with the Order. Maybe it was because it was Severus's home, and there was something very intimate about that. Severus's home was much like his study at Hogwarts. There were books lining the walls, and the furniture looked well-worn but comfortable. The kitchen was right off of the seating area, and it was surprisingly a good size. There was a small table for two tucked against the wall there, and she imagined him eating his meals there alone.

Severus turned and used his wand to start a fire in the fireplace, and the room suddenly felt cozier. He opened the blind to the window, and light filled the room. It wasn't big by any means, but since she loved books, she thought it was quite homey.

"I have enough here to read forever," she said, looking at all of the books.

"I don't intend to give you time to read any time soon," Severus said, taking her arm to pull her to him.

"Ah, I see now why you were in such a rush to leave Andromeda's," Sirana said knowingly.

"You're fortunate my strength didn't return earlier, or else they may have thought I was keeping you captive in my bed," he said, his eyes flashing at her.

"I would have made sure they didn't try to rescue me," Sirana teased.

"Let me show you my bedroom," Severus said, leading her by the hand.

"Said the spider to the fly," she quipped, following him willingly.

Chapter 75

Euphoria

Severus's bedroom was large in comparison to his living room. There were books in there as well but lining only one wall. There was a quaint reading area in a corner by the window, and a door that led into a small bathroom.

"Let me take your jacket," Severus offered.

"I see you've been working on your hosting expertise," Sirana teased.

He took off his own jacket, placing them on the chair.

"I don't plan on playing the host here. As modest as it is, it is your home now too," he said, returning to place his hands on her arms.

She was taken a bit by surprise by his words, and it touched her how good it felt for him to say them.

"I am happy to call it home, as long as you are here with me," she said sincerely.

His expression showed how much that meant to him, and he leaned in to kiss her. They had kissed over the last week since the Battle at Hogwarts, but they now kissed with the promise of their future together.

Severus felt like he poured all of the love he felt for Sirana into their kiss, and the pain and sadness from all of the nights he wanted to hold her and be with her but couldn't—the days he spent alone wishing he could talk to her, the dread he felt that he might never see her again, was all washed away. He felt her love pour in to him in turn, and he felt deep into his soul the rapturous euphoria that Sirana spawned in him, and he was driven by an intentness to make up for the unimaginable longing he had felt for her over the last year. His entire being was consumed by her, and he dared not to let her enter his mind to see the inferno inside of him that threatened to burn him alive. He noticed she was shaking, and he wondered if she was nervous or if she too felt the same fire inside of her.

Severus slowed their kiss and pulled away to see her face, and he could see it was the latter. Sirana's eyes were veiled with passion, and he could see her consumed in her own euphoria for him. They didn't speak, caught up in the torrent of their shared desire. He stroked her hair lovingly, then moved to begin removing her clothes. She reached to start unbuttoning his shirt, and he noticed her hands were shaking. He could hear her breathing, which was uniquely amplified in the quiet room, and the sound of her passion was matched by his own. He had managed to remove all her clothes while she was removing his shirt, and she stood before him in her glorious nudeness. It was only a few steps to the bed, but he leaned down to lift her up and carry her to his bed, laying her down on it.

Sirana felt the intensity of her passion filling her, and she felt Severus's passion as if it filled the entire room with an electrifying power. When he picked her up to carry her to his bed, the surreal magnitude of the moment was almost overwhelming. Severus stood at the side of the bed looking at her as he shed his trousers and shorts. He stood there another moment, returning the favor, enjoying the way she looked at him in turn. He climbed into bed over her on his hands and knees, kissing her again, holding himself up from her on his elbows, his hands wrapped in her hair, caressing her. He slid one hand down between her legs to find her already wet with desire for him, and he smiled, satisfied with the confirmation.

"Severus…" she said, looking at him as if she too felt the dreamlike quality of the moment. Yet, the dreams they had shared over the last year, as if by magic, could never compare to this vivid reality.

"Sirana…" he said softly as he settled between her legs, readying himself to enter her. She placed her hands against his chest as he slid himself into her with a slow, deep thrust. The exquisite sensation of him inside her brought out a gratified moan from each of them. He moved in and out of her in long, slow strokes, all his senses attuned to every moment of their lovemaking. Severus was engorged with his desire for her, and he heard her cry out her shock as he pushed deep into her, the powerful intimacy of their joining shocking even himself in its force. He saw her close her eyes, her expression one of alluring captivation. He moved in her slowly, savoring her obvious pleasure as well as his own. He closed his own eyes, all of his senses fighting to take forefront in his mind. She felt so good wrapped around him, and he moaned hoarsely as the strikingly fierce sensation of their lovemaking ravaged his body. He wanted to take her to the limit of her own pleasure, and he pushed himself to his own limit, hearing and feeling her quickly approaching the crest of her climax. She suddenly gasped, her neck arching back, as her body erupted in magnificent waves of her sweet crescendo. She said his name lustfully, grasping onto him. He wanted to join her in her rapture, and drove into her, unrestrained. He was met swiftly with his own orgasm, feeling all the energy in his body flow into his core, and he gasped at the jarring force of the spasms of his release. The ferocity of the emotion they had for each other culminated in their physical beings, and they met their minds, embracing wordlessly, overcome with their mutual fulfillment. They drifted in and out of sleep to hold each other, whispering their love to each other in their minds.

Chapter 76

Refuge

The contentment Sirana felt in Severus's home helped to soothe the homesickness she had after leaving Hogwarts. Hagrid had arranged to have her clothes and personal items sent to her, and she was settling in nicely.

"Although I always plan on keeping this home, I am unsure if it will be where we will make our home together in the future," Severus said at dinner.

She had wondered when Severus would finally get to the conversation about his proposal for the Order, and she also wondered how she would fit into it.

"I've often thought that there should be a more considerate option for the students of Hogwarts who find themselves without humane accommodations for the summer. In the past, students such as Harry Potter—or myself—were left without adequate options. Children who are orphaned, or who have non-magical parents that do not welcome them back," Severus said thoughtfully.

Sirana was aware of the deficit in this area, and always felt bad for those students during the holidays and summer break. She also felt touched that Severus, who many might have thought had no affection for his students, had put so much consideration into it. She was intently interested in what he was saying so far.

He looked at her for a moment as if to gauge her reaction and continued, "If we were to provide a place for them, one that offered extended education during the summer, a school of sorts, but also a home."

It was his turn to look at her expectedly. She could almost envision his plan in her mind. She loved children, and she loved teaching, and the thought of providing a refuge for these children warmed her heart.

"That sounds wonderful, Severus," she exclaimed.

"We obviously wouldn't have appropriate accommodations here in our home. I thought perhaps you could assist me in resolving that aspect—if you are interested in pursuing this path," he said.

"Yes!" she said, excited at the proposition. "I never even imagined it as a possibility, but now, I cannot envision any other path for us."

"This endeavor will not be without its challenges, and I wouldn't want to attempt it without you," he said earnestly.

She smiled at that, her heart full of aspirations for their future. "While I was traveling with the Order, I happened to meet Albus's brother, Aberforth. After Voldemort's death, I considered approaching him about a joint venture with him at Hog's Head Inn to provide a base for the Order. I know it's in an awful condition, but what if he was willing to convert it to accommodate your purpose as well?"

Severus considered her idea. He knew of the secret passage from Hog's Head to Hogwarts, and that Aberforth had provided the students with provisions when they were hiding out in the Room of Requirements. As long as they had less than a dozen students that needed accommodations, he could imagine that it would suit their purpose splendidly. The Hog's Head had a long history and being close by to Hogsmeade might be ideal, with some cleaning and with Aberforth's approval, as well as Professor McGonagall's. He thought of his last 'meeting' with Professor McGonagall. It was indeed intriguing to imagine his next meeting with her. Sirana and he could make their residence there with the students during the summer and holiday breaks, and for the needs of the Order, and then use his home at Spinner's End for their home otherwise. All in all, it wasn't a bad plan, at least in the inception.

"Agreed. We will plan on pursuing this avenue. I would, however, like for you to present the idea to the Order and to Aberforth. I believe that it must be I who approaches Professor McGonagall. Our last...*interaction*...left much to be desired, and although I don't look forward to it, we have some matters to work out between us. I would like to think that once she is made aware of the exceptional circumstances of my term as Headmaster of Hogwarts, she may soften her perception. There was a time when I would have considered us to be friends," Severus said, feeling the regret that came with the memory. He brushed that away for now, for he now was given the opportunity to write a new chapter, and he felt all of the past constraints of his life being cut away.

When they finished their dinner, Sirana poured them both a drink, and they moved into the living room. He sat in his chair by the fireplace. It wasn't quite as big as his chair at Hogwarts, but he looked forward to seeing if Sirana would still be comfortable in his lap, and he invited her to join him. She curled up in his lap and wiggled in. It was more than adequate for the duration, though he would consider arranging for his chair at Hogwarts to be brought. He put his arms around her and pulled her close. They sat and drank their drink and talked about all of the possibilities, enjoying each other's company and the warmth of the fire. He also felt the warmth of their love for each other, and suddenly felt the time may be right.

"Before the wine clouds your judgment, I have another proposition for you," he said, moving for her to raise from his lap.

He stood, taking their glasses and setting them on the table. He lowered himself in front of her on his knee and drew a small box from his jacket pocket. He looked up to her, the woman he loved more than anything in his world.

"Sirana, would you be my wife?" he asked simply but sincerely.

He opened the box to reveal a simple but brilliant ring. He was charmed when her mouth dropped open, and she brought her hands together at her chest. He was humbled and grateful when she said yes. He slipped the ring on her finger, then stood to face her. They kissed, tears coming down both of their cheeks. They could never have envisioned so much for themselves. Lily's last act of magic had brought them together in a most extraordinary work of magic. Her gift was unselfish and beautiful, just as she had been. Severus thought about all that had led them here, all of the sacrifices, both grievous and beautiful, and he vowed that none would be in vain. Their love and devotion for each other had made them whole, their souls undiminished.

www.ingramcontent.com/pod-product-compliance
Lightning Source LLC
Chambersburg PA
CBHW072023020726
47501CB00006B/1922